Touchstones

A Collection

Stephanie Burgis

For Patrick, with love.

Contents

Introduction vii

The Wrong Foot 1
Undead Philosophy 101 26
A Cup of Comfort 49
Dreaming Harry 64
Offerings 84
Dancing in the Dark 93
The Disastrous Début of Agatha Tremain 111
The Wildness Inside 148
The Art of Deception 177
Midnight 230
Clasp Hands 232
Crow 245
True Names 251
Good Neighbors 264
Love, Your Flatmate 281
House of Secrets 294

Afterword 341
Acknowledgments 343
Earlier Publications 347

Introduction

I turn to fantasy short stories, as both a reader and a writer, for a sense of wonder, for a feeling of escape—and, occasionally, for a safe way to work through some of my own most difficult and painful feelings by giving them a magical filter. In keeping with those different moods, some of the stories in this collection are as frothy and as wholeheartedly romantic as my full-length novels and novellas. Some of them are light and funny and designed purely to make you laugh. A few have darker elements, as I wrote them to help myself work through dark times...but I hope that you'll find hope and love and magic running as a steady thread through those stories, too.

My biggest hope for this collection is that some of these stories (possibly different ones for every reader!) may serve as touchstones, reminding you—no matter what you happen to be going through in your own life at any given moment—of a sense of nourishing magic and wonder that's available for all of us. These stories will be here when you need them.

The Wrong Foot

Needless to say, I didn't want to try on the slipper in the first place.

"Why should I?" I asked Mama when she came to drag me away from my books that morning. "We both know I'm not the girl they're looking for. I was standing by your side last night, remember, when she first arrived. We both commented on how taken the prince was by her. You made a rude comment about the size of her collarbone, if you recall."

"I haven't the slightest recollection," Mama said, with a typically airy disregard for the facts. She was already sweeping through my closet, tossing fresh undergarments onto my bed. Mama may look dainty, particularly next to me, but she is capable of creating an entire whirlwind of activity when inspired. Her head was buried in my closet, my finest silk stockings flying over her shoulder as she called back: "And neither have you, from this instant onward. The prince has sworn that whoever fits that shoe will be his bride!"

"A deeply impractical way to find his missing dance partner." I shook my head, setting one finger in my book to mark my place. "It certainly fits his appalling reputation, though. Has anyone suggested that he simply look at maidens' faces as a better way to recognize the girl he loves? Or was her face not actually what he was looking at last night?"

"Luckily," said Mama, "your bosom is entirely satisfactory, so he won't be disappointed. *And* your collarbone is much finer than hers anyway! Now"—as she emerged triumphantly from my closet—"put this on."

I blinked at the gown she was holding out to me. "It's an evening gown."

She tapped her foot imperiously. "We are in a hurry, Sophia."

"It's also ten o'clock in the morning!"

But of course she had her way, as always. I felt utterly absurd as I followed her into our parlor, my shoulders bare and the rose-colored silk gown only barely clinging to my famous (or at least satisfactory) bosom. The man who stood directly behind the prince, wearing a sedate black frock coat, widened his eyes at the sight of me. They were rather appealing hazel eyes, actually. I felt a momentary pang of regret as I saw them, and rather wished that I could somehow let him know I hadn't chosen this absurd outfit myself.

But the prince, standing before him, seemed to take it

perfectly in stride. He was a prince, after all. Mothers had probably sent their daughters after him wearing far less than this before. At any rate, I could tell just by looking at him that he was in a Mood. His chin was lifted in heroic determination; his handsome face looked beautifully anguished; his collar-length blonde hair, which had been perfectly slicked back last night, was now in perfectly romantic disarray.

I wondered how long his servants had had to work that morning, to disorder it quite so perfectly.

"Your Highness." Mama floated into a curtsey, and at a jab of her elbow, I followed suit, trying not to fall out of my bodice on the way. "Of course you already know my dear Sophia," Mama fluttered. "After dancing with her for so long last night..."

The man behind the prince coughed into his fist. He, I took it, *had* bothered to look at faces, unlike the prince. I could see it in his eyes.

I hadn't noticed him at the ball last night—I'd spent most of the evening either hiding behind potted palms to escape Mama's terrifyingly implacable mission to find me dance partners, or else working my way through a Cicero translation in my head as I was yanked around the dance floor by her chosen victims. Now, though, I thought perhaps I should have taken the time to look around a bit after all. The flash of humor in this man's eyes had been most intriguing—and completely absent from any of the stream of stammering young men Mama had forced me to dance with.

"Actually..." I began, speaking directly to him.

But the prince interrupted me. "Shall we?" He gestured impatiently to the footstool someone had set in our parlor. It certainly wasn't ours; it was far too impressive. Papa's incorrigible spaniel had chewed our last three footstools, and Mama had sworn off buying any more replacements until he reached adulthood and/or some semblance of common sense.

I sat down, arranging my skirts, and tried not to feel ridiculous as I lifted my foot. There was only one comfort in the whole situation, and only one reason I had finally given in to Mama's nagging: I knew this couldn't possibly work. My feet, like hers, were unusually—even extraordinarily—small. *Too* small, our dressmaker would certainly have said, if Mama hadn't terrified her into submission long ago. For all the trouble they'd caused me over the years, I blessed their oddity now.

The prince didn't seem to mind it, though. As he took off my own slipper, his fingers brushed against the arch of my foot rather too closely for comfort.

I scooted backward on the footstool, and took some consolation in the other man's presence. Somehow, even though he hadn't yet spoken a word, his sheer solidity, the breadth of his shoulders and the weary amusement on his face—amusement his expression clearly invited me to share—made my own shoulders relax a bit and the whole absurd proceedings feel more laughable than unbearable.

"You must know," I began, "I'm not the girl you're looking for."

"Mm-hmm," the prince murmured absently. "Very honored, yes, I understand, they all are. You needn't tell me."

"I didn't," I muttered.

The other man bit back a grin.

"Shhh!" Mama hissed. "Your Highness, may I offer you and your friend any—oh! *Oh!*" she squealed, raising both hands to her mouth. Her eyes misted over with tears of delight. "Oh, Sophia, it fits! It really fits!"

I stared. I blinked and stared again. But she was right. The glass molded to my foot as neatly—and as chillingly, for glass is a cold material—as if it had been made for me.

I regarded it as I would a poisonous plant that had thrown its tendrils through my bedroom window. The prince looked equally shocked, but more surprised than horrified. He stared at my foot. He wiggled the shoe. Nothing he did made any difference. The fit was absolutely perfect.

He looked up, critically, to examine my chest. I crossed my arms over it and tried my best to pull my foot out of his grip.

"This," I said, "is a most unfortunate coincidence."

The man in black took a step forward. "Your Highness, if I may..."

"Absolutely not," said the prince. "There shall be no interruption of this perfect moment." Stretching his lips into an avaricious grin, he finally dropped my foot. Alarmingly, he seized my hands instead. "My love! Forgive me for failing to recognize you at once."

"Because it wasn't me!" I said. "Just look at my face! You

took my hand for all of two seconds last night when I first arrived, and we never met again. You didn't even ask me to dance."

"Nonsense." His laugh held a distinct edge of irritation. "You needn't play coy with me anymore, my darling. I admit, it was a charming ploy to run from me exactly at the stroke of midnight—very dramatic, very striking! And to leave the shoe behind, as a challenge? Unforgettable, I agree. But I would begin to be annoyed if you tried to take the game any further." His eyes hardened. "And you wouldn't want to annoy me."

As I struggled to pull my hands from his grip, it finally struck me with some force that there might well have been a reason why the prince's dance partner had fled. From the strength of his grip, and the way his gaze had already turned back to my bosom, I began to doubt that he had drawn her aside for her conversational skills.

"My poor Sophia is *so* shy!" Mama said. Her fingers bit into one of my bare shoulders like steel. "I'm afraid she has simply taken fright, your Highness, overwhelmed by the honor of your attention. She's simply too modest to put herself forward."

Now, I felt the gaze of the man in black flick momentarily toward my exposed bosom, his expression turning sardonic. I glared at all three of them.

"I am *not* shy," I said, "and I am not a fool. This is a simple case of mistaken identity. I wish you all the best in finding your dance partner, your Highness, but—"

"You don't seem to understand," the prince said. "I made

a public declaration: whoever fit that shoe would be my bride."

"Yes, well, I'm sure any number of girls would not only fit the shoe but be delighted to do so." I finally managed to yank my hand free, but I couldn't step backward, trapped by the footstool and my long, clinging skirts and petticoats. "I, however, have no intention of marrying anyone. I have a modest inheritance of my own, you see, and scholarly pursuits to engage all my interest, so—"

"I do beg your pardon, your Highness," Mama cooed, "but my delicate Sophia is so overwhelmed, I must speak to her in private to help her settle her thoughts."

"Of course," the prince said. "Order the maids to begin packing for her, as well." He let out a bark of laughter. "But you can tell them not to bother with any books. I can't stand talking to bluestockings. I promise you, she'll have far more interesting matters than *scholarly pursuits* to engage her interest once we've had our wedding night!"

Mama dragged me from the room while I was still sputtering, incapable of response.

"Now," she said, the moment the door was closed behind us, "I want no more of this foolishness, Sophia, do you understand me? You are the luckiest maiden in this kingdom."

"Almost as lucky as the girl who got away," I retorted. "For heaven's sake, Mama! The man is a philistine. Didn't you hear anything he said? He thinks the very world revolves around him!"

"Because it does. He is a prince, Sophia. A real prince!

And someday, you will be a queen." Mama's gaze went unfocused and dreamy. "Oh, Sophia, you lucky girl. When I think of how I used to dream of being a princess one day..."

I was obviously going to gain no help from her. I crossed my arms. "We'll need to wait for Papa's consent."

Unlike Mama, Papa would understand. Papa was the one who had hired all my tutors in Greek and classical Latin. Papa was the one who had always said it would be a criminal waste for me to interrupt my studies with marriage.

Papa would be home from Florence in three weeks. All I had to do was wait until then to be rescued.

Mama's grey eyes shifted from clouds to solid ice. "For all your supposed cleverness, my dear, you don't seem to have grasped any reality outside your books. The prince has issued a royal command. It was posted in town squares across the kingdom!"

"And?"

"By the time your father returns," Mama said, "you will be a happily married woman...whether you like it or not."

Half an hour later, the prince helped me into the royal carriage with a possessive hand on my bottom. I was in too much shock to resist.

The other man seated himself across from us and took out a pencil and a commonplace book.

"My secretary, Harcourt," the prince said with a careless wave of his hand. "You won't mind his presence, my dear. Practically a servant, you know. Like a piece of furniture."

A secretary. No wonder I hadn't noticed him at the ball.

He wouldn't have been dancing, only observing from the sidelines to ensure that all ran smoothly. I wagered none of the other guests had paid any more notice of him than they had of the potted palms I'd hidden behind.

I met the secretary's hazel eyes, and he nodded infinitesimally, a moment of recognition. Had he seen me hiding from my dance partners behind those potted palms? I had a feeling that that steady gaze missed very little.

I felt an odd and most unscholarly tingle at the thought.

Then the prince set one firm hand on my chin and the other, horrifyingly, on my thigh. "And now, my dear..." he murmured, leaning towards me.

Apparently he had meant it about the furniture. The tingle disappeared, replaced by sheer panic.

"The wedding!" I bleated, both desperately and inanely. "We must discuss the wedding!"

He settled back in his seat, sighing. "Oh, I suppose so. All you ladies love weddings, don't you? You probably spent your entire girlhood dreaming through the details."

Had he heard *nothing* that I had said in the house? I stared at him in disbelief.

Harcourt the secretary cleared his throat. "If you will allow me, your Highness..." His voice was surprisingly deep. "Perhaps I might assist you both with a list of the items required for preparation. Flower arrangements, dress-making arrangements, bridesmaid selection, consultations with the Archbishop about your preferred order of ceremonies..."

"Oh, good God," the prince moaned. He tipped his head back against the cushions in despair. "What a kerfuffle!"

"...Invitations to be written, guests of honor to be selected, items of precedence to be decided..."

As the droning list continued, the prince's eyes fluttered closed...and Harcourt closed one of his own hazel eyes in a wink.

I beamed him a smile of intense gratitude. The list didn't end until the carriage pulled up in front of the palace, fifteen minutes later, by which point the prince was looking positively puce with horror, and I was feeling much, much better. With so many preparations to be made, I couldn't imagine the wedding taking place in less than a year. I would surely think of a solution by then.

Unfortunately, I had reckoned without the queen.

"My dearest girl!" She was waiting outside the carriage when the door opened, her royal robes trailing in the dirt and a toothy grin on her face. Her soft arms pressed me into her well-padded bosom before I could even touch the ground. "At last I have a daughter!" she crowed.

"I beg your pardon," I began, my voice muffled by her bosom, "but—"

"You will have a daughter," the prince said gloomily, "but not for another decade, if Harcourt is to be believed. The amount of nonsense required to arrange a simple royal wedding—"

"Nonsense," said the queen. Her voice hardened. "I am an expert at cutting through red tape."

I finally pulled free, gasping for breath. "There's been a mistake," I panted. "I am not—"

Her bejeweled hand clapped over my mouth, bands of gold cutting into my skin. Her eyes met mine and I saw the gleam of steely determination in their depths.

"My son," she said, "has finally consented to marry. Believe me, my dear, I will allow *no* mistakes."

There was very little I would put past her Majesty, Queen Hortense, after the dress-fitting I was obliged next to endure. Every time I tried to point out the logical fallacies in the situation, a dressmaker's pin just happened to accidentally stab into my skin, turning each of my attempted comments into a wordless cry of pain.

Queen Hortense smiled beatifically throughout and rattled off orders without a pause. Even Mama would have been in awe.

"...And we'll need shoes, of course," she finished. "But then, you have lovely glass slippers of your own, don't you, dear? Perhaps it would be most appropriate for you to wear that famous pair at the wedding."

I glared at her, pushed beyond the bounds of courtesy. "Unfortunately, I only own one shoe of the pair. The one your son forced onto my—*ouch*!"

"Never mind, my dear," Queen Hortense said, serenely ignoring my cry of pain. "No one blames you for losing the other one. We'll have a replacement fashioned for you in no time. Eliza?"

The most subservient of the dressmaker's assistants

rushed forward, her head down. All I could see of her was her smooth, unpowdered brown hair, pulled back into a tight knot.

"Take dearest Sophia's shoe fitting, won't you? We'll need to pass the measurements on to your father within the hour, if the pair is to be complete in just two days." Queen Hortense turned away to consult with the dressmaker. "And now, about that embroidery..."

I gritted my teeth and stood perched on one foot while my final measurements were taken. Eliza's hands, at least, were deft and quick, and she didn't carry a single pin, unlike the other girls bustling around me. One of them glanced down at Eliza's work and let out a soft cry of wonder.

"My goodness, I've never seen such tiny feet! Who'd have thought it on a such a—er..." She gulped as she glanced up at me. "Such a perfectly statuesque lady," she finished diplomatically.

I rolled my eyes and opened my mouth to assure her that there was no need for tact. But before I could speak, the other pin-wielding girl let out a startled giggle.

"Why, they're just as small as yours, Eliza," she said. "I didn't think anyone but you *could* have such feet!"

Eliza's hands clamped around my foot. My breath stopped in my throat.

Last night at the ball, of course, everyone's hair had been powdered. But unlike the prince, I hadn't limited my own perusal of the guests to ladies' bosoms.

"May I see your face, Eliza?" I asked.

Slowly, her head tilted back. Her face was pale, free of cosmetics, and very white against her plain dark gown. Her blue eyes filled with panic as they met mine. *Please,* she mouthed. *Don't.*

I gritted my teeth. "Somehow," I said, "I don't think we'll have any difficulty filling out this pair in time for the wedding."

Eliza's voice was soft and hoarse with fear. "I...my father, the cobbler, is very quick with his work, always."

"I'm sure he is," I said grimly. "Might I have a word with you in private for a moment? I have a particular favor to ask."

The other girls stared at each other wide-eyed, rustling with curiosity. Eliza rose to her feet as reluctantly as if she were walking to her execution.

Queen Hortense, all-too-sharp-eyed, called out, "Sophia, my dear, I hope you aren't thinking of trying to escape. We are just about to start working on the guest list, and I cannot have you running away from your responsibilities."

Later, I mouthed to Eliza.

Slowly, unhappily, she nodded. But it was a hollow victory.

From the look in Eliza's eyes, her flight from the ball last night had been no simple act of shyness. And even if Eliza *had* wished to reveal herself, I couldn't imagine the prince—much less the queen—taking well to the news that he had accidentally courted a mere servant. After only an hour in the queen's company, I was already confident that she would ride roughshod over any notion of class-defying romance.

I would have to find another way...and I only had two days to do it in.

It felt like a relief out of all proportion, when Queen Hortense bundled me into her writing room, to find the secretary, Harcourt, waiting there. He rose to his feet with perfect correctness. With his wide shoulders filling out his black frock coat, he looked solid and reassuring...and yet, somehow, *not*.

No, 'reassuring' was not quite the right word, after all—particularly as he met my eyes.

The unscholarly tingle was back with a vengeance. I moistened my lips. His gaze dropped to follow.

Queen Hortense said, "Ah, Harcourt, prompt as always. I trust you have a preliminary guest list ready?"

"Of course, your Majesty." He waited for the footmen to help us into our chairs, then took the seat across from me, passing a thick sheaf of papers to the queen and a stack of blank cards to me. An open bottle of ink stood on the table between us, flanked by enough quill pens to stock an army. "I've included all of the foreign dignitaries within five days' travel."

"They'll be far too late." Queen Hortense's smile could only be described as smug. "No, make a secondary list for them, and we'll send out announcements after the fact. The last thing any of us want is to give my son enough time to weasel out of his commitment!"

I coughed. "Actually—"

"Now, my dear," said Queen Hortense, "all you need do

is write the invitations. Harcourt, I leave the future princess in your capable hands. I have flowers to order!"

And with that, she bustled out, taking all but one of the footmen with her.

Harcourt looked across the table at me, in the sudden silence. I felt unaccountably shy under his steady gaze. My own eyes began to lower, like any ninnyhammer young miss blushing before an attractive gentleman.

I had never been a ninnyhammer. I jerked my chin up and met his gaze squarely. "This," I said, "is a farce, and you know it."

"Ahem." Harcourt turned to the footman, who stood against the wall with shoulders rigidly squared and gaze blank of expression beneath a powdered wig. "Jonathan," Harcourt said. "Perhaps we might come to an arrangement for your discretion. Another writing lesson?"

Jonathan's face lost its blankness to break into a grin. "Nah, Mr. Harcourt, I'll need more than that for prime gossip. You'll need to write a letter for me."

"To Rose, again? Didn't the earlier one work?"

"Not Rose," Jonathan said, and smirked. "Alice, this time."

Harcourt sighed. "Alice it is. But perhaps you might do me the favor of putting your hands on your ears, to resist all temptation?"

"As you say, Mr. Harcourt." Jonathan winked and turned away from us, putting his fingers in his ears. A surprisingly tuneful whistle emerged from his lips.

I said, "Do you resort to bribery often?"

"Only when it works." Harcourt's own grin made him look more approachable. It did strange things to my insides, too. Irrationally, I found myself wishing I could read one of the love letters he had written on Jonathan's behalf.

But that was nonsense, of course. Merely a scholar's curiosity, and I had no time to indulge it. I infused my voice with a briskness worthy of the queen herself as I said, "Unfortunately, it appears that the prince's true dance partner isn't willing to take her place in my stead."

"It would be difficult," Harcourt agreed. "I cannot imagine her Majesty taking well to the introduction of a cobbler's daughter as her daughter-in-law."

"What?" I stared at him. "You *knew*?"

He shrugged. "I have an eye for faces." His lips quirked. "And a way with open doors. I'm afraid I, ah, may have accidentally held the door open for her on her way through one of the lesser-known exits from the palace. She wasn't keen to be caught by the prince on her way out, you see."

"Only too well," I said, and groaned. "Isn't there anyone who actually *wants* to marry him?"

"At least half the ladies in the kingdom," Harcourt replied promptly. "When the prince's proclamation was announced this morning, the Marquis of Carabas's daughter, for one, declared she'd be willing to chop off her own toes to fit into those glass slippers. And as a matter of fact..." His hazel gaze rested on me curiously. "I would say with some certainty that you were the *only* young lady at the ball last night who wasn't angling for his Highness's attention."

I snorted. "I have better things to do with my life than sigh over a man who's never voluntarily opened a book."

"Indeed." He paused. "May I ask...the potted palms?"

My cheeks burned. "I had no choice. My mother is determined."

"And your father?"

"In Florence, on business." Frustration seethed inside me at the thought. "If he were here, it would be a very different matter, I promise you. But he won't be back for another three weeks."

"By which point, it will be too late."

"That certainly seems to be the plan." I stabbed one of the feather pens onto the top card in my pile, taking vicious satisfaction in the blotch of ink that spread across it. *There* was one invitation that wouldn't be sent, anyway. If I'd thought it would make any difference to the queen's plans, I would have thrown the whole lot into the fire.

I had no doubt she would simply proceed without invitations, though...and any open mutiny on my part would lead to an even closer guard. No, as infuriating as the situation might be, I would have to assume a façade of acceptance from now on, if I was to have any slight chance of escape.

And speaking of escape...

I slid a speculative glance at the man across from me. He'd held a hidden door open for Miss Eliza. Perhaps he'd do the same for me.

"I am about to hazard a wild guess," I said. "Is the queen planning to hold a supper party tonight, to introduce me to the court?"

He looked more rueful than amused. "You already begin to understand your new home."

"I've spent the last eight years working to understand ancient Greek and Latin philosophers," I said. "One modern court cannot be much more complex."

"You might be surprised." He looked down for a moment, making an infinitesimal adjustment to the sheaf of papers in front of him. "So...do I take it that you are adjusting to the image of yourself as future queen?"

I narrowed my eyes at him. "I thought you were a man of sense and intelligence."

"You did?" He looked younger, and oddly more vulnerable, as his gaze jerked back to meet mine. "I'd be surprised if you'd thought about me at all."

"You're not the only one who notices people," I said. There was something fluttering in my chest, but I tamped it down ruthlessly. "You've lived here longer than I have, though. So I'll need you to make my introductions tonight. There's someone I particularly want to meet."

I had been forced into an evening gown by my mother that morning, and forced into another woman's shoe by the prince. I refused to spend the rest of my life wearing a crown that did not fit. It only wanted an application of logic—and some unaccustomed patience—to realize exactly what I had to do.

A day and a half later, I was ready.

The prince walked me to my room the night before our wedding. That was scandalous, no doubt, but his mother shooed us on with an indulgent—and mildly terrifying—look in her eye. I was uncomfortably certain that she was already beginning the countdown toward her first grandchild. And while I could find little to say to my fiancé, he hardly seemed to take that as a problem.

"...And then I took him down with my third shot, just like clockwork. *Clockwork*—ha! That's a good one. Too bad Harcourt isn't here to write it down."

"Indeed." I sighed. As helpful as Harcourt had been, even he could not be everywhere. I would have to manage this last part on my own.

"Where did you find Harcourt in the first place?" I asked. It was an attempt at distraction, but even I knew it was hopeless. We had nearly reached the corridor where my bedroom was located, and the prince had an enthusiastic gleam in his eye.

"Who cares about Harcourt?" he said. "He's just a younger son of someone or other. Believe me, the fellow was born to be a secretary. He's always scribbling away. And he actually *reads for pleasure*, he claims. Ha!" His eyes lit on the door ahead of me...and gleamed. "I know better kinds of pleasure."

Oh, dear. We had reached my bedroom.

Seizing my shoulders, the prince pushed me against the wall of the corridor as the nearby footmen attempted to look invisible. His hot breath heaved against my neck as he muttered: "Deadly in war *and* in love, that's what they say about me, y'know. But I'll be gentle with you, I promise. At least the first time..."

I bit down hard on my tongue to hold back a retort. Then, very pointedly, I coughed.

It was a dreadful cough. A hacking cough. A cough which, when carefully aimed, let out a perfect gob of spit directly onto the prince's windswept blond hair.

"I say!" He straightened, one hand flying to his head. "What—?"

"I feel terribly, terribly unwell," I said firmly.

He smiled indulgently, leaning in again. "I daresay it's only bridal jitters. All you need is—"

"A good night's sleep," I said. "It's the only cure. The only thing that can make me ready for..." I swallowed over a moment of real nausea. "...Our wedding night. You want me perfectly healthy for that, don't you?"

"I say." His expression eased; he finally stepped back. "You may have a point. And no matter what my mother says, it wouldn't be a bad idea to celebrate my own last night of independence, eh?"

"Absolutely," I said. "Please don't abstain on my account." The worse the hangover, the better for my plan. "Don't forget, though. It's bad luck to see me tomorrow morning before the wedding ceremony. And I'll look quite different under the veil, after your mother's attendants are finished with me."

"Never mind." He smirked and flicked a carelessly appreciative thumb against my bosom. "I'd know you anywhere, my love."

I doubt it, I thought grimly, and whisked into my room before he could think twice.

Eliza was waiting for me, sitting on the bed and holding the perfect pair of glass slippers. She jumped to her feet as I walked in, and held out the shoes. "They're exactly the same, Miss, only two sizes larger, as you asked."

"Your father is a genius," I said. Then I saw the way her gaze slid away from me, and I raised my eyebrows. "Or should I say...you are?"

She nodded, her eyes lowered. "I only...I wanted to go to a real ball, for once in my life. To be one of the ladies dancing, for once, instead of—"

"You could come with me," I said. "You'd be very welcome. And for all I know, Florence might be more welcoming to female cobblers."

"I doubt it." Eliza sighed. "But thank you, miss. I'm all right here, now. Now that I know I'm not missing anything, after all."

"I wish you the best," I said. And it was true. She might have created a dreadful muddle for me, but how could I blame her? I knew exactly what it was to long for something quite different from what everyone else was expecting for you.

And there was at least one person who was desperately grateful for Eliza's deception.

Scratching sounded on the servants' door only ten minutes later. Half of my tapestried bedroom wall swung inwards a moment afterward, exposing the darkened servants' passageway beyond. Harcourt stepped into the room with a candle in one hand...and the Marquis of Carabas's daughter clinging to his free arm.

Francesca's eyes were dilated with excitement, and when she saw the glass slippers on the bed, she let out an actual mew of bliss.

"Are those really—?!"

"The only glass slippers in the kingdom now," I said, handing them to her. "You needn't even cut off any toes to fit inside them."

"Ohhh! I can hardly believe it!"

Seconds later, she was gazing at her own feet in the slippers with a look of joy that matched the look I'd seen on my own mother's face less than two days ago. I sighed, and extinguished a tiny flare of guilt.

It was too bad Mama could never be a princess. But I couldn't wear her dreams for her.

"They fit perfectly," I said. "And as we know, that's all that really matters."

"I cannot believe you're doing this for me," Francesca breathed. She really had been born for those shoes. She didn't even teeter on their high heels as she raced across to fling her arms around my neck. "It's—why, it's almost as if you were my fairy godmother!"

"Not quite." I extricated myself from her hold with some

difficulty. "But you should be safe. The queen promised I could choose which attendant would help me prepare for the ceremony, and the one I requested"—I remembered Eliza's guilty gaze—"will not hinder you. With the veil over your face, no one should even realize the truth until the ceremony is safely over."

And if they did? Well, the proclamation had been firm: like it or not, the prince would marry whoever fit those glass slippers.

It would be interesting to see if he even noticed that yet another substitution had taken place.

Harcourt coughed pointedly. "It's nearly midnight."

"I should go," I said, and patted Francesca on the shoulder. "I hope your marriage is everything you dreamed of."

"How could it not be?" She let out a giggle of pure glee. "I'm going to be a *princess*! What more could anyone possibly want?"

I rolled my eyes and followed Harcourt into the servants' passageway. When the door closed behind me, I sagged with relief. "Is everything ready?"

He pointed to a pile of clothing in the shadows. "I'll turn my back."

I could feel his presence on every inch of my skin, though, as I scrambled out of my evening gown and into the dark, subdued dressmaker's uniform. It was far easier to put on than the evening gown had been to take off.

"I'm ready," I whispered.

In the distance, I could hear the great castle clock striking midnight as I hurried down the narrow passageway at Harcourt's side.

He held open the door that Eliza had escaped through only two nights earlier. "Your carriage awaits."

"You've arranged everything perfectly."

"I thought I must." His smile looked twisted in the flickering light of the candle that he held. "I heard what you said to the prince, you see. You've never desired marriage. Why should you interrupt your scholarship for a man, when you have an inheritance of your own to support you?"

I took a deep breath. "It's true, I never intended to marry."

He nodded. "I understand. And now..." He began to turn away.

I reached out and took his arm before I could lose my courage. There would be no more hiding behind potted plants—or even my own pride—tonight. "I never wanted to be a princess," I told him. "But perhaps there are some marriages that aren't pretty cages for women. There might even be some husbands who would encourage—or share—their wives' scholarly interests."

Harcourt held himself very still for a moment. Then he turned back to me and looked into my eyes.

He was a man who had stood at the sidelines watching everyone for years. So I knew he could interpret the look on my face, even by faint candlelight.

The breath he released sounded as ragged as if he'd been

holding it for days. "I've always wanted to see Florence," he said.

My lips curved into a smile. "Shall we explore it together?"

For all my years of study, the kiss Harcourt gave me, then, in the dark, was astonishingly instructive.

Undead Philosophy 101

It's hard to tell the vampires from the students in East Lansing.

Let's face it: in a university town, at least 80% of the people on the street look young and beautiful. In a northern town gripped by seven months of winter, the only people who aren't inhumanly pale have spent way too much money in tanning salons. The ones still wearing fashions from twenty years ago are probably math majors; and in the grayest of short winter days, when darkness is only ever replaced by a bleak cloud cover, vampires can safely walk the streets both day and night.

And in every department on campus there are the PhD students who have always been there, their dissertations never quite completed, teaching a section here, a section there, but never, ever leaving. No one in their departments can even remember when they arrived and started their degrees—but with 20,000 whispering, flirting, beer-swilling, belching undergraduates to teach, the professors are only too happy to have reliable teaching assistants on hand who already have the syllabi memorized. It isn't in their interest to ask too many questions...and anyway, everyone knows that grad students keep strange hours.

So I knew exactly where to go when I couldn't ignore the vampires anymore.

At nine o'clock p.m. on a Wednesday in December, even the street lamps were covered by falling snow, and Espresso Royale was a beacon of light and warmth in the pitch-black night. I stomped ice off the soles of my take-no-shit boots as I passed the fake fire blazing outside. All the tables inside were taken, leaving five or six stragglers shivering at the outer tables...but they were all bundled in puffy coats, their gloved hands wrapped around their coffee mugs for warmth. I wasn't here for any of them.

No, my target was seated safely inside, thin blonde ponytail tied behind his head and ragged little goatee stained from his double espresso as he typed on his laptop, apparently shielded from all the noise and conversations around him by the earbuds of his iPod.

Ed Staggs was in deep cover, but I knew him for what he was.

He'd been my teacher for the last two months.

I didn't bother to order a drink. Instead, I slid into the chair across from him and waited until he noticed me. It didn't take long—and I'd have bet my first semester's student loan that it happened well before he took the trouble to look up and widen his eyes in surprise.

"Do I know you?"

"Fourth from the back, far-left row, every Thursday at nine-fifteen." I rattled off the stats. "You said my last essay on Plato's *Republic* was insightful."

"Umm...."

"And you said I should really work on my handwriting."

"Got it! Amanda, right?" He snorted out a laugh and leaned forward to share the joke. "My housemate thought, when you wrote—"

I narrowed my eyes and cut him off. "I need your help."

"Ah. Yeah, right." He settled back, sighing. "Office hours are on Monday only, two to five. You can sign up on my door."

"I can't wait that long," I said.

"Trust me, you can." He was already looking back at his computer screen, clicking on a link. "I've been teaching this class a long time, and I can tell you—"

"I know," I said, and something in my voice must have alerted him, because he looked up with sudden wariness as I finished: "You've been teaching it for forty years."

* * *

Ed Staggs's eyes did not turn red. His canines didn't flash; his face remained unchanged.

He said, "Wow. A freshman who actually knows how to use the library. Amazing."

"It wasn't that hard," I said. "You didn't even bother to change your name."

"Why should I?" He shrugged, still bonelessly relaxed in his chair. The chatter around us was unchanged, no one listening to our conversation as he said, "I like to keep things simple."

"Right," I said. "Simple. I know what you are."

His pale green eyes narrowed. "And?"

"My roommate's been bitten by a vampire," I said. "I need you to help me find out which one."

Ed Staggs blinked twice. Then he laughed. "Amanda," he said. "Amanda, Amanda, Amanda." He pushed aside his laptop and leaned forward across the table. "If you actually know what I am—"

"I do."

"—then why, exactly, do you think I'd help you track down another of my own kind?"

"Because you're different," I said. I ticked the points off on my fingers. "Stupid goatee. Bad hair. Sloppy clothes. Sitting in Espresso Royale instead of one of the bars..." His eyes narrowed. Before he could argue, I finished, "...and pretending to listen to an iPod instead of picking up undergrads."

He glared at me. "I seem to have picked one up without trying." Then he looked pointedly from my hair to my motorcycle jacket. "And speaking of bad clothes...?"

I ignored him. "You're not like the others."

"So, what? You think I'm a vegetarian hippie vampire? Stuck in the 60's forever?" He snorted.

I didn't look away. "No," I said. "But I think you have a different agenda than the others do."

He sat back, watching me. The earpods of his iPod still dangled from his ears. He should have looked harmless.

He didn't.

"Tell me about your roommate," he said. "Do I know her?"

"I doubt it." It was my turn to snort. "Aimee's fantasy is to be a model someday, if she's really, really lucky. She isn't the type to take philosophy classes."

He raised wispy eyebrows at me. "*You're* rooming with a wannabe model?"

I rolled my eyes. "You're still offended about the bad clothes comment?"

"I'm just surprised," he said.

"Don't be." I set my teeth together with a click. "Aimee and I aren't friends."

"Then why are you worried about her?"

"She's been bitten by a vampire," I said, "and she's not dead. As far as I know, it's only been once, but it might have been twice. And—"

"Aha," he said. "Third time's the charm."

"Right," I said. "I know how to use the library, remember? I looked it up."

"Smart girl." Ed Staggs picked up his espresso mug and

turned it slowly in his hands, still watching me. "So, if you're not friends, and you don't want to find yourself rooming with a vampire's servant, then why are you going to all this trouble for her? Why don't you just change rooms?"

"I tried. Housing said there weren't any openings this late in the semester."

"Got it," he said. He watched me for another minute, unblinking. Then he nodded infinitesimally. "So. Where's Aimee now?"

"It's a Wednesday night in East Lansing, and she's a freshman who wants to be a model. Where do you think she is?"

For the first time, he looked startled. "A bar? But if she's already been bitten once—"

"Exactly," I said. "That's where he—whoever he is—picked her up the first time, last weekend."

"Why'd you let her go back?"

I looked at him with contempt. "Let her? The only way I could have stopped her was by tying her up. And somehow, I didn't think getting myself arrested was going to help keep her from being bitten a third time."

"So you decided to go straight to the source." Ed Staggs smiled. It wasn't a pleasant smile, but I didn't have time to worry about it. He stood up, pulling out the earbuds. "Okay. Let's go."

"You're agreeing to help me?" I blinked. I hadn't even had the chance to make my offer yet—or my blackmail threat, if the offer hadn't worked. "What's the deal?"

"Oh, we'll figure the deal out later." He leaned down to turn off his computer, so that all I could see of him was his limp, greasy blonde hair. His voice was abstracted as he pressed buttons. "I'm sure I'll think of something."

Snow was falling through the night air in a soft, steady stream as we left the café, but some things are the same in every season: the line waiting outside the Blue Dragon stretched nearly a block down Grand River Avenue, and every single one of the waiting women was wearing a tank top or little babydoll T-shirt, without a winter coat or scarf in sight. As I looked at them—especially the ones who weren't even bothering to put on a show of cold as snow fell onto their bare arms—I shook my head in disgust.

How was it possible for anyone not to notice all the vampires in this town? And how had they become the ones in charge of fashion?

I headed for the back of the line, but Staggs set off in a different direction.

"What? You have a VIP pass?" I said.

He walked straight past the open door of the bar and into the alleyway just past it. "Not exactly."

I hesitated at the mouth of the alley. Stupid to think of it as an alley, really—it was only a short, covered passageway leading out to an open parking lot. But it was dark inside the passageway, and the line of waiting bar-bunnies outside were making way too much noise of their own to hear if anything happened...

The vampire laughed at me from the darkness. "What, you've thought better of your big plan already?"

I set my jaw hard and strode into the alley to join him. "My parents would kill me for this," I muttered.

"For which bit?" I couldn't see Staggs's face clearly in the darkness, but I could hear him smirk. "Going to a bar underage? Or doing it with an"—he dropped his voice suggestively—"older man?"

"I don't think you actually count as an older man," I said.

There was a moment of nonplussed silence.

"You're the one who looked me up. Forty years of teaching, remember?"

"Yeah, but you've been dead for all of them."

He made an irritated noise in the back of his throat. "Undead, actually."

"Whatever. That's forty years of living like a student," I said. "Sharing a house with a bunch of other guys? Wearing a stupid little goatee and jeans with holes in them and"—I thought back to how I'd found him in the café—"probably watching porn and getting into lots of internet flamewars? Personally, I don't think those forty years added a whole lot of maturity."

He didn't answer. But the air positively rippled with his irritation as he stalked out the other end of the alley in front of me.

There was a door in the wall just to the left of the alley,

looking out onto the parking lot. The only sign on it said, "No Entrance", but Staggs knocked anyway, and we only waited half a minute in the snow before it opened.

"Huh," said the man who'd opened it. "You." He was wearing a cook's apron, but his hair was lank, his fingernails looked dark with grime even in the faint light of the lamps over the parking lot, and I made a mental note not to eat anything while we were here.

He looked at me. "And...?"

"A friend," Staggs said. His lips twisted into a smile. "For tonight."

"Got it." The man stepped back to let us pass.

"You made it sound like I'm on tonight's menu," I muttered as I followed Staggs down a long, unlit flight of stairs.

The roof above the stairs was low and sloping, with weird symbols carved into the wood. Tight walls closed me in on either side. The cook shut the door above us with a click, and the last light disappeared.

"You're the one who asked for my help," Staggs said.

I scowled and concentrated on not tripping in the dark.

At least I knew the man behind me wasn't a vampire. Even in the dim light of the streetlamps, I'd seen the mark of old bites on his unwashed neck. Maybe if I showed Aimee the evidence of what another vampire's servant ended up looking like, it would frighten her into seeing sense.

On the other hand, this was the same woman who thought Britney Spears' latest comeback TV special was the most Deep and Meaningful thing she'd ever seen. So maybe common sense and Aimee just didn't exist in the same universe.

Staggs opened the door at the bottom of the stairs, and light burst through. We pushed our way through a crowded kitchen, full of workers and noise, where no one looked twice at us. In fact, at least a few of the workers were intentionally *not* looking at us. I glanced sideways at them, but they were bent over ovens and sinks, and I couldn't see their necks. The cook who'd let us in dropped away to go back to work, and Staggs cut straight across to the big swinging doors at the other end of the room. I followed after, just in time to keep them from slamming shut in my face.

Music blared straight into my ears from the speakers in the wall on either side of the doors and drowned out my groan of horror. Saccharine voices married a thumping beat, somewhere halfway between wannabe techno and bubblegum pop.

"Aimee is so not worth this," I muttered.

Staggs turned back, grinning. Vampire hearing really was excellent, unfortunately. "What, you don't like the beat?"

I stared at him. "You do?"

"Hell, no," he said. "I like the alternative scene." His gaze added the word: *Obviously*. "But this is what brings them all in, so..."

"...So this is what you guys play." I shook my head. "Is every bar in East Lansing owned by vampires?"

He shrugged. "You're the one who did all the research.

You tell me." His gaze went out across the sea of heads before us, bodies jumbled up into too-close proximity all throughout the big, open room. "So, where's your roomie?"

"No one says 'roomie' anymore," I said, but it was an empty jibe. I was searching, too. "She could be anywhere. How do these people breathe?"

"They're having fun," Staggs said. "C'mon. Don't they have any fun back where you come from?"

I gritted my teeth. "I come from Northern Michigan, not the end of the universe."

"Close enough." Staggs shook his head, looking more insufferably pleased than ever. "Lot of weirdos living up there in the wilds. Are your parents the hippie-dippie types, rednecks, apocalyptic end-of-the-world wackos, Michigan Militia nutjobs, or wannabe artists?"

I couldn't punch him if I wanted his help. So I just said as evenly as I could, "There's a lot of room for different belief systems up North."

"I bet." He looked smug. "End-of-the-world wackos, right? Holing up with shotguns and ammo and a thousand cans of food for when the UN finally invades...how did they let you come all the way down here for college?"

"My parents and I want different things," I said tightly. "Now, can we go look for Aimee, please? Because if she gets bitten again while we're hanging around here—"

"Cool down, Amanda. We'll find her." Staggs reached out and snagged the back of a passing waiter's shirt. "Hey, John.

We're looking for a girl named Aimee. She's—" He looked at me questioningly.

I sighed. Incredibly, I knew her stats. "Five-foot-eleven, two-foot-long blonde hair, size 4, 38D bust." I knew it all, because she'd made a point of telling me, the first day we moved into our room. It had been a defining moment in our roommate relationship. "She's wearing a very small pink tank top and tight blue jeans tonight."

"I'll bet she is," Staggs said. "Wow." He caught my glare and turned back to the waiter, lowering his voice. "She's been bitten at least once already."

The waiter's eyes widened. His hands were full with the two trays he was carrying, but he jerked his chin at the far end of the room. "She was over there fifteen minutes ago. I think Jeremy was on his way over to her."

"Jeremy?" I said.

But Staggs was already setting off across the crowded floor. I gritted my teeth and followed after, pushing my way through the press of arms and legs by brute force. The music pounding through the air shifted to a new, even more intrusive beat, topped by a panting female voice mimicking cries of ecstasy, and I thought that if I saw Aimee's vampire right now, I wouldn't even need a stake or holy water. I could take him out with my bare hands for putting me through this.

Throttling wasn't an option, though, because Aimee was gone by the time we reached the other side of the room. Ten minutes later, even I had to admit it: we weren't going to find her.

Damn it, damn it, damn it.

I wheeled on Staggs, balling my hands into fists. "Tell me who Jeremy is."

He shrugged, his glare still fixed on the crowd around us. "Who do you think?"

"Who do I think?" My voice started to spiral dangerously out of control. "I think he's a goddamn vampire! I think he's about to turn my roommate into his servant, if he hasn't done it already, and all because I didn't—"

I snapped my jaw shut, digging my fingernails into the palms of my hands. *Breathe, Amanda.*

I couldn't believe I was too late. And all because I'd wanted to prove a stupid, childish point to my parents, of all people, who weren't even here to see me...

"Look," Staggs said. He turned back to me, his lean shoulders stiffening with sudden resolution. "I know where we can go, if you really want to get your roommate back." He paused, cocking his head. "I know you don't think highly of her, but..."

"No," I said. Aimee might be the Queen of Vapid, but I was the idiot who'd thought I could bury my head in my books and pretend the vampires in East Lansing had nothing to do with me. I was in no position to throw stones...and even if I had been, I wasn't going to go back to bed in our room tonight and just wait for a strange vampire's servant to walk in on me. "Trust me. I want to get her back."

"Fine. In that case, come with me." He struck out toward the front exit, and, still cursing myself, I followed.

As soon as we reached the sidewalk outside, though, with

cold snow whipping through the night air, my head started to clear. I followed Staggs across Grand River to the edge of the university campus, but then I stopped and planted myself still, arms crossed. We were out of hearing of the bar bunnies across the street, and the walkway to the Union building was quiet and empty underneath the street lamp.

"Before we go any further, I want to know why you're helping me."

"Do you really think there's time for that?" He turned back to face me, hands loosely wrapped around the belt loops on his jeans. Ragged holes showed dark along the legs, letting in the snow, but for all that he reacted, it could have been a sunny July day on the beach. "Jeremy's got your roommate, and if you knew Jeremy like I do—"

"Exactly," I said. "You know Jeremy. You don't know me. So why are you helping me against him?"

He shrugged. "Because I liked your paper on Plato?"

I looked hard at him. "The fact that I'm an English major does not make me naïve or unworldly."

"Um..."

I ignored the look he was giving me. "You are not doing this as a favor to me. You don't even know what I was going to offer you in exchange."

He propped his shoulders against the lamppost, settling in. "Fine. We can stand here all night debating this if you want, while Jeremy bites Aimee a third time and takes on a new servant...or you can accept that I'm happy to score a point against the others—you're the one who said I was different from them—and we can go after your roommate. Which would you honestly prefer? Because, y'know, I'm a philosophy grad student, I live for debates like this." He snickered. "At least I used to. Now I un-die for them."

"Gahh." I closed my eyes on his smug expression. "I really hate this."

"You were the one who came after me, Amanda. I was just sitting minding my own business in my favorite café, bothering nobody, just—"

"Fine!" I said. "Fine. But I don't trust you."

"You're the one who did the research," he said, and straightened away from the lamppost with a jaunty hop. "I wouldn't trust me, either. This way." He headed off, into the university campus.

There was a deep blanket of snow covering the field across from the Union building. We trudged through it without speaking. It was only when Staggs pushed open the door of the tall building on the other side of the field, letting out a deafening blur of sound, that I wrested my gritted teeth apart to speak again.

"Jeremy takes his dates to the *music practice building* to make out?"

Staggs snorted. "Good one, Amanda. No, our Jer's a bit too smooth for that." The door swung shut behind us, and he leapt straight down the first six steps of the staircase leading to the basement, where the sounds of a hundred competing musical instruments were coming from. I waited at the top of the stairs, wincing at the cacophony.

"Then what are we doing here?"

Staggs paused on the next landing down. "This is how we get to the council."

I stared at him. "The vampire council?!"

Three girls pushed past me, holding flute cases. They didn't say anything, but their faces were pink from the effort of holding back their reaction. As soon as they turned out of sight on the stairs, their giggles burst out, floating through the air back to me. They probably thought I was insane.

Staggs just gave me a thumbs-up sign. "Got it," he said. "They're the only ones who can stop Jeremy. So come on!"

This was a really, really bad idea.

The door at the bottom of the stairs led us into a maze of white corridors lined with tiny, windowed practice rooms like cells in a beehive. Every room we passed had a piano in it, and every room had a person in it, too, looking either intent or purely miserable as they played one of a variety of instruments with total dedication, despite the fact that it was ten o'clock on the most popular bar-hopping night of the week. Obviously, the music professors had all of their students enslaved as surely as any of the vampires' servants.

I didn't have much time to think about it, though, because at the end of the second corridor, Staggs pulled out a key and unlocked the first door I'd seen that didn't have a window in it. This door was wooden and solid, without so much as a sign on it, and it swung open to reveal a new corridor—not white this time, but lined with a darker wood and carved with the same weird symbols I'd seen in the staircase leading down to the vampire's bar. It was, of course, completely unlit.

Great. The door closed behind us, shutting out the bright white light of the practice building. I said,

"And how exactly am I supposed to get through here?"

Staggs snickered. He was closer to me than I'd realized, his cold breath brushing against my cheek. "You can hold my hand, if you want."

"No, thank you." I reached into my pocket and pulled out my bulky key ring. It only took a few fumbles before I managed to press the button on the mini-flashlight that hung off it. A thin beam of light pierced the darkness ahead.

Staggs stepped away from me. "Quite the girl scout. Or is it only the boy scouts who are supposed to be prepared?"

"It's a good key ring," I said. "My parents gave it to me when I left home. It's even got a Swiss Army knife on it."

"Everything you could ever need, then." He stuck his hands in his jeans pockets and stalked forward. "I wouldn't count on a Swiss army knife stopping our Jeremy, though."

"Good to know," I said, and rolled my eyes as I followed him down the dark corridor.

We walked the next few minutes in silence, as the corridor wove around various turns. I was trying to track where we were—maybe somewhere underneath the university library?—when the corridor finally ended in a big, black door. *Completely* black: it was made of what looked like pure onyx, shiny even in the pale glow of the flashlight. Vampires can be so dramatic. I wished my heart weren't speeding up in reaction. My breath shortened in my chest.

Staggs lifted his hand to knock.

I couldn't do it.

"Wait!" I put one hand on his thin arm to stop him. "Look..." I hated how breathy my voice sounded, like some horror movie heroine. He obviously liked it, though; his lips curved in a smile as he turned back to me. "Is there any other way to get to Jeremy? Because seriously, it would be a much better idea for everybody if—"

The door swung open.

"Did someone say my name?" said the vampire on the other side of it.

Highlighted by the mellow glow of a dozen fat candles inside the room, his hair was a thick, soft blonde, the kind I immediately wanted to run my hands through; his über-preppy sweater and jeans came straight out of a J. Crew catalogue, the kind Aimee always sighed over; and even as I thought that, I spotted my roommate just past him, tied up and gagged against the pitch-black wall, her big, blue eyes filled with terror.

Hell. I really couldn't turn back after all.

Resigned, I pushed past Jeremy, who fell back, looking surprised. "Um..." he began, and then looked past me at Staggs. His voice sharpened. "Hey. What do you think you're doing here?"

I was already scoping out the diamond-shaped room and the six vampires spread out around it in various poses of coolness, disdain, and perfect style, like a collection of New York models caught in mid-photo shoot. But I heard Staggs answer,

"I've brought you guys a gift."

Aha. And there was his motivation, finally figured out.

I turned, feeling all six gazes focus on me as the vampires around me straightened into predatory interest. My eyes met Staggs's. "So much for helping me because you liked my paper, huh?"

He shrugged. "I did like your paper. That's why I thought it wouldn't hurt to have you around here for another forty years or so. I don't get to talk to that many smart people, especially in this community."

I heard a hiss behind me; next to Staggs, Jeremy's perfect features tightened in irritation.

"Ah," I said. "And that charming attitude of yours would be why the other vampires haven't been hanging out with you lately? Is that why you need to bribe them with a gift?"

The female vampire behind me laughed, a tinkling sound that grated against every single nerve ending in my body. I had to tighten my spine to keep from turning around as I felt her edge closer.

Jeremy said, "So, you've noticed what a little pain he is, too?" He started toward me, his brown eyes warming. My legs wanted to go rubbery in reaction. I wouldn't let them. "You obviously have good taste," he said, "whoever you are..."

"Amanda," Staggs said to Jeremy. "Her name is Amanda. She's from the middle of Nowhere, Northern Michigan. Her parents are wackos who won't be able to talk anyone into making a fuss...and she came to me tonight, because she'd figured out what was happening with her roommate over there." Staggs jerked his head at Aimee, who was crying silently against the wall. "Amanda already knew all about us. She's smart, and she knows how to do her research. I know you didn't think much of the last few I brought you—"

"The last thing we needed in our group were more geeks like you," Jeremy said, and his chiseled lips lifted in a frat-boy sneer. "They were barely worth using as servants."

Staggs scowled. "Well, believe me, this one's worth it."

"You know, I think you might actually be right this time." Jeremy walked a slow circle around me. His voice melted into my senses like chocolate. "She'd need a few tips on her dress sense, of course—"

"Obviously," Staggs said.

I stared at his ripped jeans. "I beg your pardon?"

Jeremy laughed. "Yeah, she's cute." He leaned in to sniff my neck, and I closed my eyes against the cloud of pure pheromones. "I vote yes." He stepped back, looking at the others. "Well?"

"Why not?" said the woman behind me. "But I want to be the one to change her."

"I don't think so," said Jeremy. He put one hand on my shoulder, lightly possessive.

Staggs said, "Hey, I'm the one who brought her in! Shouldn't I get to—?"

"Staggs!" I said sharply. "You don't want to do this."

"Yes, I do," he said.

"No, you don't." I reached inside my leather jacket, sliding my fingers toward the inner pocket. "Just help me get out, and I'll—"

They were all laughing now.

"Sweetheart," Jeremy purred, and stroked my cheek. "There is no way out."

"Oh, is she going to try to fight us off now?" the woman behind me said. "This should be fun. Staggs did say she had done her research..."

"Funny thing about that, Amanda," Staggs said. He was grinning so hard, his little goatee actually quivered with his amusement. "All those stories about stakes and garlic and holy water? Total crap, all of them. Garlic might have worked to hold off English vampires, I guess, just because they didn't like the taste..."

"My favorite flavor," the vampiress behind me murmured, stepping closer.

"Holy water only works on vampires with a serious case of Catholic guilt..."

"Not a problem for me," Jeremy said, and smiled into my eyes.

"And stakes?" Staggs shrugged. "Trust me, that's not something you even want to try. It would just be embarrassing. Think about it. You might have read up on *Dracula* or watched some *Buffy* as research, but do you really think you could try shoving some crazy, heavy wooden stake all the way through a pair of ribs and manage to aim it directly into a human heart on the first go?" He shook his head. "I don't think so."

"You're right," I said, and I looked him straight in the eye. "The only way it could ever work was if a person had spent her entire life being trained to do it perfectly. Which would be crazy, right? I mean, her parents would have to be complete wackos, wouldn't they?"

He blinked. "Well..."

"I told you there's a lot of room for different belief systems up North," I said.

And I pulled out my stake from my pocket.

I really, really hated doing exactly what my parents had wanted when they sent me down to East Lansing for college. I'd been so determined to ignore the vampires and just be a normal student.

If the vampires had ignored me back, it might have worked.

I wiped off the stake before I untied the ropes and gags that bound Aimee. There was a fresh, second bite on her neck, but not a third. They must have been saving that for the end of the evening's entertainment.

She was shaking so hard, I had to hold her up. We moved across the room at turtle speed. She let out a girly little scream when her high-heeled boots brushed against the cloud of dust that used to be Jeremy.

"Next time," I said, "please try to pick out a guy who at least has a heartbeat, okay?"

She glared at me, her lips trembling. "You are such a freak, Amanda."

So. At least our roommate relationship hadn't changed.

Hey, if I was really lucky, maybe she would be the one Housing assigned away to another room, whenever a vacancy finally opened up. I really wouldn't mind having a single for a while.

I paused before I closed the door on the diamond-shaped room that had once held the vampire council of East Lansing. The last pile of dust had a single blond speck in the middle—a fleck of hair from Staggs' goatee.

Thank goodness for small mercies, my grandma had always said, after retiring from her own hunting days.

Tomorrow was a Thursday, but for once I would be able to sleep in.

My philosophy class was definitely canceled.

A Cup of Comfort

It was the finest teahouse in Trevanne; everyone agreed on that. The ancient Dragon Queen's loyal courtiers would buy their tea nowhere else, for the quality of the tealeaves was unmatched and the blend was one that no other teahouse in the city could provide. The courtiers, all powerful men and women with subtle minds sharpened by decades of scheming, spent many a happy afternoon gathered around the central hearth, spinning political webs over steaming cups of tea while sitting in their favorite armchairs, which had worn over the years into the shapes of their familiar bodies.

The younger, wilder, and more dissatisfied members of the court, who cared far less for tealeaves than for wine, still followed the aging crown prince's lead in spending long raucous evenings at the teahouse, bypassing the fire-lit rooms inside for the pleasures of the lush, beautifully laid-out open courtyard filled with lanterns and pink–blossomed magnolia trees, where the most popular musicians in the city played nearly every night. The fires burned cozily within the teahouse, keeping it the perfect temperature, never too hot even at the height of summer; the magnolias bloomed year-round in the warm inner courtyard even when three feet of snow piled up in the streets outside.

It had been the finest teahouse in Trevanne for generations, by then. No one thought to question its magic anymore. The owner had seen to that, long ago, with promises and threats and a contract that had nearly been forgotten, by now.

But that contract had not expired.

Of course, few people had ever met its owner in this new generation. The current manager, Florian—a tall, slender man with deep brown skin and a cool, confident smile, who had spent his first years on the streets of Trevanne before being taken in by the teahouse as a child—was famous throughout the city for his dry humor, which he applied equally to all classes of society, and for his invariably calm demeanor in the face of even the most questionable customer behavior. There were stories traded, even now, of his particularly witty remarks when faced with an elephant brought in from one lord's menagerie for the crown prince's birthday five years earlier. Even those customers from the highest families in the land vied like eager children for the honor of Florian's conversation when they visited.

Some of those customers, by now, no doubt thought he was the owner—indeed, the crown prince's set even referred to the teahouse as "Florian's" sometimes, when making casual appointments for a party or a duel. The Dragon Queen's own courtiers would never be so rude or so informal; but even they would have to squint and frown for a long time to remember, vaguely, an indistinct figure in the past, hidden under layers of gauzy drapery, bowing and withdrawing—most politely—from their memories.

"A good chap," they might say at last, of the teahouse's owner. "Or...was it a lady, after all? Well, no matter. They're the only ones who sell the right blend, nowadays. I don't even know where they find the stuff, now that the ships don't leave the harbor anymore."

But they were given no explanation, for Florian only smiled mysteriously when asked those questions—and no one but Florian ever walked up the small, discreet staircase that was hidden behind the kitchen, anymore.

...until one night, in the middle of one of the crown prince's rowdiest parties yet, a plain, dark sedan chair arrived at the back entrance to the teahouse, which only the most trusted staff was ever allowed to use.

Two servants lowered the chair to the ground. One knocked on the door, after a quick glance around the darkened alleyway; the other stood by the closed sedan chair with her cloak flipped back and one hand set, waiting, on the hilt of a sword that had clearly seen long use.

In the distance, there was the sound of breaking glass, and a responsive gale of laughter. The two servants glanced at each other, eyebrows raised expressively. The woman sighed and shrugged, infinitesimally. The man glanced warily at the curtained windows of the sedan chair...but there was not so much as a twitch of the curtains to give any sign of the inhabitant's reaction.

The door to the teahouse opened, and a young girl looked out at them with watchful dark eyes.

"Tell your master—" the man began, holding out a folded piece of paper.

But the girl only shook her head, stepping back. "Her Majesty is already expected," she said quietly. "If she would follow me?"

The man's eyes widened, and he reached for his sword, his gaze darting around the alleyway in open suspicion. "How—?"

His voice cut off as the sedan chair's door opened and a shrouded figure stepped out.

"Of course I will come," said the Dragon Queen. Her voice was muted beneath the layers of dark cloth that covered her, but a ripple of amusement sounded as she added, "I should hope my old friend has not forgotten my favorite blend, after all these decades. I shall be disappointed if there isn't a fresh pot awaiting me."

"Of course, Your Majesty," said the girl, and dipped a low curtsey before leading the shrouded figure up the stairs.

The queen's servants followed close behind, jaws stiff and hands ready at their sides. At the top of the staircase, the woman held out one hand to halt her mistress on the narrow landing, and the man made to step between her and the door.

"No need for that." Heavy irony rang in the Dragon Queen's tone. "Believe me, there is no safer place for me in this city. Only point me in the right direction, and the two of you may wait out here."

"But—" the man began.

The woman put one hand on his arm and bowed, although her face, too, was tight with frustration. "Of course, Your Majesty."

The teahouse girl knocked softly on the door, then ran lightly down the stairs, skipping around the Dragon Queen and her guards.

"Come in," a voice called, from inside the room. "Your tea is waiting for you."

The heavily draped figure moved forward, guided by her female guard's helping hand...and a moment later, the door closed behind her, leaving the two guards standing alone, in simmering silence, on the landing.

Inside the room, a fire burned. A low table was drawn up before it. At the table sat a comfortably round, middle-aged woman, her skin creased with laugh lines around her eyes and mouth, and her eyes warm.

"Come now, my old friend," said the Dragon Queen. "You know you needn't disguise yourself with me." She pulled off her own layers of veils, and they slipped to the floor by her feet. A girl who looked no more than twenty stepped free of them and walked gracefully across the room.

The older-looking woman who awaited her gave a small

shrug and smiled ruefully. "Very well," she said. "If we're making ourselves *quite* comfortable tonight..."

She lifted one hand to her face, and rubbed her forehead.

Skin peeled aside under her fingers, revealing glimmering, luminescent scales underneath.

"Much better," said the Dragon Queen, as she took her seat. "I should hate not to see each other clearly after all these years."

"Oh?" Her hostess cocked her head, golden eyes snapping in the reptilian manner, from side to side, as she blinked. "Some would say that illusion is the key to true happiness. Otherwise, why wear those veils at all? Why not reveal yourself as you still are to your people?"

"And to my son?" The Dragon Queen's smile was faint. "My son, who wakes up every day hoping to finally inherit my crown...and curses every morning when he finds me still alive?"

Her hostess tsk'd. "Florian tells me he's lost nearly all his hair, now. Carelessness. He always was a whimsical boy, as I recall."

"Mm." The Dragon Queen leaned forward to lift the lid of the teapot that sat between them. She sniffed, appreciatively, her long hair falling around her face. "Bliss, as usual."

"As always," said the owner of the teahouse. "Didn't I promise you that, all those years ago? Perfect safety, forevermore. Everything you humans want."

"And the contract has been kept on both sides." The

Dragon Queen set one hand on the intricately carved teapot as she set its lid back in place. "Shall I pour, this time?"

"Nonsense. You are my guest." The dragon reached out with long, sharp, delicately curving claws and tipped the teapot once and then again, hot tea pouring into the two small cups. "A cup of youth, forevermore. A cup of comfort, to reassure you of yet another peaceful and prosperous decade."

A sudden, raucous roar of male laughter rose beneath them, echoing through the floorboards, and the dragon let out a hissing laugh, a thin line of smoke escaping her nostrils. "And, so I hear, another birthday for your son."

"He's celebrated so many, now," said the Dragon Queen softly. She lifted her cup to her lips, inhaling the sweet-scented steam. "I remember thinking of that first cup I drank as his birthday present, though he was only hours old at the time."

"You couldn't have given him a better gift." The dragon lifted her own cup. "After all, he would never have survived the month without it. You assured his safety from the outside world, along with that of all of your people."

"The outside world," the Dragon Queen mused. "Do you know what's been happening outside our city, all these years? I do find myself wondering, from time to time."

The dragon shrugged, with a whispering of scales beneath her gown. "Empires rise. Empires fall. Only yours remains beautiful and true forevermore."

"A comfort indeed," murmured the Dragon Queen,

gazing down into her cup. "For all of my people. And for you, connected to us all through my blood..."

The dragon's teeth gleamed in a smile. "Have no fear, Your Majesty. My own purposes have been served very well by our agreement."

"Indeed." The Dragon Queen swirled the pale green tea in her cup, her gaze distant. "I used to wonder, you know, why you fought so hard to persuade me to our bargain. Not that I wasn't grateful, of course. With my poor husband murdered and enemies everywhere, how could I not be grateful for the salvation you offered? It felt like a miracle."

"And I am grateful, too," said the dragon smoothly, "for this cozy home and loving bond to you and your people. That's all I've ever wanted, you know. A safe home that I can provide for my guests."

"Where everyone gathers," murmured the Dragon Queen, "from my court *and* my son's court, too. Everyone drinking your tea and celebrating their finest moments. All those fights and dramas and little worlds of human emotions..." She cocked her head. "Did you know that there used to be stories, in my childhood, about dragons who actually ate people?"

"Ha." The dragon's eyes gleamed. "Pure superstition and nonsense."

"Oh, I know." The Dragon Queen smiled. "I worked that out decades ago, in the oldest scrolls I could find in our most deeply buried archives. It's not human flesh you care for, is it?

It's human feelings...and human souls. Bound to you through me, and through our contract, forevermore."

A long line of smoke hissed out from the sides of the dragon's mouth as she considered her guest, her golden eyes unblinking. Then, finally, she smiled. "Ah, we know each other so well, do we not? We are the oldest and truest friends in this city."

"It's true," said the Dragon Queen. "No one else knows me as you do."

"And no one else knows what you've done for your people," said the dragon. "What you do every decade to renew it. And now..." She looked over the Dragon Queen's shoulder at the tall clock that stood in the corner. "It's time, Your Majesty. You wouldn't want to wait too long."

"Ah, no. That wouldn't do at all, would it?" The Dragon Queen's lips twisted, as the clock ticked behind her. "No drink before midnight...would mean no youth left for me, wouldn't it? Although it wouldn't hurt you, really, I suppose. Everyone always said, in all the old stories, that there was no way to truly hurt a dragon."

The dragon's golden eyes slitted and blinked, twice. "Even my magic is subject to the rules of our agreement." Her claws clicked, once and then again, against her teacup. "The bubble that holds your city fast, renewed here every decade. Should the midnight hour pass..." Her eyes snapped, her nostrils flaring. "You shouldn't care for the sensation of so many years passing at once, Your Majesty. Nor would your vulnerable, cosseted little city cope well with its sudden rediscovery by all those old enemies at the moment of your death."

"My old enemies. How could I forget?" The Dragon Queen sighed, her hand sinking back toward the table. "There seemed to be so many enemies, then, and so little I could do about them. Trapped in bed after childbirth with the fever raging through me, threats everywhere, my husband gone, my baby in danger, and only your tea giving me any respite..."

"You're safe from all of them now," said the dragon, her golden gaze on the queen's cup. "Don't torment yourself by thinking on the past."

"But what of you, my friend?" the Dragon Queen said. "Which enemies were you fleeing, I wonder, when you came up with your marvelous plan to hide us away from the outside world?"

"Me?" The dragon's claws tightened around her own cup. "Why would I have had any enemies?"

"Why indeed?" asked the Dragon Queen. "And yet, dragons were once feared, and stories told. There were even records kept, and warnings left, though those were buried so deeply over time that they were considered lost forever."

"Time..." The dragon's gaze moved to the clock, and her teeth set together with a click. "We have only two minutes left until midnight, Your Majesty. Two minutes for us both to drink our tea, if your youth is to be preserved and your safe rule is to continue. We must wait until later to catch up on idle gossip."

"Of course." The Dragon Queen smiled faintly. "Safety is always paramount, is it not?"

Smoke panted faintly from the dragon's mouth. Her teeth glinted, sharp and long. "One minute, now," she said, her body tense. "Will you drink, and protect your city?"

"Of course," said the Dragon Queen. "I will always protect my people."

She lifted the cup to her mouth and drank it all in one long, slow sip.

The dragon sucked her own tea down with more haste than grace. "There," she said. Her tail twitched with visible relief against the floor. "You've done the right thing, Your Majesty, and won back your youth."

"I have," said the Dragon Queen. She did not move. "But I am not a young girl anymore."

"Nonsense." The dragon grinned, her teeth gleaming, as she sank back in her chair. "No one would look at you now and think you'd aged so much as a day."

"Except for you," said the Dragon Queen. "Or have you given in to the lure of illusions, too, my old friend?"

The dragon's claws twitched. She glanced down at them, as though startled. "I beg your pardon?"

"My son celebrates his sixty-sixth birthday today," said the Dragon Queen. Her face was clear and unlined, but her dark eyes held all her years. "I haven't been able to show him my face without a veil since he was seven years old. Too many questions would have been asked, as the years passed—and not by him alone."

"Your Majesty..." The dragon blinked twice, and then a third time, her scales shivering. "Your Majesty..."

"I should have asked more questions," said the Dragon Queen. "But I was only a girl, then, and I was frightened and alone, and feverish, too...despite all that healing tea I drank. I have had decades to find the answers for myself, since then." She shook her head a fractional amount, then slumped as if the effort had exhausted her. "Those records were not buried so far after all, you see. Not for a woman who has 'forever' in her grasp...and more than one lifetime of regrets to answer for."

The dragon's claws rattled against each other as a convulsive shiver wracked her body. "What," asked the dragon through gritted teeth, "were you looking for, exactly?"

"Revenge," whispered the Dragon Queen, as her hands shook and her teacup rattled against its saucer. "I was not the only one who drank your tea, remember? You made a special blend for my husband, too."

"He was poisoned by your enemies," hissed the dragon.

"So he was." The Dragon Queen bared her teeth in a ferocious smile. "But those enemies weren't outside our kingdom after all...even if you tricked a frightened young girl into thinking so, once upon a time."

"But how?" The dragon clawed at the table as she tipped forward, but it wasn't enough to stop her slow descent. "*How?*" she repeated, in a hoarse whisper, smoke flooding out through her nostrils and ears as she fell toward the floor. "Nothing can hurt a dragon. Nothing!"

The Dragon Queen tried to shake her head, but she couldn't manage it. "Ah, my old friend," she whispered. "Perfect safety was an illusion after all, for both of us. Two weeks ago, I finally found the records I'd been hunting for ever since I first realized the truth." Her lips twitched in the faint, unmistakable attempt at a smile. "I made the dragonsbane myself...and I dropped it into our tea when I opened the lid of the pot."

"But..." The dragon stiffened against the floor, eyes flaring wide in outrage and disbelief. "But you..."

"Yes," sighed the Dragon Queen. "We are that much alike, after all. Dragonsbane will kill me, too. But you were wrong about humans. Change isn't the worst thing that can happen to us. Sometimes..."

She stopped as a gasp of pain was torn out of her, breaking through her pretense of calm. Moaning, she rocked in her seat, her face taut with pain. But she still managed to finish, in a thread of a whisper: "Sometimes...the worst thing of all...is hearing hatred in your own son's voice for all the power you've stolen from him. And knowing that that hatred will last...*forever*."

The dragon twisted on the floor. Her jaw opened. Her claws clenched...

Her golden eyes went dull, as her body began to burn.

The Dragon Queen let out a laugh that held a drop of blood. "A cup...of comfort...after all," she whispered.

She wrenched open her trembling hand. Her empty teacup fell to the floor.

Laughter echoed below the floorboards.

"Happy birthday," the Dragon Queen whispered. "Finally."

Her eyes closed and her body crumpled as the dragon across from her burned and burned.

The queen's guards were the first to smell the flames, moments later, from their position in the stairwell. They broke the door down, but it was too late.

The Dragon Queen's body was never found, no matter how many guards her grieving son commanded to search the ruins of the teahouse afterward. All that anyone ever discovered, in the seat closest to her charred veils, was a pile of strangely sweet-smelling dust...a dust that smelled to the new king, when he ran it through his fingers, strangely of the past...of safety....

...of his mother's arms wrapped around him, long ago, and of a face that he couldn't even remember anymore.

The Dragon King pulled his age-spotted hand out from the wooden box that they had brought him, full of the dust that they had found. His eyes were red from days and nights of weeping.

"Enough," he whispered, in a voice gone hoarse. "Enough."

There was no more time for searching, or for loss.

Ships had been sighted on the horizon, for the first time that almost anyone in the city could remember.

Messengers had already arrived, traveling from neighboring city-states that had turned to long-distant legends by the time of the Dragon King's youth. They bore letters offering opportunities of trade, of reunion...and of danger.

"Enough," the Dragon King repeated, turning on his heel. "I need my advisors. *Now.* And for God's sake, man, bring us all some tea!"

But when the advisors all gathered in his meeting room half an hour later, they sighed at the sight of their dull, courtly surroundings. Old and new, every one of them thought back nostalgically to the golden-tinted, perfect past, when any significant meeting could only ever have taken place in a single setting in Trevanne.

There would never be another teahouse like it.

Dreaming Harry

Making a bad night even worse, Elizabeth Nichols woke at 3 a.m. with an unmistakable feeling of nameless, creeping dread. A cold chill brushed her cheek.

Bloody hell.

She opened her eyes with deep reluctance.

An ancient, tentacled horror as old as time was lurking in the corner of the room.

She moaned and kicked her sleeping husband. "Your turn."

"Mwha?" Dan fought his way up out of the cocoon of duvets he'd buried himself in after their last wake-up. His hair stuck out in all directions; he focused blearily on the horror across the room, then flopped onto his back, groaning. "How can it be my turn? I went last time."

"You're the one who left that Lovecraft book where he could find it." Elizabeth buried her face in her pillow and squeezed her eyes shut. "You deal with the results."

She heard the scuffle of duvets being shoved aside, and then a thump followed by a yelp—Dan's bare feet hitting the floor. *That* must have been chilled by the horror, too. Elizabeth wrapped her duvet more tightly around herself, shivering at the very thought of it. Her husband's curses filled the frigid air as he stumbled down the hallway to their son's room.

After a minute, she couldn't help herself. She rolled over and cracked her eyes open to peek.

The horror was still there, exuding a miasma of turgid hopelessness and fear. Its tentacles drooped against the floor.

"You'll be gone soon," Elizabeth told it. "I hope."

She waited a full twenty minutes before it finally disappeared, though. Dan stumbled back into the room a few moments later, yawning.

"I told him they were completely misunderstood," he said. "Lovecraft got it all wrong. They're big cuddly toys, really. Terribly shy, like bunny rabbits."

"Probably vegetarian, too," Elizabeth mumbled. "Lucky for us."

Dan slid into bed, wrapping himself back up in his cocoon. His voice was muffled by his duvets. "Dr. Margo says none of his dreams can actually hurt us."

"Easy for Dr. Margo to say," Elizabeth muttered.

But the bedroom was already warming up, and when she woke up again it was nearly seven. There was a thumping sound in the corner of the room, but that only came from a gathering of bunnies, playing some elaborate hopping game with Elizabeth's shoes.

She pulled the curtains open, waited for the bunnies to disappear in the sunlight, then picked up her shoes to examine them. Apart from a few pellets in one of her Skechers, they were fine.

"Success," she said, and headed for the kitchen to make coffee.

Harry was already there, eating Weetabix with the jar of sugar sitting open beside him and a comic book lying open on the table. Elizabeth eyed the lurid illustrations with foreboding.

If any women that well-endowed showed up in their bedroom at night, she wasn't sure Dan would agree to send them away.

Still, Dr. Margo was very clear that they had to let Harry exercise his imagination, so Elizabeth didn't confiscate the comic book. She only dropped a kiss onto Harry's mussed-up brown hair and tried not to wince as he spilled a spoonful of Weetabix and milk onto the table.

"Mum!" He swivelled around, spilling more milk in an arc. "I had the coolest dreams."

"I know," Elizabeth said. Then she heard the sourness in her own voice and sighed. "Tell me about them, darling."

He did, chattering away in the background as she made her coffee and toast and peered through the window at the birdfeeder, which a squirrel was currently raiding.

Too bad they couldn't send Harry's dreams after that squirrel. See how many seeds he'd want to steal after a Cthulhoid horror came after him . . . or a hooded, dark rider, the kind who'd screamed in the corner of her bedroom all night after Harry had watched *The Fellowship of the Ring* with his friend Simon last Saturday.

Simon's mum hadn't taken Bennerol during her pregnancy. She didn't have to worry about her son's dreams.

Lucky cow.

"Mum!" Harry said. "Are you even listening to me?"

"Of course I am," Elizabeth said automatically. "You were saying—"

The doorbell rang just in time, before she had to hazard a guess. "I'll just get that," she said, and scooped the sugar jar out of Harry's reach as she left.

She was still holding it when she opened the door and found Dr. Margo standing on the doorstep, next to a dark-haired man in a tailored charcoal suit, a wide-brimmed hat, sunglasses, and the kind of gentleman's gloves that Elizabeth had only ever seen in movies.

Elizabeth glanced down at her own decidedly untailored, five-year-old M&S pajamas, which had a fresh milk stain on one knee, courtesy of Harry's breakfast. "Ah . . ."

"Elizabeth!" Dr. Margo beamed as she stepped forward, forcing Elizabeth to move back. "I'm sorry to interrupt you so early, dear, but we wanted to be sure to find you at home. Elizabeth is always so busy," she added to the man behind her, as she bustled through the doorway. "Always on the go, aren't you, dear?"

"Ah . . . I suppose so?" Elizabeth thought of the state of the living room, which she'd been too tired to tidy the night before, and rallied her energy. "I'm sorry, but we're actually in the middle of having breakfast now, so perhaps—"

"Oh, don't mind us! This is what the health service is for, you know—giving you a helping hand just when you need it. And it'll be good to observe Harry in his natural habitat, so to speak. Always meeting him in the office is so impersonal, don't you think?"

Elizabeth gritted her teeth and gave in. Dr. Margo's companion had remained on the doorstep, with punctilious courtesy; she waved him in, sighing. "Would you like any coffee?" she asked.

Dr. Margo swept ahead of her down the hallway. "Tea for me, dear. Milk but no sugar. Nothing for my colleague, though."

"Are you sure?" Elizabeth asked, trailing behind them into the kitchen. "I have decaf if you'd prefer."

The dark-haired man turned and smiled at her. "Thank you," he said. He had a heavy accent, which sounded Eastern European. "But I do not drink . . . coffee. Or tea, for that matter."

"I see," said Elizabeth, and cursed the fact that Dan had already left for work. He'd taken off the first two weeks of Harry's summer holiday while she'd stayed at the office. During those weeks, no officious health workers had shown up, and as far as she could tell, they'd spent most of the time playing video games and eating cinnamon rolls from a tin. Now, of course, it was her turn.

She pasted a smile onto her face, and said, "Harry, Dr. Margo's come to see us. And she's brought . . . ?"

"My colleague," Dr. Margo said, sitting down in the chair beside Harry. "From the government. Everyone's so interested in our Bennerol babies, you know."

At the word "babies," Harry gave her an outraged look and scooted his chair away from her. Elizabeth didn't blame him. It was a different word that had caught her own attention, though. She'd been in the middle of setting down the sugar jar, but now her hand tightened instinctively around it.

"From the government?" she said. She tucked the sugar jar up against her stomach. "Which branch of the government would be interested in Harry?"

"Oh, you needn't worry about that, dear!" Dr. Margo tittered, tipping her head back. "Why, you look as if you're thinking of some terrible MI5 conspiracy—science fiction films and the like. We're nothing like that. No, indeed! Isn't that a funny idea?" she said to her colleague.

"Ha," he said. "Ha. Ha." He drew out a chair, pulled it into the shadiest corner of the room, and dusted it off carefully with one gloved hand. "Very amusing indeed," he said, and tipped his hat to cover more of his face.

Bloody hell. Definitely MI5, Elizabeth thought. Or was it MI6? Dan was the one who would know about all that. He liked to read political thrillers when he wasn't reading terrible horror stories that sent Harry's dreams haywire.

She inched toward the telephone in the corner. "Let me just give my husband a call," she said. "I'm sure he'd like to be here for our discussion."

"Dear Dan," Dr. Margo said. "Such a good father. So involved. But you needn't drag him home from work just for us. We can explain it all to him when he comes home tonight."

Elizabeth blinked. "We can?"

"Yes, yes. This is in the nature of a surprise inspection, you see. Of course we all know that you two are doing a splendid job in terribly difficult circumstances, but not everyone in the government completely understands that—or understands just how these difficult Bennerol babies could possibly be managed in a home environment."

Harry looked across at Elizabeth with big eyes. "Am I difficult, Mum?"

"Of course not, darling," Elizabeth told him, and offered up a silent novena in apology for her shameless lie.

"You see?" Dr. Margo turned to her colleague. "Didn't I tell you she's handling it all marvellously? And that's just what you'll see for yourself tonight."

Elizabeth set the sugar jar carefully down on the counter. "I'm sorry, I don't quite understand. Do you mean that you're planning to actually stay the night? Both of you?"

"You'll barely even notice we're here," Dr. Margo said. "Well, apart from having to cover up the mirrors, of course.

But that's just a silly little preference of my colleague's, nothing to worry about. We won't interfere at all in your routines—we're only here to observe, you know. Think of us as being like that TV show—*Big Brother*, isn't that the one? Only without the cameras, of course."

"Of course," her colleague echoed. "Ha. Ha. Cameras. As if we would want any of those turned on."

"Ahem." Dr. Margo gave him an admonishing look and turned back to Elizabeth. "We all want to lay those silly official worries to rest, don't we?"

"But we're not really prepared—I mean, we don't have a guest bedroom, and the living room isn't—"

"Oh, don't worry about any of that," Dr. Margo said. "My colleague doesn't sleep much anyway."

"Bennerol babies are creatures of the night," her colleague said. "So we must spend the night awake to understand him, must we not?"

"Of course," Elizabeth said faintly. She reached into the sugar jar and dug out a spoonful for her coffee that would have made even Harry quake.

She was going to need it.

"What the hell is going on?" Dan hissed, eight hours later. He'd dragged her into the kitchen, promising the others tea, and closed the door behind them. "Why is Dr. Margo making Lego towers with Harry in our living room? Who's that bloke dressed up like the Invisible Man in the corner? Why's the hallway mirror covered with a pillowcase? And damn it, why didn't you warn me about any of this before I got home? If I'd known social services was visiting, I wouldn't have been carrying a case of cider when I walked through the door. Now they probably think we're alcoholics!"

"I couldn't help it." Elizabeth pushed the kitchen door back open so that she could hear Harry's piping voice. Reassuringly (under the circumstances), he was cackling with manic glee. She heard the telltale crashes of Dr. Margo's Lego towers being bashed over by his newest inventions: giant multi-coloured Lego frogs of Doom. She dreaded to think how much space one of those might take up in the bedroom at night. For once, though, sleep was the least of her concerns.

"They've been here all day," she whispered. "I thought about trying to ring you from the toilet, but Dr. Margo looked at me like I was a pervert when I said I wanted to take Harry in with me, and I didn't want to leave him alone with them while I went. I'm bursting now, though, so if you could just keep an eye on the situation for a moment—"

"No chance." Dan clamped his hand around her arm. "First, tell me. Harry had an accident, didn't he? How bad was it? One of his dreams must have spilled over. Or he had one in the daytime. Or—did the neighbours see something and complain? For God's sake, when you think how many times their dogs have kept us up—"

His voice was rising. Elizabeth pressed her free hand against his mouth to stop him.

"It's not the neighbours," she hissed. "It's the government."

Dan lost his grip on her arm. "Bloody hell," he whispered against her palm.

Then they both turned, as the silence coming from the living room finally struck them. The crashes of falling towers had ended. The only sound that carried was a soft murmur—Dr. Margo's voice, speaking too quietly for them to hear. Their eyes met in a moment of perfect understanding.

Dan took off for the living room so quickly, Elizabeth was surprised not to see flames erupt underneath his boring black loafers. When she joined them five minutes later, carrying the tea tray, she found him standing behind Harry like a bodyguard, arms crossed and legs spread apart, glaring at Dr. Margo's colleague across the room. She elbowed him in the stomach as she passed.

"Be nice," she whispered. "Don't offend him."

Dan bared his teeth in a menacing smile. The other man smiled back, with a courteous nod of his head. Elizabeth blinked at the sight.

She had never seen teeth so bright white and . . . well, sharp-looking, before. Even in the fading light of early evening, in his shadowed corner of the room, they positively sparkled. And was it just a trick of the light, or were his canines a bit longer than was usual?

Dr. Margo cleared her throat loudly. Her colleague closed his mouth. Dan widened his stance by at least an inch.

"You're standing funny, Daddy," Harry said. "Do you have something wrong with your—"

"What would everyone like for supper?" Elizabeth asked brightly, speaking over Harry's final word as she handed out the cups of tea.

Dr. Margo said, "Oh, anything, dear. Except for any food with preservatives in it, of course. Or anything that's been frozen, or come from a tin. Or anything with red ingredients. You can never really trust red ingredients, can you?"

"Well . . ." Elizabeth mentally ran through their kitchen cupboards, feeling her heart sink.

"But I wouldn't want to put you to any trouble," Dr. Margo said.

"Of course not." Elizabeth smiled tightly. "And . . . ?" She started to turn to the man in the corner.

"Oh, you needn't worry about my colleague," Dr. Margo said. "He isn't hungry."

"Are you sure?" Elizabeth asked, trying not to sound hopeful.

He nodded regally. "I do not eat . . . supper. But should you not be going to bed, very soon? You need not stay awake for us, you know. Dr. Margo and I can look after your son very well without you."

Elizabeth didn't have to look at her husband to know that their thoughts were in perfect unison, possibly for the first time since their wedding ceremony.

Still, with the health service—not to mention the government—watching, there was no excuse to keep Harry up late.

Elizabeth supervised his tooth-brushing under the silent, looming observation of Dr. Margo's colleague, and Dr. Margo beamed maternally from one corner of Harry's bedroom as Dan sat down to read him his bedtime chapter of *Captain Underpants*. She winced, though, at the first fart joke, and looked more and more pained as the chapter went on.

"Isn't there something a bit more traditional that Harry might like?" she whispered to Elizabeth. "One of those nice *Narnia* books, perhaps? Or—"

"Trust me," Elizabeth said. "Waking up to find the White Witch in my bedroom is not an experience I want to repeat. And Aslan may be friendly in the books, but that's not terribly reassuring at three a.m., when he's keeping us all up with his roaring."

"I'll find out what that's like myself, tonight," Dr. Margo said, regaining her cheer. "I must say, I can hardly wait! Nighttime really has become so much more interesting ever since Bennerol was invented, hasn't it?"

Elizabeth smiled weakly in return. It wasn't until five minutes later that she finally lost control.

She was leaning over Harry's bed to kiss him goodnight when he said, with sleepy consideration, "I don't think I like those pills Dr. Margo gave me, Mummy. They're making everything look a bit funny."

"What?!" Elizabeth straightened with a jerk. "Dr. Margo gave you pills? When?"

Dr. Margo rose from her seat in the corner. "Now, dear . . ."

"It was while you and Daddy were in the kitchen," Harry said. "And again just after dinner, when you were clearing away. She said it would be instead of pudding. But then you gave me pudding anyway, so that was all right."

"Let me get this straight," Dan said to Dr. Margo. "You gave Harry two different pills, without asking us? Without even telling us?"

"Oh, Harry." Dr. Margo shook her head sorrowfully. "Didn't I tell you those pills were our little secret?"

It was a long moment before Elizabeth could trust herself to speak. "You did just right to tell me, Harry. You're a good boy. Now go to sleep." She leaned over and pressed a second kiss against his tousled brown hair. "If you start feeling really ill from those pills, just call us. We'll be close enough to hear." She turned to Dr. Margo and was glad to see the other woman step back under the heat of her gaze. "We'll be in the living room, having a little chat with Dr. Margo about ethics and the law."

She stalked out of the room, her spine rigidly straight. Dan waited, pointedly, for Dr. Margo to leave before he followed.

The other man was already sitting in the living room when they arrived, flipping through one of the horror novels that Dan kept on the top shelves of the bookcases in almost every room of the house, well out of Harry's reach. He looked up questioningly as they walked in, but Dr. Margo ignored him.

"If we can all please refrain from overreacting—"

"Overreacting? You drugged our son!" Elizabeth kept her voice low for Harry's sake, but it shook with rage. "How do you think the General Medical Council is going to feel about that? When we report what you've done—"

"Oh, I really don't think you want to do that, dear."

"Why not?" Dan demanded. "If you think you can walk all over us now, just because Elizabeth let one brainless midwife talk her into taking those pills in the first place—"

"I beg your pardon?" Elizabeth stared at her husband. "You and I both agreed I should try the Bennerol! Everyone said there weren't any side-effects. They said—"

"Children!" said Dr. Margo. "Please. The pills I gave Harry are completely harmless. All they're intended to do is strengthen the results of his dreams."

Elizabeth didn't say a word. She couldn't. Distantly, she heard Dan say, "Why in the name of God would you want to do that?"

Dr. Margo sighed. With her carefully-curled grey hair, pink silk blouse, and patterned scarf, she looked the very definition of a kindly grandmother. "You see? This is why I couldn't discuss it with you ahead of time. Parents are always the same. So conservative. *So* narrow-minded."

Elizabeth said, "I'm ringing NHS Direct right now, to find out how to register a complaint. Dan—"

"Do it," he said. "And as for you two—"

"If you do," said Dr. Margo, "you will regret it. Because those pills work . . . and the Government would be very interested in discovering that."

Dr. Margo no longer looked in the slightest bit vague or harmless. For the first time since Elizabeth had started taking Harry to his monthly sessions with her, four years earlier, she looked past the air of kindly, fluffy condescension. There was a scientist behind the candy-pink blouse, and behind Dr. Margo's old-fashioned, cat's-eye glasses, her hazel eyes shone with far more ambition than Elizabeth had ever recognized before.

"I thought *he* was from the government," Elizabeth said, gesturing to the heavily-swathed man in the corner. He had moved on from the horror novel to one of Harry's *Calvin & Hobbes* collections and was sniggering over the pictures . . . but with an alarming expression of hunger on his face.

Was that drool slipping down from one of his sharp teeth?

"It made things simpler for you to think so," said Dr. Margo. "But trust me, dear. I'm the only one standing between you and a whole host of exciting government agencies, all of whom would love to know that our Bennerol babies could turn into real weapons. Without me, Harry and all the little children like him would have been taken away from their parents years ago. You can hardly begrudge me a few experiments of my own, can you? Just for my own personal satisfaction—as a small payment, you might say, for my protection?"

She smiled gently, as Elizabeth and Dan said nothing. "No?" she said. She sat down on the couch, patting down her trousers. "I thought not. Now, I'd like some tea, please. Elizabeth?"

Elizabeth met Dan's eyes. They looked darker than usual against his pallor. He shrugged, the gesture despairing.

"Fine," Elizabeth said flatly. "Milk?"

"But no sugar," Dr. Margo said, as she opened up her notepad. "It's so unhealthy, don't you think?"

Elizabeth couldn't think of any answer that didn't involve cursing.

Luckily, Dr. Margo didn't seem to expect a reply. She was already tutting softly over an earlier page of notes. Harry's parents, it was clear, were old business.

Elizabeth didn't bother to ask Dr. Margo's colleague, this time. She already knew what the answer would be.

As she filled up the electric kettle in the kitchen, her eyes went to the darkness outside the window. It felt like a palpable force, pressing in on her chest until she could barely breathe.

She couldn't see the birdfeeder in the dark, nor the squirrel who'd driven her so wild that morning. Was it really less than twelve hours since she'd stood here idly wishing she could send Harry's dream-creatures after that pitiful little animal, to frighten him away? It already seemed like a different world. This morning had been just another day of summer holiday. Harry had been safe, warm, and protected in her kitchen, chattering about his dreams, and her biggest worry had been the comic he was reading, because she knew how it might affect them.

Cold water overflowed from the electric kettle. It

splashed across Elizabeth's hand as she stood unmoving, her mouth open.

She might not be a scientist, like Dr. Margo. But she had learned something important all those years ago, after she'd let that damn midwife reassure her about the Bennerol. She'd learned to never, ever again let anyone intimidate her out of listening to her instincts, especially when it came to protecting her son.

And Harry wasn't the only one who had an imagination.

When Elizabeth stepped into the living room ten minutes later, carrying her best tea service on a tray, Dr. Margo didn't even look up. She was too busy making notes. Excitement glittered in her eyes. Ten minutes ago, that would have sent alarm flaring deep in Elizabeth's gut.

Now, Elizabeth lowered her own eyes submissively and set the tea tray down on the coffee table. It was laid out exactly as her mother-in-law had taught her one excruciating Sunday afternoon, like a souvenir from the Victorian era. Normally, it would have elicited a sarcastic comment from Dan. Tonight, though, Dan sat with his head propped on his fist, staring hopelessly into the empty fireplace. He didn't move to pick up his tea, or comment on the leaf that fell off Elizabeth's hair as she stepped back from the coffee table.

She shifted casually in place to cover the leaf with her shoe, and ran one hand over her hair to check for any other giveaways. For the first time ever, she felt deeply grateful for just how quiet Harry could be when he was sneak-reading a book in bed after lights-out . . . especially one that had always been off-limits, hidden on the tallest shelf of the bookcase in his parents' bedroom.

He had been so thrilled to finally get hold of this one, he hadn't even asked why Elizabeth was climbing in through his window to give it to him, along with her mini-torch.

When Elizabeth turned around, the man in the corner was leering at her neck. Rather than showing any embarrassment as he met her gaze, he waggled his eyebrows meaningfully, tilting his head toward the kitchen. His eyes seemed to burn with urgent invitation.

Heat swept across the room. The scent of temptation filled her senses. All she had to do was give in.

Elizabeth smiled serenely and sat down beside her husband, patting his knee affectionately. Sometimes, it was good to be a mother.

If Mina Harker or Bella Swan hadn't managed a single full night's sleep in six years, they wouldn't have had the energy to be mesmerized by a vampire's stare, either. Daniel could have warned the other man about that issue, if he'd been asked.

She picked up a magazine from the table and began to read about the season's latest fashion innovations. Across the room, she heard a mournful sigh.

"Harry's dreams always manifest in your bedroom, don't they?" Dr. Margo asked half-an-hour later, when she finally looked up from her notes.

Dan only grunted. Elizabeth looked up placidly from her magazine and said, "Yes, always."

"Well, then, I'm afraid we'll have to use that room tonight. You won't mind sleeping on the couch, will you, dears?"

Elizabeth sighed heavily. "If you insist . . ."

It was three a.m. when the first scream sounded. Dan jerked out of sleep, still sitting upright on the armchair. "Wha—? Was that—?"

"Shh," said Elizabeth, and put one hand on his arm to hold him back. "They wouldn't want us to interfere."

It was seven-thirty when she finally opened the door to her bedroom. Harry was still fast asleep, of course—he always slept in after staying up to read a particularly gripping novel.

Powerful though they might have been, his dreams had still dissipated in the morning sunlight. Harry had, after all, had only two doses of Dr. Margo's experimental pills. She could only imagine how many more doses had been used on some poor child to create Dr. Margo's "colleague" . . . or what might have happened before Dr. Margo took over his supervision.

A small pile of ashes lay on the floor next to Dr. Margo. Elizabeth made a note to clear them up as soon as she emptied out the vacuum cleaner.

Dr. Margo herself sat on the bed, glassy-eyed and staring. Her pulse was rapid, but her eyes were glazed. As Elizabeth walked into the room, she repeated, as if by rote, "I will not create vampires. I will not . . . I will not . . ."

"Shh," Elizabeth said. "Of course you won't. You won't ever do anything to any of the children again."

She patted Dr. Margo on the back. The other woman, still in a deeply hypnotized state, didn't even blink.

Good for Harry, Elizabeth thought. *And good for Dr. Van Helsing*. He had always been her favourite character in the Dracula book and movies. She was pleased she'd been able to convey her abiding love for him—and all of his varied abilities, from hypnotism to vampire-staking—in the five-minute pep talk she'd given her son last night.

"Come along," she said to Dr. Margo. "I'm making breakfast. You can drink a cup of tea while you tell me exactly how long it'll take for Harry's doses to lose their effect. Because . . ."

She smiled. Of course, Dan might have his own ideas, but surely he would agree that tonight was her turn?

". . . I think today might be the perfect day to introduce Harry to Jane Austen. Starting with *Pride and Prejudice*—the Colin Firth edition."

Offerings

That Wednesday, the witch found five silver paperclips laid across her doorstep, next to an apple and a sharpened No. 2 pencil. She regarded them gravely as the breeze from the lake swept up through the pine trees and ruffled her upswept black hair. Then she turned to see if she could spot any signs of who had left them.

The dirt road was empty behind her; a single squirrel raced back and forth across her front lawn, chittering manically as he hunted for food.

The witch shrugged. "'Back to school,' I suppose." She scooped up the offerings and carried them with her into the small wooden house.

As usual—as the rules required—she set the day's offerings on the altar in her living room before she even shrugged off her jacket, and she said a blessing spell across them for whoever had left them to her. If she'd been more certain of their meaning, she could have made the spell more focused; as it was, she wished the giver luck in new ventures and an open mind for knowledge, and she hoped she hadn't missed the point entirely.

Once she'd finished the spell, though, she couldn't dismiss the offerings as neatly as usual from her mind. Sitting on her back porch, drinking coffee with her high-heeled work shoes kicked off and her hair released from its clips, she gazed into the rippling waves of the lake that bumped up against her sloping back yard and found herself thinking back to her own school days.

Apples, paperclips, multiple-choice tests...simplicity. Order. Her lips curved, ruefully.

Alexander had always said she had a mind as rigidly shut to opposing theories as any Victorian school textbook.

The witch's smile snapped off as quickly as a light bulb going out. She flipped her loose, long black hair over her shoulder and stalked back into the house, clenching her fingers around her coffee mug.

A long, low wave swept the lake behind her, in her wake. Ducks fluttered up out of the water to avoid it, squawking.

The witch's door was already closed.

The next day, she had to stay late at work, dealing with a crisis. She was still muttering to herself, her shoulders tense, as she walked across the neatly-trimmed grass of her front lawn, side-stepping the squirrel in his usual hyperactive race. She almost tripped over the tiny pile of offerings that had been left that day on her doorstep: a long, narrow candle that looked like it had already been lit at least once before, and seven candy hearts, pink, yellow, and orange, neatly arranged into a tiny "U". She stopped herself just in time, before the tip of her shoe could crush the bottom heart—that would have broken all the rules—and she looked down at them, baffled.

"'Love,' I suppose," she murmured. Her eyebrows drew together. "But why the 'U'?"

There was no one to answer her except the squirrel, chittering as he scurried up the trunk of the closest pine tree.

She picked up the offerings carefully, keeping the hearts in their proper order, and carried them into the house. At the altar, she dutifully offered a blessing spell to the giver, wishing him or her luck in love. But she felt oddly itchy as she did it, and she found herself glancing out the big front windows to make sure that no one was watching her. Only the squirrel's beady black eyes looked back at her from the prickly branches of the pine.

Yesterday's offerings had already been transmuted into a part of the altar, cool and finished. They offered her no help.

She sat down in the kitchen instead of going to the back porch. The sky outside was already beginning to darken. The candy hearts lay in their 'U' formation on the altar in the living room, where she'd left them. She nudged off her high heels but left her hair firmly clipped up as she gazed into the depths of her coffee cup.

It had been a long time since she'd wished for love for herself. That had been the point of accepting the old witch's offer of this house and all the responsibilities that came with it. That was the reason behind the house's rules.

Upstairs, in the attic, there was a box that held photograph albums from her college years. She hadn't looked at them since a week after graduation, almost three years ago.

She would not look at them now.

The squirrel's chittering sounded through the kitchen window. With a flash of irritation, the witch pointed her finger at the radio on top of her refrigerator. It burst into sound, covering up his noises and her too-uncomfortable thoughts.

But it couldn't cover up her growing conviction, which she would have preferred to drown out: the same person had left both days' offerings. That meant her first blessing spell hadn't worked—or it hadn't been enough. That meant, somehow, she had missed the underlying message.

The witch didn't like making mistakes.

For the first time in years, she found herself reluctant to come home to her safe, quiet house, the next night after work. She'd left the office early, to make up for her long hours the day before. Instead of coming home, though, she wandered through the downtown area, gazing idly at expensive jewelry and useless crafts she didn't want. Her reflection in the display windows was cool and professional, blending in neatly with the early evening crowd. No one would know, from looking at her, what she truly was. Only Alexander, of all the men she'd ever met, had known her for a witch. But that, of course, was only because he himself came from a long line of wizards.

Stupid, hard-headed wizards. She ground her teeth together, grinding old hurt into anger.

She wasn't the one with a closed mind. She wasn't the one who'd given ultimatums. She wasn't the one who'd left town the week after graduation and never come back.

The shop assistant gave her an odd look through the window, and the witch realized she had been glowering. She lifted her chin and stepped away. It was time to go home.

The evening air was cool as she walked across her front lawn. The tangy scent of pine mingled with the fresh, sweet smell of the lake. As always, the dirt road was empty. Her closest neighbor lived half a mile away, and even supplicants so desperate that they would drive hours to the witch's house never dared linger to see her accept their offerings. Were they really afraid of her, she wondered? Perhaps they were more afraid to admit what they believed. Only the squirrel was there when she arrived, running back and forth across her lawn, searching desperately for...something. She dismissed him from her mind as she saw her front doorstep.

A bright orange life jacket, limp and deflated, lay propped against her door. Frowning, she scooped it up.

"'Help?'" she asked.

No one answered her.

She walked into the house, closing the front door firmly behind her. As she set the life jacket down on the altar, her fingers brushed against a set of tiny holes in the fabric.

Teeth marks. Very, very small teeth marks.

The witch kept her mind utterly blank as she spoke the blessing spell for safety and aid in great endeavors. She kept her mind blank as she changed out of her professional clothing into a bathing suit. She chose her most modest and all-covering suit, despite the fact that she had no neighbors to see her. She walked out the back door, across her carefully-tended back lawn, and dived into the lake.

The water was cold and piercing, like knives, or knowledge. She swam deep under, trailing her fingers through the thick, slimy weeds. When she surfaced, gasping for breath, her hair lay cold and clinging against her shoulders. The squirrel was running up and down the steps of her back porch, looking frantic.

A strong, cold wave swept through the water, sending birds and insects fluttering away from it in alarm. The witch didn't move as it swept over her, stinging against her open eyes.

It was time to face the truth.

The next morning, she called in sick to work. She put on her most expensive black blazer and skirt, pinned her long hair neatly atop her head, and drove out of sight of the house. Then she cloaked herself in silence and stillness, and walked back to sit, invisible, on her front lawn.

She didn't have to wait very long.

It took a great deal of effort for the squirrel to drag all the different sticks he'd gathered across the yard. Even more effort, chittering and anxious, to arrange them into letters, nibbling at the ends of the sticks to shape them properly. The witch watched, her anger rising and falling from moment to moment. She waited until he had stepped back, preparing to jump into the safety of the trees.

Then she undid her cloaking spell.

"So you've given up on symbolism?" she said.

The squirrel froze. His beady black eyes stared at her. His big, bushy tail twitched.

The witch stepped up beside him to read the awkward number and letters formed by sticks.

4give.

"The rules say I have to take these to the altar," she told him. "The rules say I have to say a blessing spell over them, whether I want to or not."

He stared up at her, his black eyes shining.

The witch said, "I only agreed to the rules because of you. To keep anyone else from hurting me the way that you did."

He looked up at her, shivering. She couldn't tell if it was from the breeze or from nerves.

She ignored the sticks. Instead, she scooped up the squirrel. He froze in her hand for a moment, then raced up her arm to stand on her shoulder. She set her mouth in a grim line and walked into the house, to the altar. He hopped onto it, looking nervous.

On the altar, all his offerings were frozen into place around him, fixed for all time.

The witch took a deep breath and remembered cold water, sharp and bracing against her skin. She did not let herself remember the albums upstairs. She closed her eyes and said the spell.

She heard the altar shatter before she opened them.

Alexander was thinner than he had been three years ago, and he stood naked before her. His human eyes were dark and focused with intensity, and she had to look away from them to keep hold of her breath and righteous anger.

"You couldn't just phone me?" she snapped. "If you finally changed your mind about your stupid ultimatums—"

"I changed my mind less than a week after I left," Alexander said. "Do you know how long it takes a squirrel to cross the country?"

"If you hadn't been careless enough to turn yourself into a squirrel—"

"I wasn't the one who did it," he said.

"Well, I certainly didn't—" She stopped. "Wait. Is this some family curse? All those wizards in your family..."

Alexander shrugged, flushing. "I turned my back on love, so my ancestors jumped in to teach me a lesson. I agree with the message, but I wouldn't have chosen their methods."

"Well," the witch said. Her lips twitched. "Well."

She looked down at the offerings, fresh again and unfrozen, scattered across the floor with the remnants of the altar.

Paperclips, pencil, apple. *I want to learn.*

Candle, candy-hearts in a U. *I love you.*

Life jacket. *Help.*

And, outside: *4give.*

She felt a shiver in the air around her, signaling changes underfoot. The rules had been broken. Anything could happen.

The witch said to the wizard, "You'd better come into the kitchen with me. It's warmer there. We'll have coffee."

Dancing in the Dark

I have three uncles, but one of them is dead.

He's the funny one.

The afternoon that Mom and Dad didn't come home, Uncle Rom was the one who took care of all the details. He stood as solid as an oak in the kitchen of our house, making phone calls all through the evening. There were four chairs in the kitchen, but he ignored them all. Even as Billy and I were being herded up the stairs to bed that night, I could still hear his voice, endlessly calm and reasonable, talking our future into place.

Uncle Kev isn't like that. He was the one who picked me and Billy up from school that day and cried as he told us the news. He hugged us both hard before he turned off the lights that night, and he swore he would be waiting downstairs in the morning. He promised that we would never be alone.

But in the middle of the night, even Uncle Kev couldn't hold off the darkness. Billy woke up crying after midnight and crawled into bed with me. I'd already been awake for hours, staring into the dark, imagining everything Kev hadn't told me. I'd passed a bad car accident on the highway, once. I'd seen the ambulances gathered around, the woman sobbing on the side of the road. At seven years old, I already had what my teachers called "an active imagination".

Uncle Jack was the one who saved us that night.

He was wearing a ripped T-shirt when he appeared, but it didn't look old or grubby. It looked stylish. My mom had always told us that Jack was the rebel in the family, which made him sound wild and dangerous, but he just looked like a regular grown-up to me. Nineteen looks old to a seven-year-old, I guess.

Jack had floppy hair and a goofy grin, and when Billy saw him, he was so surprised, he stopped crying.

My breath caught in my throat, but I wasn't scared. Not exactly. I knew who he was, right away. He was Mom and Uncle Rom's little brother, the one from the picture in the living room.

And if he was here, then maybe someone else was, too.

"Can you bring Mom and Dad?" I asked. My voice quavered as I said it, but I gripped the blanket hard in my hands so I wouldn't cry.

Uncle Jack's smile dimmed. He shook his head.

"I want Mom and Dad!" Billy said. He started crying again.

Jack put one hand to his mouth, miming the message that he couldn't talk. Then he turned his back on us, and I thought he was going to leave.

"Wait!" I said.

But he'd already started dancing by then. It was a funny, awkward little shuffle-step, like a penguin dancing on slippery ice, and at the end of it, he took a fall so long and comic, Billy started giggling even through his tears, and we both scrambled down to the end of the bed to see. Jack reached out for the toychest to pull himself up, but his hand passed straight through the wood, and he fell right back down onto the floor, opening his mouth and eyes wide in such exaggerated shock, I had to bite my own hand to keep myself from snorting with laughter.

He stayed all night, even after Billy fell back to sleep. I finally closed my eyes, too, but I couldn't sleep for more than fifteen minutes at a time. Every dream turned into a nightmare of fire and screams...but every time I opened my eyes, I saw Uncle Jack sitting on the floor with his back against the wall. He'd wink at me and put a finger on his lips to remind me not to wake Billy up, and I'd keep my eyes on his face until I started to feel calm again.

He finally faded away as the sun came out, but by then Uncle Kev was awake, already cooking in the kitchen. I could smell the scents of fresh coffee and baking sugar drifting through the house, Kev's own best cures for sleeplessness and grief.

I asked Uncle Kev about Jack over breakfast.

"I never met him, sweetheart. He was before my time." Kev pointed at my pancake, rolled up with strawberry jam and thickly frosted with sugar on top. "Now take a bite before it gets cold, okay?"

"Okay," I said. I cut off a piece, but I couldn't force myself to raise it to my mouth. There had been a hard fist clenched inside my stomach since yesterday afternoon, and the thought of putting any food down there made me feel sick. So I rubbed my forkful into the plate as if I were trying to soak up extra sugar, and said, "Rom and Mom talked about Jack, though, didn't they?"

"Oh, sweetie." Kev sighed. "You know your uncle. I'd been dating him for almost a year before I even found out he'd ever had a younger brother. I didn't find out about what happened to Jack until after we'd moved in together, when I saw the old newspaper articles." He frowned. "It's not that Rom doesn't care. You know that, right? He cares too much. That's why he has a hard time talking about things."

"I know," I said. Rom hadn't said a word to me and Billy about the accident yesterday. All he'd done was give us hard hugs and tell us, gruffly, to eat the dinner Kev had made us.

But Rom hadn't eaten last night, either. I was pretty sure he would understand if he knew how my stomach was feeling. I didn't always want to talk about things, either.

So when Kev stepped out of the kitchen for a moment, I cut off two thirds of my pancake and dropped it onto Billy's plate. Billy didn't mind—he was already nearly done with his first pancake anyway. By the time Kev walked back into the room, Billy was almost finished with everything on his plate, and I'd settled my fork and knife neatly across the last few inches that remained on mine.

"I can't eat any more," I said. "I'm sorry."

Kev looked at my plate and then at me. He sighed. "That's all right, Becca," he said. "Maybe at lunchtime you'll feel hungrier."

It took weeks, not hours, though, before the fist in my stomach finally unclenched. Months before I grew used to Rom and Kev sleeping in the room that had belonged to Mom and Dad; before I woke up in the morning simply knowing what had happened, instead of having to remember it like a cliff falling on top of me, every single day.

But Uncle Jack stayed with us every night. Sometimes he danced for us, the way he had the first time. More often, he just sat by the window, keeping us silent company through the night. Keeping us safe.

Two weeks after the accident, I stole the photo of Jack from the living room. He was grinning in it, standing with his arm around some girl I didn't know. I hid the photo in the top drawer of my chest of drawers, so no one could see it and take it back. Whenever I was alone in the room during the day, I took it out and set it next to me on the bed. Whenever I left the room, I put the photo back in the drawer and covered it in a layer of clothing to keep it safe.

My secret only lasted two days. On the afternoon of the

third day, I walked into the room and found Rom standing over the open drawer, staring down at the photo in its frame. A pile of clean clothes lay forgotten on my bed as he looked down at his brother's face, tracing it through the glass with one big finger.

I froze in the doorway, too startled even to run away.

Rom looked up at me. He didn't say a word. But he picked up the frame and set it carefully on top of the chest of drawers, propping it up so Jack grinned out at both of us.

The photo stayed there from then on, without any discussion required. And that was how I recognized her, when she came.

The doorbell rang on a Saturday morning, eight months after the accident. Billy was out shopping with Kev, but I'd been allowed to stay home and watch television. Rom was in his workroom in the basement with his music playing, so I was the only one who heard the doorbell ring.

I opened the door, keeping it on the latch the way we'd learned in school. *Stranger danger*, my teacher had taught us, and I knew the moment I saw the woman on the doorstep that I had never met her before.

She was younger than Rom and Kev, younger than my parents, but older than Uncle Jack would ever be, and dressed in what I thought of as serious grown-up clothes, even though it was a Saturday. I really hoped she wasn't here for my parents. It had been months since I'd had to tell anyone what happened. Everybody was supposed to know, by now.

I stood behind the cracked-open door and watched her warily. "Yes?"

She looked down at me and her eyes widened. "You...oh, my goodness. Are you Rom's little girl?"

"No!" I said. Just hearing the question made my stomach hurt. Rom and Kev lived with us now, but that didn't make them our parents.

I'd spent all morning in the living room, as if life were normal again, but now all I could think of was getting back to my bedroom and to safety. I started to close the door, but she stepped forward, pushing her hand into the crack to hold it open.

"Wait! Is Rom at home?"

"He's busy." I scowled up at her. I didn't want to invite her into the house or listen to her tell me what a shame my parents' deaths had been, once she figured out who I really was. All I wanted...

Oh. As she turned her head, some trick of the light caught her face and triggered memory. My grip on the door loosened with surprise.

I might not have met her before, but I had seen her—seen her at least a thousand times, although I'd never paid her any attention. She'd only been the girl in the photo; the girl with my uncle's arm around her.

She wasn't a girl anymore. Her hair was still blonde, but instead of hanging in a long, shaggy sweep around her shoulders, it was swept up in an elegant knot, and there were lines around her blue eyes and wide mouth now, even though she'd tried to hide them with make-up. She looked tired, and she looked as if she'd been crying recently...and maybe for a long time before that.

I said, "Rom's in the basement. I'll go get him," and at my words, she stepped back and finally let me close the door.

I turned around and had my second shock of the day.

Uncle Jack stood in the hallway. I'd never seen him in daylight before.

"Jack?" I said.

But he wasn't looking at me. He was staring past me at the panel of thick, leaded glass at the top of the door, where the wavering outline of a blonde head showed through.

"Jack!" I said again.

He didn't smile at me, or wink. There was an expression on his face that I'd never seen there before, and I didn't like it at all.

I turned around. I was going to tell the blonde woman that Rom couldn't come to the door, and then I was going to get rid of her and make things right again.

Before I could move, though, the door to the basement swung open. "Becca?" Rom rubbed a hand over his thick, dark hair, and wood shavings fell onto his flannel shirt. "Is someone at the door? I thought I heard the bell."

He didn't see Jack, and Jack didn't look away from the door. I didn't say a word, but Rom looked past me and saw the woman's outline in the glass. He sighed and put one hand on my shoulder. He looked like he might say something else, but he didn't. He just his head and went to open the door.

"Hello?" he said. "Can I help you?"

"Rom?" The woman's voice wavered, like she might start to cry again. "It's me, Susan. Do you remember me?"

"Ah..." As I stepped up beside him, Rom shook his head. "I'm sorry..."

"Susan," she repeated. "Jack's—I was with Jack when —when..."

"Susan," Rom said, and shook his head again. He looked staggered. "I...right. Yes. Susan." He stepped back, tucking his hands into his pockets as if he didn't know what to do with them. "Ah...do you want coffee? Or tea?"

"I'll take something stronger, if you have it." Her smile wobbled.

Rom blinked and looked past her into the sun-drenched street. "Aren't you driving?"

"Oh..." She waved a hand, flapping away the question. The gesture made her stagger slightly on her low heels. She caught herself on the door frame.

"I'll make you coffee," Rom said firmly. He caught my eye as he turned, and winced. "Becca, maybe you'd better—um..." He looked back toward the living room, where the TV was still playing. "Weren't you watching cartoons or something?"

I shrugged and followed them into the kitchen. Jack followed after, standing in the doorway with his gaze on Susan. She couldn't see him any more than Uncle Rom had. Her gaze passed right over him as she drifted through the kitchen, turning over knick-knacks on the windowsill and touching all the magnets on the fridge.

The sight of it made me itch with irritation. Rom didn't look happy, either, as he poured out the coffee. He kept glancing at the clock—hoping Kev would get home soon, I bet. Kev was always the one who entertained guests.

Kev wasn't due back for at least half an hour, though.

Rom spoke again just as Susan was pulling off one of Kev's to-do lists from the fridge.

"Do you take milk, Susan?"

She turned, setting the list back down. It missed the fridge and drifted to the floor, but she didn't notice. "Just sugar," she said, and crooked her mouth in a rueful smile. "Lots of sugar."

"Okay." He dug out a bag of sugar from the cupboard, looked at it doubtfully, then set it on the table with a spoon, next to a mug of coffee. "Ah, I'll let you measure it yourself."

"Thanks, Rom. You're a sweetheart." She sat down and wrapped her hands around the coffee mug. She didn't bother to add the sugar, just cupped her hands around the mug like she was soaking up its heat.

Rom poured me a cup of milk and sat down beside me. He didn't have a drink of his own, but he didn't seem to realize that until he was already sitting. He looked blankly at his empty hands for a moment, then laced his fingers together on the tablecloth and glanced at the clock again.

"Jack said that, you know," the woman said abruptly. "He said, 'Rom, he doesn't talk much, but he's got the kindest heart of anyone you'll ever meet.'"

"Ah." Rom unlaced his fingers to rub the back of his neck. "Did he?"

"He did. He was crazy about all of you, though. You and Carol and your parents—is Carol still living around here? I heard she got married, had a couple of kids."

Rom didn't turn, but maybe he felt the sudden intensity of my gaze. "She's not in town right now," he said, and my shoulders melted with relief. "We're looking after the kids for her and Sam."

"That's nice." She picked up her spoon, stirred it idly through her black coffee. "I always thought I'd have kids by now. But...you said 'we'? So you've met someone, too?"

Rom gave a quick, jerky shrug. "Mm."

"That's nice," Susan repeated. Her eyes glittered with tears. "That's really nice."

I glanced at the door. Jack was staring at her with such intensity, I felt my cheeks burn. I looked away.

Rom said, "Susan, is there anything I can do for you?"

"Do for me?" She choked on a laugh. "I'm not...I know your family doesn't think much of me."

Rom closed his eyes. "That's not—"

"No, I get it," she said. "If it hadn't been for me, he'd have been safe on campus where he was supposed to be. It was my idea to skip class and drive out to that festival, my idea to stop in that stupid gas station even though he said we didn't need to. He said we could make it another fifteen miles, and we could have, but I was so paranoid and so fucking *stupid*—!"

"Ah, Susan..." As her voice rose, Rom nodded his head in my direction.

She put one hand to her mouth. "Sorry," she said, behind her hand. "Sorry, sorry. I didn't mean to...I didn't mean any of it," she said, and a sob caught in her voice. "Please. I really want you to know. If I could go back in time, be the one who went into that station to pay—if you knew how many times I've wished—"

"You don't have to do this," Rom said, cutting her off. I could see the lines of tension on his face, but his deep voice was steady. "No one thinks it was your fault. You weren't the one who shot him."

"But I'm the reason it happened." She pushed her chair back, sent the chair legs scraping against the floor, and scrambled to her feet. "I'm sorry. I shouldn't have come here. I just —it was ten years this week, you know—of course you know—and I just wanted you to know how sorry—how very sorry..." She wiped one hand across her face, smearing her make-up. "And then there was the fire, and—"

"A fire?" Rom said. He'd stood up too, more carefully. "Were you hurt?"

"Oh, no," she said. "It was just my asshole ex—excuse me," she added, glancing at me. "God, I keep forgetting she's in the room, she's so quiet. No, I wasn't in the house when he set it, thank God. But all my pictures, Jack's old T-shirt, the one he gave me...anyway." She took a deep breath and lifted her chin. "That's not your problem. But I wanted—I just wanted you to know I haven't forgotten him. Won't ever forget."

"That's...fine," Rom said after a moment. "That's fine. I don't think you should drive yourself home, though."

She laughed, bitterly. "That's not a problem. I told you there was a fire, right? There isn't any home to go to. I mean, there is, but it's half-full of ash. The landlord's clearing it out for me, but until then I'm staying with a friend."

"Good," Rom said. "Good. Why don't I just call her, let her know where you are?"

She fumbled with her purse. "I can drive. I've got keys—"

"Can I see them?" Rom closed his big hand around them. "Why don't you sit down, finish your coffee first? You can give me your friend's number in the meantime."

They kept arguing, but I stopped paying attention. Jack was gesturing to me, for the first time since Susan had arrived. When he saw me looking, his face lightened with relief. He pointed into the hallway, then back to Susan. I frowned at him, not getting it.

He looked frantic as he pointed again and again. Finally he slapped his forehead, and started to mime. He was moving around a room—a bedroom, I realized, as he stumbled and fell into a bed. My lips curved, and I had to bite back a laugh. I loved Jack's mimes. Then he was pulling himself up, opening drawers, coming to the top of the chest of drawers, and then—

"No!" I said out loud.

Rom and Susan both stopped talking.

"What is it, Becca?" Rom asked.

I couldn't answer. I was staring at Jack's pleading face in the doorway as he mimed holding up a photo. A photo that belonged to me.

"No," I repeated, and I turned my back on him.

My eyes were burning now, and there was a prickling pain in my chest, like betrayal.

"Becca?" Rom said.

I clenched my hands into fists, holding back tears. "I think she should go," I said. "She said she wants to. We should let her." I felt Jack's gaze on my back. "No one wants her here anyway."

Rom's shoulders sagged. For the first time I could remember, my uncle looked at me with real disapproval.

"I think you'd better go to your room, Becca."

His voice was quiet, but it stung. I gritted my teeth and walked out of the room. Jack didn't even bother to step aside to make way for me—he obviously couldn't bear to take his eyes off Susan, even for a moment. I walked straight through him, then hurtled down the hallway at a run. I slammed the bedroom door behind me.

On top of the chest of drawers, Jack grinned out at me confidently, exuberantly.

He was my uncle. He belonged to me and Billy, not to *her*. We were the ones who needed him. She was a grown-up. She should be able to take care of herself. And anyway, she'd said it was her fault he'd been killed. She said...

I picked up the photo, carrying it with me to the bed. I curled up like a baby around it, tucking it to my chest and studying it while tears burned against my eyes and choked my throat.

She was grinning just as exuberantly as Jack was. His arm was around her shoulder; her arm was around his waist. They were wearing T-shirts for the same band. And I realized something for the first time as I studied it. They didn't just happen to both be happy. They were making each other happy.

I remembered feeling happy like that.

The tears stopped choking me, then. They ripped out of my throat like knives as I remembered.

Jack drifted in at the very end, as I was finally gasping my way to a halt. He sat back against the door and shut his eyes. He didn't look at me. He didn't beg. He only looked infinitely weary and a hundred years older than he had in the photo, even though it had been taken only a few months before he died.

I uncurled my legs and pulled myself up off the bed. I walked over to stand in front of him, the way he'd stood in front of our bed that first night.

His eyes opened. He looked up at me. I put one finger to my lips, the way he had a thousand times, reminding me to be quiet for Billy's sake.

"Shh," I said. "It's okay. It'll be okay."

Rom was helping Susan into a tiny, dented blue car when I came out the front door. Another woman stood next to them, shaking her head. They all looked up at me as I came out, even Susan, whose eyes were bleary.

"Becca?" Rom said. "I thought I told you to stay in your room."

I walked straight up to Susan. "Here," I said, and held out the photo. "This is for you. He wants you to have it."

"Well, isn't that sweet," the other woman cooed.

Rom said, "Becca?"

Susan took the photo in her free hand. Her lower lip trembled. She looked down at it, and then at me. "He *wants* me to have it?" she whispered.

I nodded. "He does."

"Thank you," she whispered. "Oh, thank you."

I tensed, waiting for her to lunge at me with an unwanted hug, the way adult women always seemed to. But she didn't. She just slid into the passenger seat of the car, holding the photo. She was still staring down at it as her friend drove her away a few minutes later.

Rom and I stood together, watching in silence as the car drove down the street.

Finally, he said, "'Wants'? Not, 'would have wanted'?"

I shook my head. "*Wants*," I said.

We stood there for another moment. Mr. Miller, down the street, was mowing his lawn. Cars passed slowly up and down the street, veering to avoid the soccer game some of the boys at the far end had set up.

"Well," Rom said. "I guess we'd better go back inside."

He reached out his big hand, and I took it.

That night, I waited after the lights went out. I kept my

eyes open as the hours ticked by on the clock by my bed. But Jack never appeared.

In the middle of the night, Billy woke up crying. Jack still wasn't there.

I got up out of bed as he whimpered and rubbed his eyes.

"Jack," he said. "Where's Jack? I want Jack!"

I waved to catch his eye. He looked up at me, through the darkness.

And I began to dance.

The Disastrous Début of Agatha Tremain

At the age of sixteen, Agatha Tremain let down her skirts, pinned up her hair, and set herself to running her father's household. Her first step was to forge her father's signature and dismiss her hated governess. Miss Blenheim left with her perfectly straight nose held high in the air, trailing bitter premonitions of disaster like wriggling serpents in her wake.

Agatha's second step was to teach herself magic, using the books in her father's library as her guides.

The first time Agatha entered the library to find an introductory text, her father looked up at her with vague approval from his customary seat by the fireplace. When Sir Jasper's eyes focused on the book she took from the shelves, though, his normally mild face darkened into anger.

"Do take great care with that work, my dear. There are no fewer than five different points of contention in his arguments, and three outright fallacies. I should hate to see you taken in by such folly."

"I'll take care, Papa," Agatha promised. She stepped off the wooden stepladder, brushing dust off her fingers. "I shan't believe anything without proper evidence."

"I'm very glad of it. But, I say..." Sir Jasper blinked. "I don't mean to be rude, but are you permitted to be in here at all? I thought that creature Blaggish—Blagmire—"

"Miss Blenheim?" Agatha waited for his nod. "I sent her packing this morning. I'm old enough to look after myself now."

"What a relief. I never could abide that woman." He began to subside back into his chair, but an expression of sudden surprise halted him mid-movement. "Good Lord, I am hungry. Have I missed luncheon, by any chance?"

"You've been in here for two days, Papa." Agatha sighed. "I've ordered a hot supper for you. The servants should bring it shortly."

"Oh, good. I was afraid I might have to leave."

Her father settled happily back into his book. Agatha pulled up a second armchair beside him. Carelessly crushing her skirts beneath her, she set her booted feet upon the footstool in front of the fire and began to read with a feeling of vast contentment.

The Tremain land was set fifteen miles out of town and nearly three miles from their closest neighbors. As a young girl, left to the sole care of Miss Blenheim and her malevolent admirer, the butler Horwick, Agatha had frequently regretted the distance. Keen-eyed adults might have been salvation to her then.

As she grew into her own, however, free of Miss Blenheim and able at last to cow Horwick into a sullen form of near-submission, she realized that isolation had its benefits. With no irritating supervision or near neighbors to gossip, Agatha was free to forget all the oppressive rules of dress and proper maidenly demeanor. After all, what were such fripperies to her?

As Miss Blenheim had explained hundreds of times over the years, Agatha's unfortunate nose, unnaturally red hair, and general lack of grace meant she would certainly never be capable of winning any man's heart. Only her dowry could ever appeal to a potential husband...and Agatha refused to ever marry any man who took her on such terms.

She understood only too well what it was to live with one who scorned everything about her; she would never repeat the experience.

With no prying eyes upon the spacious lawns of Tremain House, Agatha was free to practice her spells in perfect ease, ignoring he irrational social law that deemed the practice of magic unladylike. The only people ever to be alarmed by her experiments were a few of the weaker-spirited maidservants, and by the time that they finally fled the house, Agatha was nearly seventeen. She had learned by then to summon and control her own helping spirits, who filled their places to a nicety.

Moreover, the sight of the dark spirits moving about the

house, eerily silent and obedient, miraculously transformed Horwick's complaints from snarls of contempt to mere unintelligible muttering underneath his breath, which suited Agatha far better.

By the time Agatha turned eighteen, she had become so accustomed to her freedom that she no longer feared to lose it. So when an imperious knock sounded on the front door of Tremain House one morning, it never even occurred to her that it might be the sound of approaching Doom.

In fact, engrossed in one of her more challenging experiments in her own private study, Agatha barely noticed the sounds of bustling arrival in the rest of the house. It was only when Horwick appeared, looming in her doorway, that she even remembered hearing the knock.

"Well, Horwick?" As she spoke, Agatha kept her commanding gaze fixed upon the inch-high imp who slouched on the desk before her.

This was her first attempt at multiple transformations and by far the most complex set of spells she had ever attempted to master. The imp, who was a startling bright blue and currently engaged in making horrible faces, had begun its life as a common field mouse. If Agatha spoke every word of the spell correctly, it would next become a housecat and remain one, too, a sensible and useful addition to the household. As Agatha hadn't yet recited the second (and intimidatingly intricate) spell, though, the imp was still enjoying its first, highly dangerous transformation. She couldn't afford to take her eyes off it for an instant.

"What is it?" she asked impatiently.

"A caller for you, Miss Agatha," Horwick intoned. "A *lady* caller," he added dolefully.

"Well, tell her I can't attend on her, for heaven's sake." Agatha narrowed her eyes at the imp. It had far too mischievous a look on its blue face, almost as if it knew something she did not. Of course she did not believe that for an instant, but it made her uneasy nonetheless.

Agatha realized, with a sudden flash of irritation, that Horwick had not moved from his pose of ominous warning. "Tell whoever it is to go away," she said. "I don't have time to wait on some gossipy neighbor who wants to nose about the house. Get rid of her!"

"Now, my darling girl, you cannot possibly mean that." A rich, velvety female voice spoke from the doorway, rippling with amusement. As Agatha half-turned, caught by surprise, a woman wrapped in floor-length furs swept past Horwick into the study.

"Dearest Agatha. Don't you remember me? You were only a little tiny girl when I saw you last. I'm your aunt Clarisse, finally back from Vienna. Now, take off that silly gaping look from your face, my love, before it freezes there!"

Chuckling, she patted Agatha's face, which was stiff with shock. "My goodness, I can see you have been in need of a proper woman's influence, haven't you, my poor child? Oh, I've worried so much about you! You wouldn't believe how many sleepless nights I've spent agonizing over the injustice of your situation, a beautiful young girl like you trapped out here with my absurd brother for years on end with no season in Town or eligible suitors in sight."

"I don't—"

"No, of course you needn't worry any longer, dear. I'm here now, and I shall take marvelous care of everything. I've come to live with you and your father and take all the burdens from your shoulders. Now, doesn't that sound perfectly wonderful?"

Slim, scented arms closed around Agatha. Soft fur pressed into her face and covered her eyes. The imp leaped off the desk with a yip of glee and darted toward freedom and mischievous adventure. It would undoubtedly cause nightmarish catastrophes all throughout the household, and even more of the maidservants would resign their posts.

Agatha couldn't bring herself to worry about any of that, though. She was too overwhelmed by the far greater and more terrifying disaster that had closed her in a loving auntly embrace.

"My dearest Jasper." Clarisse swept into the library ten minutes later, still draped in furs despite the heat. Agatha trailed behind her, speechless with horror. "Aren't you utterly delighted to see me?"

"Ah..." Sir Jasper blinked over his book. "I say, Clarisse. Is that you?"

"Of course it is, you absurd creature. Didn't you read my letters? I told you I would arrive today."

"Letters?" Agatha croaked.

As a matter of course, she read every letter that arrived for her father. It was a question of necessity rather than interference, as his post piled up on every available surface otherwise, ignored for years as their estate accounts languished. She had learned to pass on only those notes to which he was likely to pay attention: fat packets of argumentation from scholars in Germany and the Netherlands, written in spidery scrawls with every line crossed twice as they fiercely debated the most abstract theories of magic.

Estate management and personal gossip were both equally tedious to Sir Jasper, and Agatha had learned long ago that it was best to simply forge his signature on any cheques, business letters or notes of polite regret that had to be posted on his behalf.

"Oh, I sent piles of letters." Aunt Clarisse smiled ruefully. "How could I help myself, missing home and family as I did all these long years?"

Agatha said, "They never arrived."

"Those dreadful continental mail carriers." Clarisse shook her head sadly. "But never mind that! I'm here now, at last. And of course our first order of business must be your social début."

"My *what*?" said Agatha.

"But what else, my dear? Jasper, I am ashamed of you." Her

furs rippled as she made a *mouë* of disapproval at him. "It's one thing to bury yourself down here for years on end, but to bury your young and"—she looked Agatha up and down, managing to look both skeptical and kindly at the same time—"not *entirely* unattractive young daughter along with you? There is that nose of course—and that dreadful hair—but a multitude of sins can be concealed by her dowry. Still, how in Heaven's name is she to find a husband and home of her own out here in the wilds?"

"This is my home," said Agatha.

"Nonsense," Clarisse said. "Every young girl dreams of an establishment of her own and a husband to give her status in Society. I shall launch you upon Town immediately. We must thank our blessings that the Season is not yet over. Jasper, all that I require from you is your chequebook—but if you don't immediately surrender it to me, I promise I shall nag you unmercifully for weeks until you give in."

"I beg your pardon," said Agatha, "but this is absurd. I don't wish to be launched into Society. I have no interest in going to dances or to London, and I certainly do not desire a husband. All I want is to stay here and study—just like you, Papa."

"Just like my brother?" Clarisse let out a tinkling laugh. "My dear, haven't you yet learned? You are a young lady now, not a child to be so willful. Your duty to the family is to marry, just as your grandmother, great-aunt and I all did before you —and I can tell you that *studying* is hardly required for that vocation. Gentlemen are none of them so very difficult to understand."

"Papa!" Agatha said. "Pray tell my aunt that I do not need to be launched upon London!"

"Jasper," said Clarisse, "do you really wish me to settle myself here in your hermit hole for the next full month, talking non-stop until you finally agree with me? You know it is my right to chaperone your daughter into matrimony. It was promised to me by our own parents, all those years ago."

Clearly, the weapons had been drawn. Agatha pulled out her own most ruthless stratagem. "If I leave, Papa, who will take care of all the practicalities? Who will listen to the housekeeper's complaints and deal with the estate manager? You will have no time to devote to your own studies."

"Well..." Sir Jasper looked pained. "It is true that I shouldn't like—"

"We will only be in Town for a matter of weeks," Clarisse said. "A few months at the absolute most. That is the longest it could possibly take me to find our dear Agatha a fiancé. I am certain you can allow the practicalities to pile up that long, Jasper—indeed, I am more than certain that you have done so in the past. And our dear old Horwick may see to all the rest."

"That is true," Sir Jasper said, with obvious relief. His gaze lowered stealthily toward his book.

"Papa!" Agatha said, and snatched the book from his hands. "Aunt Clarisse means to marry me off. If she succeeds, I will be gone *forever*."

"Have no fear," said Clarisse, and smiled kindly. "I shall remain here, Jasper, to look after everything for you. It will be as if nothing had changed—except that you had done your duty to your daughter, and to me, at long last."

"Oh, well," said Sir Jasper. "That does make a difference, I suppose."

Agatha stared at him. "Papa? Haven't you heard a word I said?"

"Yes, yes, my dear," Sir Jasper said peevishly. "Indeed, I haven't been forced to listen to so much tedious debate in a very long time—not since Clarisse left the last time, I suppose." He sighed. "You do not know how difficult your aunt can make it for a man to study, Agatha. And Clarisse is right—marriage is what young ladies are meant for, particularly in our family. If only you had been born a boy, it would have been different...but there are promises, you know, that must be kept, whether we care for them or not."

"But—"

"You forget, my dear," said Clarisse softly, "you are entirely in your father's care until you find a husband. You must abide by his decisions—and I shall stand as your guardian in his absence." She smiled warmly. "Have no fear. We shall make the decisions that are best for all of us, even if you are too young to understand them now. You will be grateful in later years, when you have a daughter of your own."

Agatha fisted her hands and did not reply.

It might have been two years since she had finally escaped Miss Blenheim, but she had not forgotten how to fight. Her aunt would soon discover just how little Agatha Tremain could be cowed.

It did not take long to think of a plan. That night, supper was served in the dining room for the first time in years. Agatha allowed her aunt's stream of scandalous continental gossip to pass over her unheard, while her father sat looking miserable and casting longing glances in the direction of the library.

There was no expecting Sir Jasper to stand against his sister, that much was clear...and unfortunately, Clarisse had the right of it: according to law as well as custom, Agatha was her father's property, little though she might relish the reminder. She might be the heiress to his estate, but at the moment, her only legal possession was her dowry. Sizable though that was, she could not even touch it—that privilege belonged to her future husband.

Should her father and Clarisse desire her to be forced onto the marriage market, Agatha had no legal or financial means of resistance.

Fortunately, she had spent the last two years developing every magical recourse available. It was time to make clear to her fashionable aunt exactly what sort of young lady she really was.

The first shock of the evening came when she slipped out of her bedroom and down the corridor to her private study, which she'd left unlocked in the confusion of her aunt's arrival.

The handle refused to budge...and her key, as she remembered only too clearly, sat inside upon the desk, beside a stack of unused candles and all of her notes.

"Blast," Agatha muttered.

It was the imp at work, of course, causing trouble as she'd expected. She turned with a swish of her dressing gown and strode into the next room—a guest bedroom, never used—to give the bell-pull an imperious tug.

For once, Horwick did not make her wait. Indeed, he slipped through the servant's door hidden in the tapestry as swiftly as if he had been waiting nearby for the summons.

"Yes, Miss?" His normally doleful tones sounded suspiciously self-satisfied. To Agatha's shock, she saw the corners of his narrow lips twitching as if he were repressing a grin, the first she'd seen on his face in years.

She had poor memories of his grins. They had generally coincided with some new witticism Miss Blenheim had made at her expense, or a particularly humiliating punishment the two of them had devised for her.

Now Agatha scowled at him and reminded herself that she was a mature eighteen years of age. She was no longer a child to cringe before her old tormentor. "I require your assistance, Horwick," she said.

"Indeed, Miss." Horwick's jaw moved convulsively; under Agatha's disbelieving stare, he even rubbed his hands together in delight. "Always happy to be of assistance in any way I can, Miss."

"I am glad to hear it," she said. "If you would simply unlock my study using your copy of the key—"

"It can't be done!" Horwick caroled the words with open glee. "No, I can't do that, Miss."

"Why on earth not?"

"Because I don't have that key anymore. No, Miss, I don't. Your aunt, Miss Clarisse as was, had it off me this evening."

"But—"

"Every copy to be in her keeping," he said happily. "That's what she said, and that's what she did. The key from the desk and the key from my ring, and I saw her lock the door herself. 'Much better for all of us this way, eh, Horwick?' she said. Oh, that Miss Clarisse. The memories she brings back..."

Chortling happily to himself, he backed away and closed the hidden door behind him while Agatha stood numb with shock.

Every note, every grimoire, every carefully-prepared brazier and specially-ordered candle she possessed sat behind that closed office door. Without them, she was as helpless as...

No. Agatha set her jaw. She might not have magic at her command anymore, but she was no longer a helpless child. Miss Blenheim and Horwick might have found a young, motherless girl an easy target, but Clarisse would not find the same.

She stalked down the corridor to her aunt's room and threw open the door without a knock.

"My goodness." Clarisse looked up with amazement from the dressing table where she sat. A maid stood with her back to Agatha, brushing Clarisse's rippling, waist-length golden hair. Even dressed for bed, Agatha's aunt was still draped in lush furs—this time, a lavishly fur-trimmed satin dressing gown in royal blue, with skirts that spread in draping folds around her chair.

A fire blazed in the hearth, raising the temperature in the room near boiling point. Clarisse's maid stepped back, turning away discreetly as Clarisse shook her head in amused disdain.

"We really must work upon your manners, mustn't we, dear? In polite society, you know, it is customary to knock before entering a lady's bedroom. Or a man's, for that matter, although perhaps we'll wait until your wedding night to discuss such delicate questions."

"In polite society," said Agatha, with icy control, "it is customary not to steal other people's keys. *Or* their homes, for that matter. I don't know what may have brought you home now after all these years abroad, but if you think you can bundle me off like an unwelcome parcel just so that you can take my place—! Well, you do not know who you are tangling with."

"Oh, don't I?" Clarisse raised perfectly arched eyebrows. "What do you think, Blennie?"

The maid's shining dark head tilted up. She turned to meet Agatha's gaze.

Agatha's breath stopped in her throat.

The maid was smiling with open amusement. The same expression was mirrored on her aunt's face, but Agatha barely noticed it. All her attention was fixed on the maid's glittering green eyes and her perfectly straight nose.

...Just as she remembered them.

"Oh, you are just as my dear Blennie had described to me," Clarisse said. "I cannot begin to express how helpful it was, all those years, to have a faithful friend in my old home, keeping me apprised of everything that mattered. And of course she knew just where to come when you staged your childish little rebellion."

"*Blennie?*" Agatha mouthed. But she couldn't say the name out loud, not with Miss Blenheim grinning at her over her aunt's fur-trimmed shoulder.

Agatha knew that grin, even after two years of freedom.

"Oh, you might be surprised at how well I know you already, my darling niece," Clarisse said. "But never fear. Once we leave for London next week, you shall grow to understand me as well...and you may be surprised by just how much we have in common."

Agatha couldn't answer. All she could do was stagger out of the room before the strength in her legs deserted her.

The helping spirit who assisted her in lieu of a proper lady's maid never made its appearance in her room that evening, but Agatha took no note of its absence. All that her senses could encompass was the sound of her aunt and Miss Blenheim's mingled laughter, ringing in her ears all night long.

Many new visitors to London notice first the miasma in the air, a thick, dark substance pumped out from the thousands of chimneys and coal stoves that fill the capital. The unsavory pollution can stagger noses still accustomed to the more innocent countryside, especially in addition to the overwhelming and inescapable aroma of horse dung.

Other newcomers gasp first at the sheer size and variety of the crowds pressing about their carriage, from the pedestrian throng that chokes the streets to the peddlers who sell everything from eels to china, and the thin children who sweep the dung away and dart through the crowd in rags more fit for the Dark Ages than a supposed Age of Progress.

Clarisse, needless to say, ignored it all. She maintained a steady stream of chatter about the Great Exhibition that was taking place in the Crystal Palace, to show off the technological advancements of the age...and Agatha, with Miss Blenheim's sardonic gaze resting upon her, sat silent and icy cold on her side of the carriage, numb to the press of humanity and the sights outside.

Over the past four days, she had come to understand the full extent of her aunt's new dominion. The helping spirits Agatha had summoned so carefully over the years were all dismissed like smoke blown through the air; the grimoires she could have used to summon reinforcements were locked out of her reach; and worst of all, when she had stepped into her father's library the day after Clarisse's arrival, Sir Jasper had reacted with an embarrassed cough.

"I say...should you really be here, Agatha?"

Agatha stared at him. Her armchair still sat beside his in its regular position; her footstool stood prepared before it. "Why would I not be?"

He looked pained. "Well, as a young lady...that is, if any of those gossips got wind...I mean to say...well, it's not quite the done thing, is it?"

Agatha folded her hands together to keep them from curving into claws. "Has my aunt Clarisse instructed you not to allow me in here anymore?"

"I wouldn't say *instructed*," said Sir Jasper. "But you know, if anyone in London did ever find out that you'd been practicing magic out here, as an unmarried female—well, if Clarisse hasn't managed to snag you a husband first—that is—oh, blast it, Agatha, you simply can't be here anymore! I cannot have Clarisse breathing down my collar for allowing it despite all the promises our parents made her. You have no notion of how she can discompose a fellow!"

"No?" Agatha asked, her spine rigidly straight. "You think not?"

But Sir Jasper had already turned back to his books...and Clarisse's carriage took both ladies to London four days later.

When the carriage finally drew up in front of a row of red

brick terraced houses in a relatively quiet London square, after eight full hours of travel, Agatha lunged for the door like a sailor reaching dry land after a year at sea.

"My, such undignified haste." Clarisse clucked disapprovingly and pulled her furs tighter around herself. "You may wait for a footman to hand you down, dear. And don't take too long about making your toilette; we must sally out once more as soon as possible, to visit the modistes at Cranbourne Street before the end of the day. Our first engagement is tomorrow evening, you know, and we cannot have you still looking like such a country yokel. Not when so many gentlemen are waiting to meet you there."

Agatha felt, more than saw, the curl of Miss Blenheim's upper lip and the quick flick of Miss Blenheim's gaze cataloguing her features, no different now than they had been throughout her childhood.

She kept her mouth shut despite all temptation. She would not humiliate herself by protests that were clearly futile.

The next evening she entered Lady Sherington's glittering drawing room in a new gown of deep golden silk, with a domed skirt that swept two full feet in either direction of her nipped-in waist, sustained underneath by uncomfortably thick and heavy horsehair petticoats. Her hair was, of course, still unmistakably copper, but it was also carefully teased into silly ringlets and puffed over her ears before rising to a *chignon* behind her head.

("This is all useless anyway," Miss Blenheim had

muttered, as she'd held the hot curling tongs by Agatha's face. "We can't disguise the color, can we?"

And Clarisse had sighed in regretful agreement.)

The drawing room was richly lit by candles, and a dozen mirrors flung the candlelight's reflection onto the velvets and silks of the assembled company. The reflected light flashed against the diamonds and garnets on the bare skin of the women and the ornamental dress swords strapped to the sides of the officers.

Agatha lifted her chin and glared defiantly at them all. She refused to duck her head to hide her nose or her hair. All the better to frighten off any would-be suitors and save her the trouble of refusing them.

"My dearest Clarisse!" Lady Sherington rustled toward Agatha's aunt, emeralds and rubies glinting on her outstretched fingers. "How delightful to see you home at last. And this is your dear niece? Oh, yes." She exchanged a conspiratorial glance with Clarisse, as Agatha's back stiffened. "I do see what you mean. Well, I may tell you that every gentleman on your list is here tonight, and they are most impatient to make her acquaintance." She turned a kind smile on Agatha. "You needn't worry about being a wallflower tonight, my dear."

"I wasn't worrying," Agatha said, through gritted teeth.

Lady Sherington's eyes widened. Then she and Clarisse both burst into laughter as they linked arms and steered Agatha into the room.

Two hours later, Agatha took ignominious shelter in the

lady's retiring room. Thankfully, it was empty, but she could still hear the laughter and voices from the dance nearby ringing through the walls and grating against her ears. She tipped her head against the cool glass of the mirror and closed her eyes.

I am ice. I am stone. This cannot affect me.

"Oh, where has that foolish girl got to now?" Her aunt's voice sounded through the door of the retiring room, and Agatha gave a start that rapped her head against the mirror. As she straightened with a jerk, her aunt continued, "Have no fear, Captain de Lacey. She shall be only too delighted to dance with you a second time—couldn't you see how ecstatic she was to be noticed by you in the first place? Just let me...."

The door handle began to turn. Agatha spun around. Her gaze landed on the servant's door hidden in the wall. She lunged for the crack in the wallpaper, slipped through into darkness—

—and bumped hard into another girl already hiding there.

"Oof!" Agatha's breath knocked out of her.

"Quick!" hissed the other girl, and pushed the door shut just in time.

"Agatha?" Clarisse's voice sounded in the retiring room. "You aren't trying to hide somewhere in here, are you? Because you know there's no use...ah well." Her voice softened to wry amusement. "Probably gone to the library," she murmured. "Not that that fool will care. All the better not to let her muck it up, anyway."

Footsteps moved away. The door opened and shut.

Agatha finally breathed again.

In the unlit, windowless corridor, she couldn't make out any of the other girl's features, only a general impression of warmth, soft breathing, and a shape a little smaller than her own. Their domed skirts were so bulky, they took up all the width in the narrow corridor, and Agatha could feel her silk skirts being crushed by the enclosing walls. Thinking of Clarisse's irritation at the sight was her one consolation for the indignity of her position.

"Your mother?" the other girl asked sympathetically. From her matter-of-fact tone, it might have been a perfectly customary experience to have a casual social meeting in a darkened servant's corridor.

"My aunt." It came out as a growl from Agatha's throat. "She's determined to marry me off."

"Aren't they all? Well, apart from mine, anyway. She gave up on me ages ago."

"Why?" asked Agatha. Then she realized, too late, all that the darkness might be hiding. She winced. *Graceless as ever, Agatha.* She could almost hear the amused, scornful words spoken in her ex-governess's voice. *This* was why she was better off alone with her studies, not trying to make conversation with party guests. "I apologize," she said stiffly. "You needn't answer if—"

"Oh, I'm not deformed," the other girl said cheerfully. "Only hopelessly poor, and not beautiful enough to make up for it. Worse yet, I'm bookish, to round it all off. In fact, I'm a naturalist, like Mr. Darwin."

There was a pause as Agatha assimilated the news. An inexplicable feeling of warmth and ease was slipping through her, relaxing the muscles in her back for the first time in five days. The dark, narrow corridor felt seductively safe, the close air like a protective bubble that held the two of them separate from reality. She felt a dangerous urge to reveal all her own secrets in response to that warm, cheerfully open voice.

As she struggled with herself, the other girl spoke again, this time sounding subdued. "You probably think it's unladylike or absurd to call myself a naturalist, don't you? I shouldn't have told you, I suppose."

"No!" Startled, Agatha reached out. Her fingers found the other girl's gloved hand. "I think it's wonderful, actually."

The other girl's fingers felt warm and strong through the fabric of their gloves. The weight of their skirts seemed to push them closer together in the narrow corridor. Suddenly dizzy, Agatha said, "I practice magic. That's not ladylike either."

"Do you really?" The other girl sounded delighted. "I knew there was something about you! From the moment I saw you in that doorway..."

Agatha dropped her hand as if she'd been burned. "I know," she said. Her shoulders hunched as her voice turned flat. "My features and my hair color and my deportment. You needn't remind me of my appearance."

"I beg your pardon?" Agatha could feel the other girl's astonished stare, even though she couldn't see it. "What are you talking about?"

Agatha gritted her teeth. "Large. Red. And awkward. That is what you meant, isn't it? Believe me, I harbor no illusions about my lack of attractions, so you really needn't—"

"That's not what I meant at all. Who was ever mad enough to call you unattractive?" Warm fingers closed around Agatha's gloved hand in the darkness. "But there is something about you, something different. I didn't know what it was until now. It's the magic, isn't it? I can feel it sparking in your skin. It's amazing."

Agatha swallowed. Her throat was dry, her pulse oddly rapid. She could feel sparks, too, suddenly racing up and down her skin, but they didn't feel like magic. They didn't feel like anything she recognized. "That's not how magic works," she said. "Magic is all about using the proper grimoires, with exactly the right words in Greek. It has nothing to do with talent, only diligence, and using the right supplies. You can't even use normal candles, they have to be specially prepared. They're very expensive..."

Her voice trailed to a halt. The air in the servant's corridor felt so hot, she was tingling and light-headed. She spoke almost at random as she finished: "My aunt stole all my grimoires and supplies, so I can't do magic anymore."

The other girl laughed, a shockingly intimate sound in the darkness. "Who told you that?"

Agatha blinked. "Everyone! All my father's treatises say—"

"Well, isn't that what gentlemen always say? And no wonder. If you need to mouth exactly the same Greek phrases some man came up with three hundred years ago, you'll need money and education to get hold of the texts and make use of them, won't you? And if you've been told you can't even try it without expensive supplies..."

"The treatises all say it would be too dangerous," said Agatha.

"Then that keeps women and the lower orders safely in their place, doesn't it? Leaving the magic to the gentlemen who rule the empire." The other girl snorted. "No wonder they don't want anyone else sharing their power. They wouldn't let me into university either, even though I'd taught myself Latin and Greek as well as any Eton student. But do you think I'm going to let them stop me?"

"No?" Agatha said. Somehow, they were standing even closer now. She could feel the other girl's breath brush warm against her cheek. It felt like a warm breeze waking her at last from the icy chill of helplessness that had gripped her for the last five days. Every inch of her body tingled with reaction.

"Never," said the girl. "If they won't let me study at Cambridge with the gentlemen, I'll simply teach myself. That's the message of the Great Exhibition, isn't it? Times are changing, at long last. And when I start publishing treatises about my discoveries, no one will care whether or not I ever sat in a university classroom with a whole crowd of wealthy idiots."

"I believe you," Agatha said. And she did. She felt wider awake than she had in days, and wild with curiosity. "What's your name?"

There was a long pause. Then... "Isobel," said the girl. "Isobel Cunningham. I'm Mrs. Wesley Stanhope's companion, for my sins. She's probably calling for me again by now." She sighed, her fingers relaxing their warm grip around Agatha's. "I should go. But thank you. It was lovely to meet you, whoever you are."

"Agatha Tremain," said Agatha. She moved forward when Isobel stepped back. "Wait," she said. "Can I call on you tomorrow? If I can escape my aunt—"

"Mrs. Stanhope doesn't like me to receive callers," Isobel said.

"But—"

"We'll be at the Tennants' ball tomorrow," said Isobel. "Who knows?" She moved closer, her voice lowering to a whisper. "Maybe you'll find me in a servants' corridor again, where no one else can see us."

Her breath brushed against Agatha's mouth. Agatha felt her heart begin to race. She held perfectly still, waiting for...for...

"Goodbye, Agatha," said Isobel softly.

She opened the door and slipped swiftly into the retiring room, revealing only the back of her rich brown hair and her modest gray bombazine dress in the candlelit doorway. By the time Agatha forced herself out of her trance to push the door open again and search for more, Isobel had vanished from the room.

* * *

Agatha moved through the rest of the evening in a daze, dancing without protest with each gentlemen her aunt presented to her, but making only monosyllabic, distracted answers to the conversation that sounded like buzzing insects around her ears. No matter how she craned her head over her various partners' shoulders, she couldn't catch sight of that plain gray bombazine gown anywhere in the crowd.

All she lived for, in the endless hours that remained, was the moment when she would be allowed to return to her room in the rented townhouse, to turn over every memory of that brief, electric meeting in her mind. As she and her aunt rode back in their carriage, she let Clarisse's icy stream of words wash over her, as harmless as rain against a sturdy umbrella.

The Tennants' ball would be tomorrow. She would have another new gown by then, the modiste had promised. Not that appearances mattered in a servants' corridor, of course. But still...

When she started down the corridor toward her bedroom, Clarisse's hand shot out as quickly as a striking snake to fasten around her arm. "Oh, no, my dear. We have important matters still to discuss."

Yanked out of her thoughts, Agatha pulled her arm free. "I'm sure tomorrow will be soon enough."

"Tomorrow," said Clarisse, "we shall announce the news of your betrothal. I will compose the notice to the newspapers tonight."

"What?" Agatha stared at her. "But I haven't—no one has even proposed to me yet."

"Goodness, what a romantic you are. I had no idea of it!" Clarisse tittered as she walked gracefully into her own bedroom, her vast skirts and petticoats rustling and her Indian shawl wrapped tightly around her shoulders. "Your fiancé arranged it with me himself, of course, just as mine did with my own parents. You have nothing to do with the decision."

"But..." Stopping short in the doorway, Agatha stumbled to a halt. Miss Blenheim stood at the dressing table, holding Clarisse's fur-lined dressing gown. Under her ex-governess's gleaming gaze, Agatha's instinctive urge was to freeze or, better yet, retreat to safety.

She remembered Isobel's words. *"Do you think I'm going to let that stop me?"*

No, Agatha told herself, and her shoulders straightened. "I believe," she said coolly, "it is customary for a gentleman to ask a young lady's consent as well."

"Oh, well, in love matches, perhaps..." Clarisse waved a careless hand in dismissal.

Miss Blenheim tsk'ed compassionately. "Did you really expect someone to fall in love with *your* face, Miss?"

Even as Agatha started to shrink, she remembered that warm, delighted voice. *"Who was mad enough to call you unattractive?"*

Of course Isobel had only seen her for a moment in the doorway; the words meant nothing, really, not when she thought logically about them. Isobel might well change her mind in the light of day. But still...

Agatha's chin lifted. "The law may not allow me to choose a husband without my father's consent," she said, "but you cannot force me to marry against my will. I will say no all the way to the altar itself."

"Now, my darling girl." Her aunt sank down in front of the blazing fire, as Miss Blenheim wrapped the dressing gown around her solicitously. Tucking her chin into the lush fur collar, Clarisse said, "I believe it is time for you to understand the truth about the women of our family."

As Agatha saw her aunt shiver and lean into the fire, her newly-wakened senses grated at her.

"It's as hot as a furnace in here," she said. "Why are you wrapping yourself up so tightly?" She frowned, thinking back. "You always do, don't you?"

Miss Blenheim's lips curled as she leaned over to stoke the fire higher. "It took you this long to notice, Miss?"

"Now, Blennie. I told you she must be clever enough to put together the pieces eventually, did I not?" Clarisse gave her niece an unfriendly smile. "Well done, my dear. But I would attempt a bit more compassion, as you'll be sharing my condition yourself soon enough."

"What do you mean?"

Clarisse rolled her eyes. "Why do you think all your little magical experiments at Tremain House were so successful?"

Caught off guard, Agatha answered with involuntary honesty: "Because I had nothing and no one to distract me from my studies. They're the only thing I've ever been good at." Then she felt herself flush, as she realized the truth of it...

and exactly who she'd said it to, as Miss Blenheim let out a soft snort of contempt.

Still, it was true, wasn't it? And it had been all she'd wanted...or all that she'd allowed herself to want, at least. She frowned.

She had believed all that Miss Blenheim had told her about herself. She'd sworn never to be humiliated again by trying for anything she couldn't have.

Agatha remembered again Isobel's warm voice; the soft breath whispering across her mouth.

I can have more, she thought suddenly. *I can believe what I want about myself. I don't have to settle for less.*

But her aunt regarded her with a jaundiced eye. "It is all that makes you valuable, I agree," said Clarisse. "But then, you are a Tremain female, and that means you have an affinity for magic, just as I have, and my aunt and my grandmother before me. How do you think your great-grandfather acquired Tremain House and all his fortune in the first place? That is why you have a duty to the family to marry, for the sake of your older female relatives; it is why a particular sort of gentleman will pay so well for the privilege of having you to wife; and it is why you *will* marry, dear girl, whether you like it or not, and you will marry with some speed, too. It is your turn now to step into the breach, and I have waited quite long enough for a younger Tremain female to finally pay me back what I am owed."

"For what?" Agatha gaped at her. "What have you ever done for me?"

"It is the sacrifice all the females in our family have to pay," said Clarisse. "Magic ripples through our veins, you see. If you were a man, you could make use of it. As a woman, you were born to be a source of power, just as I was for far too many years to contemplate. But just think..." She gave Agatha a look of mock-sympathy. "Your husband may make marvelous advances for the British Empire using the power he draws from you. In return, he will give me what I need with the first magic he extracts. And then..." She sighed, leaning closer to the fire. "I shall never be cold again."

Agatha's head spun with more than the heat of the room now. She held still, refusing to retreat. "Why can't you take for yourself what you need? Why do you need my future husband to do it?"

"Because those spells are never taught to women," said Clarisse wearily. "You've never come across them in your father's library, have you? No, Jasper may be the most useless and impractical creature ever born, but even he is not so careless as to allow any of those texts to be kept in public view on his shelves.

"But none of that matters now." Clarisse shook her head dismissively. "All you need to understand, dear, is that my magic was drained out of me over and over again across the years while my husband rose ever higher in the Austro-Hungarian Court. Simply dismissing your creatures from Tremain House took nearly all that I had left." Her lips curled into a smile. "Nearly...but not all."

Slowly, sinuously, she rose to her feet, while Miss Blenheim smiled behind her, a smile of deep satisfaction.

"I have been waiting for this day for two long years, Miss," said Miss Blenheim. "Did you really think you could dismiss me so easily? Knowing all that I do about you and your family?"

Agatha could only shake her head numbly.

"It was tremendously helpful of you to keep all your books and supplies so carefully organized in your little office," Clarisse said. "When combined with the supplies that my dear Blennie found for me in Vienna, I am more than prepared to take on this last spell. And I think we can agree, can we not, that I am the only person in this room with both magical power *and* the spells and supplies that are needed for it?"

Agatha looked from her aunt to Miss Blenheim. Her chest tightened.

She had wanted so badly to believe herself free.

"What are you planning?" she asked, through dry lips.

"That," said Clarisse, "is entirely up to you. If you are a good girl and follow your part in the plan like every Tremain girl has before you for the past hundred years, I won't need to do a thing—and you may have your payment in return as soon as your own daughter is old enough to be sacrificed.

"If not, though..." She shrugged gently. "I have both the supplies and the spellbooks to make you mouth any words I wish until you are safely wed and drained. I could not care less which choice you make."

Agatha stared at her aunt's face, so similar in shape to her own father's. "And you would really do that to me, after everything you went through yourself?"

Her aunt's blue eyes were cold and hard as sapphires. "My darling niece," she said. "I would do anything, and sacrifice anyone, only to be warm again. In twenty years, I daresay you will feel exactly the same."

Bright, hard flames leaped in the fireplace, and Agatha tasted the bitterness of defeat. If only she had managed to salvage a single grimoire, a single sanctioned brazier...

Wait. She closed her eyes. Suddenly, with the flames shut out, she was in the darkness again. And in that darkness, she was not alone.

She heard Isobel's laugh echoing in her ears. *"Who told you that?"*

Agatha had always believed she could do magic only by mouthing an expert's words. But Clarisse said magic rippled in her veins...and unlike her aunt, great-aunt, or grandmother, she had been allowed to devote two full years to the uninterrupted study of her father's grimoires. She understood the very essence of the spells she had performed, better than any Tremain girl before her.

Sparks ran up and down Agatha's skin, and this time, she knew that Isobel had been right. The sparks were magic—*her* magic, sparking through her. Her own personal magic, which she had never believed in until tonight.

Her magic, which she would never allow anyone to take away from her again.

"This is an Age of Progress," she said. "Things are changing for all of us, now. We don't have to follow the old ways anymore."

She opened her eyes and looked from her aunt to Miss Blenheim. "Do you know what the last spell was that I worked on, back at Tremain House?"

Clarisse frowned. "I can't imagine that it would be relevant, dear."

Miss Blenheim sneered. "Do you think we care about any of your little games, Miss?"

"No," Agatha said. "But I'll tell you anyway..."

She smiled as she finished: "Transformation."

She lifted her arms and magic swept out from them, changing the world around her.

The Tennants' ball was packed with ladies in sparkling diamond tiaras, ropes of pearls, and gowns that swirled across the crowded floor. Footmen bellowed out the names of each new arrival. Officers smiled down at admiring girls and black-coated gentlemen swept their dance partners around the room.

Agatha ignored them all. Whispers rustled around her as she forced her way, unchaperoned, through the crowd, but she barely even noticed.

Her hair was pinned into a plain bun with no ringlets or waves. It was all that she could manage without the help of a maid. Her corset was undoubtedly laced too loosely for an absolutely perfect waist; her new blue gown didn't fit as well as it had in the modiste's fitting room.

In the dark, though, none of that would matter. If only she was still in time...

She stepped into the ladies' retiring room and forced herself to wait for the giggling, excited crowd of other girls to finish fixing their appearances. The moment the door to the main corridor closed behind them, she pressed her hand to the crack she had glimpsed in the flowered wallpaper. More female voices were coming down the corridor. She rushed headlong into the darkness before they could arrive.

Warm, ungloved hands caught her, and pressed the hidden door shut behind her.

"You came!" Isobel said.

"You waited," said Agatha.

"I've been waiting for an hour," Isobel said, so softly that Agatha could barely hear her. "I had to take off my gloves after the first half hour—it's so hot in here. Mrs. Stanhope probably thinks I've run away by now. I suppose it was silly to hope you would really come, but..."

"I hope you will run away from Mrs. Stanhope," Agatha said. "I mean..." She stopped, gathering her breath. Her corset laces might be loose, but she still felt light-headed. She was gasping for air. She could feel Isobel only inches away; could feel their heavy skirts brushing against each other.

She had never been so frightened in her life. But she couldn't give up now.

"I'm going back to Tremain House," she said. "I hoped... will you come with me? Please?"

There was a pause. Agatha couldn't see Isobel's face, couldn't guess at her expression.

"When you say I should come with you," Isobel finally said, "do you mean as a companion? As I am to Mrs. Stanhope?"

Agatha swallowed hard. "If you want," she said. "That is, I could do with a friend, and a companion. I think I've spent too much time alone. But also..."

She closed her eyes in the darkness.

She had sworn never to humiliate herself by asking for what she couldn't have. But she had also made a vow to never hide again.

Agatha leaned forward, holding her breath.

Isobel's lips were soft and full.

Magic sparked between them.

A long time later, Agatha drew back. She was breathing quickly now, flushed with a warmth that left her unsteady. She wanted to laugh, or cry, or dance in the darkness. She forced herself to hold perfectly still instead as she waited for Isobel's reaction.

"Well," Isobel said consideringly, "in that case..." She laughed suddenly, and her voice was bright with joy. "Yes. Yes, yes, yes!"

"Really?" Agatha caught hold of the rough wall to support herself as her legs turned limp with relief. "You'll really come? You really want to..."

"Well," Isobel said teasingly, "as a committed naturalist, you know, I can't take any of my first observations on faith. So perhaps..." Her warm, bare fingers curled around the nape of Agatha's neck; her words whispered against Agatha's lips. "Perhaps I ought to repeat the experiment one more time, for Science's sake. And then again, and again, and again..."

* * *

Even Sir Jasper seemed pleased, in a vague sort of way, to learn that Agatha had brought Miss Cunningham home for good.

"Good for a young girl to have someone to talk to, isn't it?" he said. "She seems like a very decent companion for you, my dear. Very quiet. Doesn't bother a fellow in his library. Understands that it's the right place for a man to take his meals." He beamed, settling more comfortably into his armchair. "Thank goodness Clarisse gave up and took herself off, so we can all be comfortable again. Did she go back to Vienna, did you say? Or was it Paris this time?"

"Somewhere warm, I believe," said Agatha. "I'm certain she'll be happier now."

"Yes, yes," Sir Jasper said. "I'm sure you're right, my dear. But you brought back a set of animals from London, too, you say? What on earth did you do that for?"

"Only two animals, Papa," said Agatha, "and they won't bother you, I promise."

"Oh, no," Sir Jasper said, falling back into his book with

relief. "No, I am quite sure of that."

Agatha closed the library door behind her and went, with a spring in her step, to find Isobel. Her dearest friend would be walking in the woods at this time of day, as she did every morning while Agatha worked on her own magical studies; the woods of the Tremain estate were apparently bursting with interesting animal life.

Agatha had finished her studies earlier than usual, though; something about the scent of her latest experiment had reminded her of Isobel.

A smile deepened on her face; she lifted up her skirts to run, and magic sparked in the air around her, carrying the sound of her laughter to the woods before her.

Isobel was waiting for her there...and they were both distracted from their work for the rest of that morning, in the most delightful manner possible.

The two animal additions to the household, as promised, disturbed Sir Jasper not a whit. The housecat, a sleek black creature with an oddly straight feline nose, kept to the kitchens, where her bad temper made her a perfect mouse-catcher and a useful addition to the household...

...and the elegant, golden-blonde cocker spaniel with her coat of thick, soft fur rarely moved from her preferred spot in front of the fireplace. As Miss Tremain had given explicit orders that a fire always be lit for the dog's comfort, regardless of what heat might bake the house, she could be certain of at least one thing:

Clarisse would never be cold again.

The Wildness Inside

Nick woke up because the dogs were barking, down on the beach below the cottage. Probably a flock of Canada geese, he figured, or a weirdly-shaped piece of driftwood that had spooked them; this deep into the forested outskirts of Michigan's Upper Peninsula, strangers weren't even a possibility. He would have gone back to sleep if he could, but the barking just kept on going, Greta's deep-throated bellows mingling with Mimi's higher, nervous shrills. After about five minutes of it, Nick groaned, rolled out of bed, pulled on a pair of jeans, and strode out of the cottage, down toward the beach. The top of the horizon was still dark blue with night; the sun was only starting to creep up over Lake Superior.

The dogs crouched shoulder-to-shoulder, about ten feet

from a dark shape Nick couldn't make out. He clapped his hands.

"Greta! Mimi! Leave it."

Greta, the German shepherd, gave in first, loping back to press her big shaggy body against his side and grin up at him. Mimi took longer, her tiny poodle body quivering as she barked alone in high-pitched yips then leaped straight backward and tore toward Nick as if her life depended on it.

Nick rolled his eyes. "C'mon, you two. Let's..."

But his voice trailed off as the dark shape moved. He blinked, wishing he'd taken the time to find his glasses before he'd left the cottage. His long-distance vision sucked. Could the dark shape be a hurt animal? Coyote, maybe? No, too big. There had been a few reports of wolves spotted in the last few months, but Nick had laughed them off. Wolves were vanishingly rare up here nowadays despite all the conservation efforts, hunted to near extinction. They only ever appeared in the fairy stories told by people like his older sisters in big cities down in the lower peninsula, trotted out every time they wanted an excuse to summon him back down again to Lansing, to human society, to *Real Life.*

Still, if it was a real wolf and it was hurt, he'd have to find some way to take care of it. Wolves weren't hostile to men by nature, but injured animals were always defensive. He walked toward the dark shape slowly, just an inch or two at a time, keeping his gaze carefully averted. Cool sand crunched underneath his feet.

"It's okay," he murmured, as gently as he could. "S'okay, sweetheart, I won't hurt you, there's nothing to be scared of."

Something blurred in the corner of his eye, sudden movement. *Damn.* He turned his head with aching slowness.

He almost tripped over his own feet when he saw her. Not a wolf, not at all. A woman, lying crumpled and naked on the beach. Her head half-raised to meet him; her eyes were wide green sparked with splashes of yellow, as wild and as wary as if she really were the creature he'd somehow taken her to be.

Nick leaped back, his heart racing. "Sorry!" His breath felt constricted in his chest. He really did need to wear his glasses more often; his vision must be worse than he'd realized. He wished, belatedly, that he'd put on a shirt. Of course, she wasn't wearing anything at all, but then...

He'd been so busy *not* looking at her nakedness after that first sweeping glance, it took him a whole minute longer to react to the long, dark spot he'd seen on the beach below the curve of her bare thighs.

Blood. He looked again, saw it clearly: a jagged wound in her right thigh. She'd been shot.

Her voice was husky, barely more than a growl.

"Help me," she said. Her voice faltered. "Help me?"

"Of course," Nick said. He leaned over to lift her to her feet. Her skin was warm and tough, her grip on his hand strong and firm. She leaned against his shoulder, took a step, and gasped with pain.

"Here," Nick said. He turned and met her green, wild eyes. "Let me carry you."

The dogs padded behind them all the way up to the cottage. Tall pine trees closed around the house. Greta growled softly as they crossed the threshold; Mimi let out periodic, unhappy squeaks.

"Shh," Nick whispered.

He wasn't sure if he was really talking to them or to himself, his own raging heartbeat loud in his ears. He hadn't held a woman's naked body—hadn't so much as brushed hands, except with his sisters—since Sara's death, over two years ago. He hadn't even wanted to.

The woman in his arms held a scrap of fur clutched in her right hand. She didn't let it go even when Nick helped her down into the single kitchen chair and brought her one of his big flannel shirts to wear. She struggled into the shirt, her lips pursed in concentration, but her right hand remained clenched in a protective fist. Her other hand held the towel he'd given her to staunch the wound.

The dogs sat three feet away, eyes trained on her intently. When Nick filled up their food bowls, usually their signal for ecstasy, the two dogs didn't even glance around. Nick straightened, set down the bag of dog food, and took a breath.

The woman looked at him expectantly.

Nick had to clear his throat twice before he could speak. "The closest doctor's office is about an hour's drive. That's closed till three o'clock, though. There's a hospital, about two hours from here, so we could—"

"No," the woman said. "No—hospitals."

"Do you not have health insurance? Money?—No. No, of course not." Nick shook his head and looked out the window. The sky was lightening outside. He'd moved here for the view over the lake in the mornings, the sense of absolute peace and safety. The solitude. He felt like the gravity had gone missing underneath him as he looked back at the woman watching him. "Do you know if the bullet's still in there?"

"No." Her face settled into stern lines. "I took it out."

"You—?" He looked at her hands, bare of blood. She lifted the towel for him to look closer. He could feel her stiffen as he approached. Her legs were unshaven, thick with hair, the opposite of Sara's silk-smooth skin. The edges of the wound were raw and jagged. They looked as if sharp teeth had gnawed at the edges, delved deep inside.

He looked up, fighting a shiver. Her full lips were slightly parted; her teeth, smooth and even. He shrugged aside the superstitious images his imagination had conjured. Maybe his sisters were right, after all. Maybe he had spent too much time on his own, these past two years. Maybe it was starting to make him a little bit crazy.

He stood up and looked away. "I'll get my first aid kit and clean it out. Once we've got a bandage on it, it might heal up on its own." He paused in the doorway and made himself say the rest. "You can stay here as long as you need, to rest up."

She nodded solemnly. Greta let out a quiet whimper of distress, the sound disconcerting from her big throat.

"Shh," Nick said, to Greta, to himself. "Everything's going to be okay."

He fled the kitchen before anyone could argue.

Apart from the weekly phone calls with his sisters, Nick hadn't spoken to another human being for—how long? Weeks? Months? When he thought about it, he realized that he couldn't even remember. He did all his work online; it was just as easy to work here, from this cottage, as it ever had been down in his and Sara's house in Lansing. Far easier to do it here, now that their old house had filled with stabbing memories. In email messages, you couldn't see the pity in people's eyes, or hear the encouraging, maddening tones of their voices: *Poor man. Buck up!*

He didn't know how to talk to the woman sitting in his kitchen; how to move, how to act in his own house with her green gaze fixed on him.

He cleaned and bandaged up her leg as well as he could, found her some breakfast, and retreated to his laptop in the corner of the living room. The two rooms were linked by a wide archway and an open hatch. He couldn't stop listening to her movements as he worked at typing in code or just stared at the screen, reading and re-reading the same page of script.

After half an hour of it, he gave in and just let himself watch her through the kitchen hatch. She was moving slowly but thoroughly through the whole room, limping but determined, picking up one object at a time, frowning down at each and then—he couldn't avert his gaze—sniffing each object deeply. She sniffed with an intensity he'd never seen in anyone but his dogs. Her eyes drifted closed as she lifted the coffee canister and inhaled its scent; he saw the exhalation of her breath all along the line of her throat and chest.

Nick stood up hastily, almost knocking his chair over. She jerked around, eyes flaring. They stared at each other through the kitchen hatch.

"I'm, uh, just going to clean out the kennels," Nick said. "Through there." He pointed, needlessly, at the back door.

She nodded, eyes still wide. He saw that she had scooped up her scrap of fur. She held it pressed close to her chest.

It was a relief to escape outside to the fresh air and hard physical work. Greta and Mimi both stored all manner of forbidden treasures in their outdoor kennels, from rotting trash to ball point pens. Normally, whenever he cleaned out their stashes, the two dogs hung about behind him, helpless but concerned. Today, they didn't budge from the kitchen.

Nick was hosing down the clean kennels at the end, back aching, when he heard footsteps behind him on the gravel drive.

"Are you hungry? I could—oh." Nick stopped as he turned around.

A gray-haired, stocky man in camouflage, a baseball cap and an orange vest stood between him and the cottage, holding a gun. *Hunter*, Nick thought, with a twinge of distaste. He'd never felt any urge to kill animals for sport, even before he'd lost all ability, two years ago, to think of death in a calm manner.

Then he looked again at the gun and felt his chest tighten.

The curtains in the cottage were drawn. He hoped they'd stay that way.

"Morning," the hunter said affably. "Nice weather."

"Good enough." Nick switched off the hose. "Can I help you with something?"

There were no signs of another car. The man must have walked here through miles of forest.

"Sorry to bother you, sir." The man's eyes were intent. "I came to ask if you'd seen any wolves in the area."

Nick looked pointedly at the gun. "Last I heard, it was illegal to shoot wolves. They're an endangered species, aren't they?"

The man nodded. "So we can't go hunting for them—but we sure can shoot them in self-defense if they attack us. So it's only smart to carry a gun around them, right?" He shrugged, smiling.

Nick didn't smile back. "Wolves don't attack people. That's a myth."

"You might be surprised how many myths are true. You're not from around here, are you?"

Nick looked back at him for a long moment. "I haven't seen any wolves," he said, finally.

"Pity. There's one got shot last night—attacked some poor guy outright, I heard—but got away."

"I didn't hear anything in the news about that."

"Oh, it wasn't local, but wolves can run for miles. It's a long, hard end for an animal, bleeding to death." The man's eyes narrowed. "I'm sure a man like you, with pets you care about"—he nodded at the kennels—"wouldn't like to see an animal in agony. Better to give it a good, clean death with a single shot."

"I don't have a gun."

The man shook his head gently. "Pity. But I'll thank you for your time anyway. Sorry for trespassing on your patience, sir."

"You're trespassing on my land," Nick said. "These thirty acres of forest and beach belong to me." Behind the man's back, he saw the back door of the cottage open and the woman look out. His stomach clenched. He added, more loudly than he'd intended, "And I don't allow hunting on my property."

"Is that so?" The hunter spun around as quickly as a snake uncoiling.

The back door was closed. No signs of life showed in the cottage.

"That's right," Nick said. He tried to slow his racing heartbeat.

"Well, then. Good to know." The hunter touched the tip of his baseball cap and turned away. "Maybe I'll be seeing you again."

"Not on my property, you won't."

The other man's voice floated back to him as he walked into the woods. "Pity..."

Nick stood still, watching, until the other man had disappeared. Then he turned and walked, deliberately slowly, into the house. The woman sat with her good leg curled up beneath her on the big faded-blue sofa in the living room. Greta and Mimi lay on the floor in front of her. As Nick walked in, he saw Greta lift her big head to lick the woman's hand, tail thumping in submission.

"He's gone," Nick said. "I told him not to come back."

The woman nodded. "Thank you."

Nick looked at the scrap of fur, which she'd left on the coffee table. He felt her sudden tension, as she saw the direction of his gaze.

Nick took a deep breath and rolled his shoulders out. "I'm going to make some coffee. D'you want some?"

Maybe it's time to read up on myths, he thought, as he turned toward the kitchen.

He drove into town the next day, Tuesday, his usual day for a grocery run at Bronner's General Store. This time, along with his normal supplies, he stocked up on bandages and antibiotic ointment and some wood for carpentry. He took his time picking out the wood, even though he was already thinking about the library trip ahead, planning where to start his search even as he walked up to the cash register.

The woman who owned the shop—Mrs. Bronner, he assumed—rang his items up without comment, as usual. As she passed him back his change, though, she said abruptly, "There was a fellow in here yesterday, talking about you."

"Sorry?" Nick took the coins and looked closely at her for the first time in the two years he'd been shopping there.

She was about sixty, small but solid and tough-looking, with short-cropped white hair. Her blue eyes narrowed thoughtfully as she looked back at him. "It was you, all right. He described your place real well."

"What did he say?"

Tension built between Nick's shoulders. Over the woman's head, he saw her husband step out of the shop's back office and lean against the wall, listening.

"Said you were keeping a full-blood, wild wolf as a pet." Mrs. Bronner snorted. "Told us all about how illegal that was. Thought we should hear about it and maybe pass the story around."

"Oh." Nick pulled the grocery bag across the counter, gathering it to his side. The bandages slipped off the top; Mrs. Bronner passed them to him without a flicker of nuance in her expression.

"Friend of ours had a wolf as a pet once," her husband offered. "Cutest little pup you ever saw, but it didn't work out so well when he grew up. Never does. They may look like dogs, but no matter how much love you give 'em, you can never take away the wildness inside. They just can't be happy settling in a human house."

Nick said, "Right."

The woman in his house had taken the sofa instead of the

bed, by preference, last night. When he'd stepped into the living room that morning, he'd found her curled up on the cushions, asleep, a tangle of long limbs and dark hair. Her eyes had opened the moment he'd looked at her; he'd stood like that, just holding her green gaze, for a full minute before he'd been able to make himself speak.

"Right," Nick repeated. "Ah...do you know how many other people this guy talked to?"

"Doesn't matter," Mrs. Bronner said. She turned and exchanged a look with her husband, who nodded. "You've been here a while now," she said. "Him?" She shrugged. "No one's ever seen him before."

"Thanks." Nick felt a strange, hot prickling behind his eyes. He turned to walk away.

"Son?" The man behind the counter called out to him as Nick opened the door. "If you did happen to know anyone with a wolf..."

Nick paused. "Yeah?"

"I'd keep it safe inside for a while." Bronner's gaze was steady. "That gun looked pretty serious. And the man holding it—he didn't seem like the type to take a 'no' and go away quietly."

Nick ran all the way to the car. He gunned the engine, hitting ninety on the long, empty road home, cursing himself for stupidity. Library trips? Research? *Idiot.* He should have taken her with him, should have...

Gravel spattered as he pulled into his driveway far too

quickly. He heard a stifled yelp, saw a blur of grey fur, heard a slamming door at the back of the house.

He launched himself out of the car and into the house. The front door was unlocked. As he'd left it. Stupid, brainless...

"Hello?" the woman called, from the living room.

She was sitting upright on the sofa, hair disheveled, breathing hard. She clutched one of his flannel shirts to her chest; the scrap of fur had fallen to the ground beside the sofa.Greta and Mimi paced around her, tails wagging low to the ground with worry.

Nick closed his eyes a moment just to breathe in the sweet relief. When he opened them again, she was wearing the shirt, and the scrap of fur had disappeared into one of her pockets.

"That hunter," Nick said. "He hasn't left. He's been going around town, trying to stir things up. He might come back any time. So it would be a good idea..." He met her eyes, feeling light-headed. "It would probably be a good idea if he didn't see a wolf outside the house."

Her eyes widened. Her hand crept up to touch the right-hand pocket of her shirt. "You—know?"

Nick shrugged. "We'll keep the doors locked from now on, too. I'll give you the spare key, so you won't be trapped."

"But..." She stood slowly and limped toward him, her green gaze intent. "You *know*."

"It's all right," Nick said. "I won't tell anyone."

She shook her head. A wondering smile tugged at her lips. "I believe you," she whispered.

She leaned forward, put one hand on his shoulder for support, and wrapped the other in his hair. Then she kissed him.

Her lips sent sparks across his as they kissed; her smooth teeth nipped his lower lip playfully. Laughing, she released him. Nick licked his tingling lips and looked at her. She was just as tall as him; her green, wild eyes on a direct level with his.

"Come on." She took his hand and pulled him toward the kitchen. "I'm hungry!"

Nick followed her in, past the open windows. The feeling in his chest was so unfamiliar, it took him a long time to recognize it. He only finally worked it out halfway through lunch, as she laughed and talked and made him talk too, making him explain exactly what all the different appliances did, how everything worked and what all the different words he used meant. When he realized what the feeling was, it startled him so much that he stopped talking for a moment and closed his mouth entirely, until she reached over and tugged at his hair and made him answer another question.

It had been a long time since he'd felt happiness.

His sister Christine called two nights later as Nick was working in the kitchen, building a new chair and a stool for the wolfwoman to stretch her injured leg onto. The wolfwoman herself—Kyra, she'd decided—was frowning over a book in the living room, her forehead knotted in concentration. Somehow, at some point, someone must have taught her to read, but who her teacher had been, Nick didn't ask, and Kyra didn't volunteer any answer. They talked about everything, it seemed, except the past...and those moments when she used her key to slip outside on expeditions she didn't invite him to join.

"Nick?" Christine's voice sounded brittle and slightly impatient, the telephone call just one in a steady line of tasks in her busy evening, dealing with her three kids and her husband after her job and still taking the time to check in on her brother.

She worried about him, Nick knew; still, he sighed when he heard her voice, and settled back against the cupboard to listen patiently to her weekly lecture.

In the living room, Kyra sighed, too, and tossed her book down. Greta crept across the floor to her, head averted in submission, stomach brushing the carpet. Kyra murmured softly to the dog in a low, husky growl and stroked her fingers through Greta's shaggy ruff. With a sigh of contentment, the big dog rolled over and presented her chest for petting. Mimi raced over to join them, nearly shrieking with excitement, and Nick had to choke back a laugh. Kyra looked up and met his gaze; her own face was filled with affectionate amusement.

"Nick? Nick, are you even listening to me?" Christine asked.

"Of course I am," Nick said, and tried to summon up her lost words. Since he couldn't remember them, he fell back on a safe guess. "I'm sorry, Chris, but I'm not moving back. I'm happy here."

"Happy?" Christine laughed shortly. "How could you be happy living like a hermit?"

"I've got the dogs," Nick said lightly. "And friends." He held Kyra's gaze with his own. She winked.

"What friends? You won't even talk to anybody unless we call and force you into it." Christine sighed. "This is pointless." A thread of real unhappiness entered her voice. "It's been long enough. For God's sake, it's been over two years. Aren't you finally ready to let go?"

"Let go of what?" Nick asked. Discomfort twisted through his chest.

Christine's voice was unexpectedly gentle. "The pain. I'm sorry, Nick, but you can't keep mourning Sara forever. You need to let it go."

Nick took a deep breath and released it. Kyra and the dogs were watching him from the living room. He lowered his voice. "I *have* let go. I'm not sitting up here feeling sorry for myself. Not anymore."

"Are you sure? Because it sounds to me—"

"Just *let it go*, all right?"

There was a dead silence. Nick realized he'd nearly shouted the words.

The pressure in his head threatened to overwhelm him. He pressed one hand against his forehead and closed his eyes.

"It's been two years," he said dully. "It used to hurt all the time, it did, but...it hasn't hurt like that for a while. Months. Maybe even a year."

But he had never realized that, until now. How long had it been since he'd thought, *really* thought about Sara? Since he'd summoned up the image of her face on the pillow next to his in the morning, and remembered the sweet slide of her soft skin against his? Since he'd smelled the vanilla scent of her perfume, imagined the sound of her helpless, snorting laughter over those ridiculous cartoons that she loved...

It had happened as gradually and as naturally as the passing of the seasons, and he hadn't even noticed.

Nick felt the muscles of his back and arms clench, then start to shiver as if he had been caught in a sudden snowstorm.

"I'm sorry, Chris," he whispered. "I've got to go."

He set the phone down in its receiver without opening his eyes. When it began to ring again, a moment later, he ignored it.

How could he have let Sara go?

He felt a warm hand cover the hand he held to his forehead. Slowly, he opened his eyes.

Kyra was kneeling in front of him, frowning. She looked at him steadily, in silence. The tumult of feelings inside his chest was too strong for Nick to speak.

He reached up with his free hand to cover hers. Her fingers were warm and strong. For that moment, it was enough.

He woke the next morning feeling strange and unmoored, as if he'd been cut loose from reality. He blinked, trying to capture the difference. Sunlight slanted through the windows, higher than usual. He'd slept in.

Then he turned his head and saw Kyra watching him from the second pillow, her dark hair tangled around her face, her eyes gleaming. Her grin deepened into a smirk.

"I knew I could wake you if I watched you long enough."

Nick blinked. Memories flooded him, filling him with tingling warmth...and uneasiness. He reached out to stroke the side of her face. "I feel like I'm still dreaming."

Kyra turned her head and kissed his fingers, nipping them gently. "Maybe you are." She rolled over until she was on top of him, warm and solid. "Do you want to check?"

"Yes," Nick said, breathlessly. He reached up to kiss her. Guilt clenched his chest as their lips touched, until he couldn't even taste the musky warmth of her mouth.

Sara.

What was he doing?

He rolled away, dislodging Kyra, breathing hard. "I can't —I..."

She stared at him. "What's wrong?"

Nick took a deep breath. "Let me take you out to breakfast. We'll drive into town, go to a restaurant. It'll be great."

Kyra frowned. "Nick—"

"Please." Forcing a smile, he reached out to stroke his hand along her bare shoulder. "I just need to get out of this house for a while, okay?"

She sighed, her eyes closing against him. "If that's what you want."

He pulled on clothing, skipped all the morning rituals. Normally, he would have let the dogs roam free while they were gone, but he shut them safe in their kennels today, in case the hunter came back. He rushed Kyra into the car, talking loudly the whole time to silence his own thoughts. She followed him, nearly as silent as on her first day, watching him with worried eyes. Only when they had been driving for twenty minutes did she suddenly gasp and run her hands over her pockets.

"We have to go back!"

"What? Why?" The windows were rolled down; wind ruffled through Nick's uncombed hair. It was good to let the wind blow over him, blowing away his twisting, painful thoughts.

"My fur. I forgot to grab it! I was so worried..." Kyra's voice drifted off; she bit her lip. "We have to go back," she said again.

"I can't," Nick said. "Not yet." He tightened his hands around the steering wheel. "We won't be gone long, I promise. Just three or four hours."

"You don't understand." She put her hand on his thigh, squeezed. "This is important!"

"It's okay," Nick said. "It'll be safe in the house. The doors are locked and the dogs are there. No one's going to take it."

"But..."

"Please," Nick said. "I need to go out and just...pretend we're a normal couple." *Pretend I'm not cheating on my wife. Oh, God!*

This didn't count as a real betrayal, though. Did it? He couldn't think straight. The idea of going back to the house right now—that house—felt like a shroud pressing down over his face, suffocating him.

"We *are* a couple," Kyra said so softly that he barely heard her over the roar of the wind through the windows. Her hand fell from his leg. She shifted away. "Aren't we? Sometimes I still don't understand things in your world."

Nick pulled the car over to the side of the road. He turned off the ignition and stared down at the steering wheel, still gripping its leather curves.

"I'm sorry," he said. "I know I'm being an ass. It's just..." He turned his head to meet her wary gaze. She'd wrapped her arms around her chest defensively. As Nick looked into her eyes, he felt another barrier break down, with painful liberation, inside him. "Last night was great," he told her. "Better than great. Wonderful. But...the truth is, that scares the hell out of me."

Her face was stiff, holding back tears. "Because of what I am?"

"No." He swallowed hard, but made himself finish. "Because I was married, and my wife...my wife died. Two years ago. That's why I moved up here. To be alone with the memories of her. It's why I've stayed here all this time."

"I knew someone else before, too," Kyra whispered. "But

he wasn't honest. My family warned me, but I ignored them. I didn't want to believe what they said about him...about men... but they were right, that time. He wanted to take something from me."

"I don't want to do that," Nick said heavily. "But I don't know what I do want, either." He looked at her, his fingers flexing against the steering wheel. "I'm sorry. I wish...I wish I wasn't so confused. I know it isn't fair."

She looked at him steadily, her eyes wide and grave. "I think I'm falling in love with you," she said. "That scares me, too." She paused, closed her eyes, and took a breath. "But I would have left by now if I wanted to give in to fear. My family knows where I am and knows I'm well enough to go back and join them again—but I told them I don't want to leave you. Not yet."

Relief shuddered through him. "I'm glad," Nick whispered. "I don't want you to go, either."

She gave a firm nod. "Then we can go into town now, if you need to. If you tell me that my fur is safe, I *will* trust you."

"Thanks." He started the car again. This time, he drove more slowly. She put her hand on his leg, anchoring him with warmth along the way. Every time that he could, he set his own hand on top of hers. It felt strong and steady, like the promise of real hope.

They started at a pancake restaurant in the center of town and shared two different orders. Then they walked around town, drifting into the few shops, holding hands. Nick bought a Great Lakes wolf calendar, with 'wolf facts' written for each month. Kyra snorted and read through it with her eyebrows arched in skepticism. They paused in front of the library. Kyra looked at Nick.

"You want to go in?"

Nick shook his head. "No," he said. "No need."

They drove home with warmth filling the car. Kyra fiddled with the different radio stations and periodically read Nick 'wolf facts' from different months of the calendar, adding her own pointed commentary. Nick pulled the car into the gravel drive.

The front door of the house hung open.

The dogs were barking frantically from their kennels behind the house. That meant they were alive and unhurt. Nick switched the engine back on, shifted into reverse, and kept his voice steady with an effort. "Okay, this is what we'll do. We'll drive back to town, go to the cops, and they'll—what are you doing?"

Kyra was already wrenching her door open. She leaped out while the car's tires were skidding through gravel. "He's hunting for my fur!"

"Kyra!" Nick grabbed for her. He missed. "It's too dangerous!" he yelled after her.

She disappeared into the house. Cursing, Nick switched off the engine and ran after her through the open door.

He stumbled to a halt in the living room, nearly bumping

into her. The hunter stood in the center of the room, his gun leveled at them.

"Get out of my house," Nick said.

The hunter laughed. "What, because you scare me?" He shook his head. "I'm not going anywhere until I've got this girl's fur safe in my hands. I've been waiting for an opportunity like this."

"What are you talking about?" Nick's lips felt numb. He took Kyra's arm and stepped up beside her, his gaze fixed on the barrel of the gun.

"Hard enough to find a normal wolf in the wild nowadays. But to find a genuine shapeshifter? Now, that takes patience and cunning."

Nick yanked Kyra behind him. "Change," he said. "Quickly! I'll keep him here. You can run."

"No, I can't," Kyra said softly.

"She hasn't told you much, has she?" the hunter said. "I bet you don't have the slightest idea how much power you could have had, if you'd only known it."

"I can't change without my fur." Kyra's fingers bit into Nick's arm. "I am trapped."

Nick swallowed bitterness as the pieces all fell into place. "I'm sorry," he said. "I should have turned the car around this morning, when you asked. If I'd known..."

"Like she was ever going to tell you?" The hunter snorted. "The man who holds a shapeshifter's fur holds her forever. She can't even *ask* him to let her go. You think a wild thing like her would ever trust anyone enough to tell them that?"

He aimed the gun. "So tell me, honey, where exactly did you put this fur? If you don't tell me, first I'll have to shoot this idiot, and then I'll shoot out your other leg. You won't be doing any more running after that."

Nick lunged forward. The gun fired with a crack like lightning. Pain exploded in his left arm. Nearly blinded, he charged forward and knocked into the other man's stocky body. As they collided, Kyra howled. The sound was piercing, filling Nick's ears. Outside in their kennels, the dogs went silent for a moment. Then they raised their own voices in howls to match hers. Three voices mingled hauntingly, sending a chill across Nick's skin. He grappled with the hunter, throwing all his weight into it, but the other man was too strong. The howls intensified, rising even higher, louder. More joined in.

"Shut up!" The hunter slammed Nick down onto the floor and kicked him hard in the stomach. He started toward Kyra. "I'm warning you, I'll—!"

Four gray shapes flowed into the house, through the open front door into the living room...but none of them were Greta and Mimi. None of them were dogs at all.

From the floor, Nick watched them sweep around Kyra's tall body like waves around a rock. Lips curled back over sharp white teeth; muscles rippled. The hunter pointed his gun—

—And Nick slammed his booted foot into the other man's ankle. The shot fired into the cottage wall.

The wolves were on the hunter before he could fire again.

"Stop!" Nick yelled. He forced himself to his feet and lunged toward the mass of gray, shaggy bodies. "Stop!"

Still standing, Kyra let out a guttural bark. The wolf pack froze. Massive heads lifted to look up at her.

"What's wrong?" Kyra asked him.

"Don't kill him," Nick's voice came out as a croak.

She stared at him. "He attacked us. He shot you! He—"

"That doesn't justify murder." Nick looked down. The four wolves held the hunter in place. The man's eyes squeezed shut; his lips moved in whispered prayer. "He broke into my house, and he shot me. He'll go to prison for it. That's enough."

"That's not all he wanted to do." Kyra's face flushed. "He wanted to make me his slave. Don't you care?" Her face worked. "Or is that what you would have done, too, if I'd told you the truth about my fur?" She stepped closer to the group of wolves, reaching out to bury her hand in gray fur. The wolf she touched turned to gaze at Nick, its eyes predatory. "Is that really the only kind of love any human man can want?"

"It's *not* what I want," Nick said. "But he'll be punished, and you'll be safe."

"Not as long as he's alive."

"Once he's in prison, he won't be able to hurt you. Trust me!"

"I trusted you before, when you told me my fur would be safe in this house!"

Nick closed his eyes. The wound in his arm burned, dragging at him. "I'm sorry," he said, "but I can't stand here and let you kill him. Death is... I can't do it. Not to anyone."

"Then I can't stay here anymore."

"What?" Nick opened his eyes. "But—last night..."

Kyra wrapped her arms around her chest. "I need my fur. *Now.*" Her face tightened. "I could have sworn I left it on the couch last night."

Three of the wolves kept the hunter pinned down while the fourth sniffed the floor and furniture, helping Kyra search. Nick wrapped a kitchen towel around his arm and slipped out through the back door when Kyra and her helper went into the bedroom. The other wolves watched him leave impassively.

Outside, a cool breeze blew up from the lake. Blood trickled down Nick's arm as he walked to the dogs' kennels. Dizziness threatened to swamp him. He forced himself to keep on walking.

He'd known where the fur had to be even before Kyra began her search. Luckily, Greta hadn't started chewing on it yet. Nick pulled it out of her treasure hoard in the back corner of her kennel while she whined and licked his wounded arm.

"Bad dog," Nick whispered, without force. If Greta hadn't taken it, the hunter might well have found it. And then...

A woman who can never leave.

Nick's fingers tightened around the fur.

She couldn't even ask him to give it back.

He imagined her leaving with the wolves. Her half-built chair left empty. His house returned to silence, bleak emptiness, and pain. The way it had been for the past two years, ever since...

Nick remembered his sister's voice.

"Time to let go," he whispered, to Greta and to himself.

By the time he reached the house again, he was woozy, and the towel around his arm was soaked through. Kyra stood in the living room waiting for him, her eyes wide and glazed. The smile she gave him—bland and empty—made nausea swirl through his stomach.

Nick handed her the fur. He had to close her fingers around it.

"Here," he said. "This belongs to you."

Kyra blinked and took a shuddering breath. Her eyes cleared. "Thank you," she whispered, pulling it close. "Thank you."

The wolves held the hunter down while Nick and Kyra secured his hands and feet. Kyra wrapped a real bandage around Nick's arm to stop the bleeding.

"Will you be safe?" she asked as they walked outside together.

"When I call the cops, I'll tell them I need a medic," Nick said. He tried to shrug. He couldn't. He swallowed down the words that wanted to spill out.

Stay with me. Don't leave me alone in here. Please.

"I have to go," Kyra said. "He could get away from the

police and come back to steal my fur. They might not even send him to prison after all."

"They will," Nick said. "He shot a local. He'll go to jail."

"Well..." She shrugged unhappily and stepped back, toward the wolves. "You don't understand," she said. "You can't. The idea of being trapped..."

"I understand," Nick said hoarsely.

He'd locked himself inside his own trap by choice two years ago, over the protests of everyone who loved him...and he had shrunk within his cage. He wouldn't do that to her, too.

Still...

"I don't have to stay here anymore," he said. "I mean, I will stay until the trial, I guess, but after that..." He took a deep breath, forcing his feet to shift back instead of forward; to entice with his words, not trap her in his arms.

She'd had enough men doing that already.

"I just want you to know," he finished quietly, "that if you don't feel safe here, in this house...that matters to me. What you want matters to me. I promise I won't ignore your needs again. And I can learn more about your world, too."

The other wolves growled warningly at his words—but she lunged forward and kissed him, flinging her arms around his neck, her tongue warm and probing as it swept through his mouth. She tasted like passion and freedom and home, and she made his head spin. He had to force himself to let go when she pulled back at the end, instead of drifting helplessly after her wild scent.

"Will I ever see you again?" he asked, despite himself, as she stepped away.

Kyra looked at him in silence for a moment, her green eyes wild and utterly inhuman. Then her lips tugged into a mischievous smile. "You really should have gone into that library today—or at least read that silly calendar for yourself."

Nick's eyebrows rose. "What did it say that I should know?"

Her warm breath brushed tinglingly against the vulnerable skin behind his ear as she leaned in to whisper, "The month of May. Interesting wolf fact number five: *wolves mate for life*."

She stepped back, eyes gleaming, and pressed the fur against her throat. The air blurred around her.

Five wolves ran into the woods together. The fifth wolf limped as she ran, and turned at the edge of the pine trees to look back with yellow-splashed green eyes.

"For life," Nick whispered after her as he let her go.

The Art of Deception

There are three moves every true swordsman should know. First, the Shagomir Defense, as taught by every minor proponent of the art; second, the whistling attack, suitable for advanced students only; and third, the Hrabanic Deception, a lethally difficult move which turns a seeming defense into the neatest of stabs, clean into your opponent's chest, piercing the heart in an instant. The Hrabanic Deception is always fatal.

Considering that Niko Hrabanic had invented the move, he should have been more prepared when it was used against him. But he had never been as gifted in the art of verbal swordplay as he was with the blade; and at any rate, he was attacked at an inopportune moment.

* * *

"What do you mean, 'useless'?" It's hard to carry off any semblance of dignity while naked, but Hrabanic did his best, pulling the sheet up to his chest and directing an outraged glare at his bed partner, who also happened to be his landlady.

She sat up in bed, disregarding the sheet, and crossed her arms. Her dark hair tumbled invitingly across her shoulders; her jutting elbows emphatically refuted the invitation. "Useless: lacking in use, ineffectual, unable to accomplish that which—"

"All right, all right! We all know you were raised in a library." Hrabanic set his teeth. "I've never heard you complain before."

"I never had to leave anyone else in charge of you before."

"I will pay my rent. Soon! All I need is a few more students, and then—"

"You've been saying that for the past nine months."

"Don't I make myself *useful* in other ways?" He dropped his sheet.

She snorted. "Well, you aren't going to be doing that with the friend who's taking over for me."

He narrowed his eyes at her. "You think not? If you find me so useless, then perhaps—"

"It's my friend Miriam. The one with the husband who won five wrestling championships."

"Oh." He pulled the sheet back up. "Well. There's still the matter of everything else I do around here. I stop fights from breaking out at the bar every night, I take care of all the heavy lifting for you—"

"I'm fairly certain Miriam's husband can deal with those matters himself."

"I also have a reputation, in case you've forgotten."

"You did, once."

Hrabanic let out a growl. "That's low, Julia. Even for you."

"Well?" She shrugged. "You used to be the most famous swordsman in Plötz, yes. But you've been hiding out in a rundown tavern in a little backwater town nobody's ever heard of, ever since the Archduke fired you."

"I was not fired. I was—"

"You were fired," Julia said. "So you ran away to lick your wounds, and like the soft-hearted fool I am, I took you in. But now Miriam and her husband are doing me the kindest of favors by taking over while I'm gone, and I can't leave them with a tenant who's useless to them, just because he's afraid to go back out into the wider world."

"Why do you have to leave at all? You still haven't explained that part."

Julia's eyes, for the first time, slid away. "That doesn't matter."

"Ha." Hrabanic pushed himself up to a sitting position. "You're the one running away, aren't you? Maybe the tavern's not doing as well as you say. Maybe you're afraid of how you feel about me. Maybe—"

"I have to go home for a while," Julia said.

"To the White Library?" He blinked. "What are you meant to do there? That's—"

"I've been called back, and I can't ignore the summons. But it's dangerous. I don't know how long it'll take—or even if I'll be coming back at all. So I have to set things in order here, first."

"Nonsense. Just don't go."

"I have to. If I don't..." She took a deep breath. "They'll send their minions to come and get me. And that would be much, much worse."

"The White Librarians can send as many of their creatures as they like after you. Do you truly think I'd let them past the front door?" Hrabanic had never seen vulnerability on his landlady's face before. He reached out awkwardly and pulled her into his arms, speaking into her soft, tousled hair. "Come now, Julia. You know that none of them could get past me."

"Really?" Her voice was muffled against his chest. "You could protect me, even from them?"

"Of course," he said. "With me around, you don't need to be afraid of them. I'll keep you safe. I promise."

"Perfect." Her voice was as smooth and rich as cream. Or, more like, a cat who'd just swallowed a whole pitcher-full. Hrabanic stiffened as she tipped back her head and smiled. "Well, then," she said. "That's settled. Miriam and her husband will take over the tavern, and you'll come along with me to keep me safe at the White Library."

"But—what—?" Hrabanic took a hold of himself. "Look,"

he said. "I don't leave this town anymore. You know that. I don't like going out into—"

"You promised you would keep me safe," Julia said. "And so you shall. I feel much better, now." She gave him a quick kiss, which he barely felt, and slid down under the covers beside him. "You'd better go to sleep now, Hrabanic. We'll be leaving in two days, and you have a lot of packing to do before then."

The Hrabanic Deception is always fatal.

He was still reeling at dawn two mornings later, when he and Julia set off from the tavern with little Miriam and her hulking husband waving their cheerful farewells from the doorway. Julia, of course, looked as coolly confident as if she were preparing for an ordinary morning of bartering with the local butcher, rather than setting off on foot for the near-mythical building about which a thousand children's cautionary tales were told, of unnatural creatures and strange powers at work behind the fabric of the world. Five miles down the road, though, she startled Hrabanic once again.

There were no other travelers in sight along the dusty road that stretched up through the hills, into the mountains. Only hill farmers and their goats picked a living out of the dry, rocky outcroppings to the side of the road, and even they were nowhere to be seen under the pale blue sky that morning. Julia looked around, set down her pack, and loosened the fastenings of her cloak.

"Too much for you?" Hrabanic said. "We can still turn around, you know. Or—auugh!"

With one pass of her fingers across her face, Julia's whole appearance had changed. The hawk nose—so arresting and oddly attractive in her own face—remained, but the curving cheeks had hollowed, the face turned from an oval into a rectangle, and, worst of all, a light spattering of hair covered it all, that of a man who'd forgotten to shave that morning. Another pass of her hand across her chest, and...

"We are not sleeping in the same bed tonight!" said Hrabanic.

"Oh, don't be a ninny." A man's voice came out of her mouth, deeper and fuller, but still quintessentially Julia's in its authority. "You know perfectly well that I could talk you into liking it if it were real. As it is, though, it's barely one thin layer of illusion, and I did it for both our sakes."

"Not mine," Hrabanic said, eyeing the newly-straight form beneath her cloak. "Trust me. If we have to walk all across Plötz together, I would much rather—"

"Why fight more battles than you need?" Julia said. "This way, you won't have to worry about fighting any drunken louts over me in the inns we stop at, and I won't have to deal with innkeepers thinking they can take advantage when I negotiate our rates."

"Ha. Little do they know. Poor fellows." Hrabanic looked mournfully at her/him, as she/he undid the familiar, thick, dark hair and retied it in a simple man's queue. "How long have you been able to do this, anyway?"

"I told you where I was raised." Julia swung the pack over her shoulder. "I haven't done this for nearly twenty years, because I didn't want to take the risk of attracting their attention. But now that I've been summoned anyway..." She shrugged. "You can't grow up in the White Library without learning how to perform a simple illusion or two."

"Huh." Hrabanic narrowed his eyes at her. "So, you really think you need my protection there, do you, Madame Illusionist?"

"I can deal with illusions," Julia said. "But they're not the only dangers at the White Library. I might be able to fool a man's eyes into thinking I was wearing armor, but I couldn't stop his blade from piercing my skin."

"What a pleasant homecoming you've invited me along for." Hrabanic sighed. "Just tell me one thing. All those stories whispered about the White Library—how many of them are true, exactly?"

"Oh, only about half of them," Julia said cheerfully, and strode forward, her newly-masculine boots scuffing up with dust. "Most of the really bad secrets don't ever leave the Library. They're very careful about that."

"Hmm," Hrabanic said, as he fell into step beside her. "But you left."

"So I did," Julia said, and re-settled the pack against her back. "A fine day for a walk, isn't it?"

"Hmm," Hrabanic repeated thoughtfully.

* * *

Only two assassination attempts enlivened the rest of the journey. One of them was aimed at him, by a young blade who recognized him in the main room of an inn they'd stopped at, and wanted to prove himself to the swordfighting world through Hrabanic's death; that, Hrabanic had expected and didn't mind, beyond the loss of the wine he'd spilled when the youth had jostled his arm. But the second attempt, in the middle of the night, was aimed straight at Julia, sleeping in the bed beside him in her own true form.

Hrabanic woke at the sound of the opening window. His sword was in his hand a moment later. The Shagomir Defense blocked the man's first blow and sent his sword spinning across the room. The rest wasn't even worth opening his eyes for.

"So," Hrabanic said, as he pushed the limp body out the window. "They're expecting you, are they?"

"Apparently." Still sitting in bed, Julia turned over the seal they'd found in the assassin's cloak—a glittering white star. It glowed in the darkness, casting a pale light up onto her face.

"Why did they bother to summon you, if they only wanted to kill you? Why not send an assassin in the first place?"

"There's more than one White Librarian," Julia said. "They don't all want the same things." Her voice was as cool as ever, but by the light of the assassin's seal, Hrabanic could see the unaccustomed strain on her face. "Layers of illusion, Hrabanic. Remember?"

"Right," he said. "Well, your particular illusion doesn't seem to have worked on them. They knew exactly where to find you."

She shrugged, tracing the star on the seal with the tip of one finger, as gently as if she feared to rub it off. "The illusion was only meant for our fellow travelers."

"I see." Hrabanic closed the window. "Is there anything else you'd like to tell me before we arrive there tomorrow?"

Julia shook her head, still staring at the seal. "No," she said. "No. Right now..." She tore her gaze away from the seal and looked up at him. "Right now, I think I'd like to sleep. To save my strength."

Hrabanic looked at her shadowed eyes and sighed. "All right," he said, and crossed the room to take the seal out of her hand. It tingled against his fingers; he dropped it face-down onto the floor beside the bed to hide its glow, then gathered Julia into his arms. "You sleep," he said. "I'll keep a look-out. I could do with some time to think, anyway."

Hrabanic had expected an impressive building—and an impressively large, white building, at that. What he hadn't expected was an impossibility.

The White Library climbed all the way up the side of a mountain, like the shining white carapace of a monstrous snail, curving round and round itself. Its higher regions disappeared behind the mist at the very top of the mountain. Hrabanic was not a man given much to fancy, but when he tipped his head back to peer through the cloaking mist, he found himself wondering if the Library itself had any top, any limit to its vastness, or if it truly spiraled into the heavens forever.

Illusions, he reminded himself, and shook his head sharply. But he found himself breathing quickly, as winded as if he'd just fought a hard battle. When he looked down, he saw Julia returned to her own appearance and neatly plaiting her dark hair into a crown around her head.

"So," he said. "The illusion's ended, then?"

"Hardly," she said. "Come along." She pinned the last braid into place. "We shouldn't keep them waiting any longer."

"Did you tell them a particular time we'd arrive?"

"No," she said. "But they'll have been watching us for at least the past hour. If they think we're dawdling, they'll see it as a sign of weakness."

"Ah," Hrabanic said. "Um. An hour ago or more—"

"Not while you were naked," Julia said, and rolled her eyes. "They only watch this last stretch of road, to prepare for visitors."

"Very sensible," Hrabanic said, and frowned at the impenetrable white, curving walls, which were—yes, he'd remembered correctly—completely free of windows.

Ah, damn.

"Well, then," he said, "we'd better hurry."

Half an hour later, and only twenty feet away from the shining snail-shell, there was still no opening to be seen. But Hrabanic had had long practice training his expression to confidence even when he didn't feel it, and he matched Julia step for step as she strode straight toward the white wall. The closer they came to it, the less Hrabanic liked it. No stone or any other building material he knew could be fitted together so smoothly, without a single join, nor would it gleam so, untouched by any of the veiling, swirling dust from the road that led up to it.

Julia swung her hand out at the last moment, just before her arrogant hawk nose would have smashed into the wall, and turned her fingers in the air as if turning a door handle. With a groan, the snail-shell surface opened before them, revealing a hallway that glowed with unnatural, almost blinding white light—and a white-cloaked figure standing in the center of it. Water stung Hrabanic's eyes; he had to squint to make out the cloak, but no amount of squinting could catch him any glimpse of the face beneath the hood. The voice that spoke from underneath it was a woman's voice, cold and clear.

"I see you haven't forgotten all your training, after all."

Hrabanic kept his mouth shut. Julia's chin lifted. "You'd be surprised at how much I remember," she said. "Good morning, Lafka. Do you think you might tone down the light a bit? My companion would like to be allowed to see."

"Julia. Polite as always." The light dimmed, revealing a

corridor full of elegant, curving white arches and pale gold lattice-work, and Hrabanic saw a narrow face beneath the Librarian's hood, remotely beautiful as a mountain sunset. The large, gem-like green eyes blinked slowly. "And Niko Hrabanic. You will be welcomed here."

Hrabanic bowed and restrained the impulse to set one hand on the hilt of his sword. "I am honored that you know me, Madam."

"Oh, I am not the one who knows you," Lafka said. "But we have—shall we say, an old friend of yours here. *And* her husband."

Hrabanic's jaw clenched. He saw her narrow, pale-pink lips curve into a satisfied smile.

"Yes, the Archduke and Archduchess are also guests here,"said Lafka. "We can all hardly wait to witness your happy reunion."

Don't pull out the sword. Don't pull out the sword.

"Julia?" Hrabanic said, through gritted teeth.

"A delightful surprise indeed," Julia murmured, and set one hand on Hrabanic's arm. It might have looked, in this temple of illusion, like a ladylike gesture of support, but he felt the strength of her warning pinch, and winced. "Show us to our rooms," she said. "Now."

With an enormous effort of willpower, Hrabanic managed to wait until Lafka closed the door of their suite of rooms behind him before he spoke again.

"How long have you known?"

"Hrabanic..."

"I said..." He lowered his voice to a hiss. For all he knew, every one of the gilded mirrors that lined the apricot-and-gold walls of their front bedroom might serve a double function as window and listening station. "*How—long—have—you—known?*"

"That the Archduke and Archduchess would be here?" Julia shrugged and set down her pack on the double bed. "I didn't know it. Not for certain."

"You suspected."

"It made sense, given the circumstances."

"It made sense," Hrabanic repeated. "It made—!" He whirled around, swinging back his cloak. His sword, released at last, slashed through the crimson covers of the bed. Stuffing exploded out of them, inadequate replacement for the blood and guts he would have preferred. "It made gods-damned *sense*?"

"Control yourself!" Julia's voice was nearly as cold as Lafka's had been. "I've never seen you like this."

"You've never trapped me with the bloody Archduke and that harpy!"

"That's not a kind way to speak of a past lover. If I were an insecure woman—"

He lowered his sword, breathing hard. "I wouldn't say one more word about that, if I were you."

"Fine." Julia sat down on the bed, ignoring the piles of loose stuffing. "Then I'll only say this. The new Head of the White Librarians is about to be chosen, as the current Head has reached his maximum allotted term of rule. It's not surprising that the Archduke and his wife would be here for such an important political event, is it?"

"And you didn't see any need to mention this to me beforehand because...?"

"Because you wouldn't have come. Obviously."

"Obviously," Hrabanic repeated. "Well. How about another obvious move now, from simple, obvious me? I'm leaving."

"Oh, for pity's sake. It's been three years! You've spent enough time licking your wounds by now, you can surely face the two of them for a few minutes in public. I know it must have humiliated your pride to be fired, but if you are going to sleep with your employer's wife, you can hardly expect—"

"Expect what you like," Hrabanic said. "Good-bye, Julia."

"Hrabanic!" She jumped up from the bed. "Where are you going?"

"Anywhere but here." Hrabanic sheathed his sword with a jerk. "Don't worry—I won't foist my uselessness on Miriam and her husband. I've spent far too much time already in your tavern. *Obviously.*"

Her face paled. "You promised you'd protect me."

"That was before I knew the truth."

"I would have told you if I'd thought you'd be reasonable about it. But I knew, as soon as you heard the Archduke's name—"

"And there you go, saying it again." Hrabanic bared his teeth in a smile. "You can say it all you like once I'm gone.

Hell, say it to his face, for all I care." He swept a bow. "Your servant, Madam. Or rather, not anymore."

Julia crossed her arms. "You gave me your word."

"You lied to me."

"I did not lie. I simply didn't tell you all the truth."

Hrabanic's voice erupted into a bellow. "Is every gods-damned word in this building an illusion?"

Julia met his gaze steadily. "Yes," she said. "Every single one. That's why I need you."

"Oh, for—" Hrabanic clenched his jaw and shut his eyes so he wouldn't have to see her face.

"Please," she said. "You've never broken your word in your life. Don't start now."

He opened his eyes and glared at her for a long, pulsating moment. Then he said, "Fine."

"Well, thank the gods for that." Julia's face relaxed into a smile. "I must say, Hrabanic, you do have an impressive temper after all, don't you? You actually had me wondering—wait, where are you going now?"

Hrabanic strode past her, toward the inner door of their suite of rooms. "To the second bedroom," he said. "We're not sharing a room here. Not anymore."

He was in step just behind her for that afternoon's formal reception, though, his sword strapped on over his finest blue satin breeches, his knee-high boots polished to gleaming brilliance, and his expression schooled to bland, professional watchfulness. Julia, of course, looked as unruffled and confident as ever, her lips curved into an arrogant half-smile, as she stepped into the crowd. No one, looking at her, would have guessed that she was nearly as irate as Hrabanic himself, and that their rooms were still vibrating from their unfinished dispute.

Of course, for all he knew, the people around him might be far better than him at recognizing every shade of her different expressions. It seemed there was a great deal he didn't know about Julia, after all.

The Diamond Room, where the reception was held, was at least the width and height of Julia's own four-storey tavern. Rich chestnut shelves of books covered all six walls, rising up to a rounded ceiling magnificent with frescoes in sky-blue, crimson, and gold. Novices, identifiable by their cream-colored robes, circulated through the glittering crowd, passing out glasses of wine that bubbled and popped; here and there Hrabanic spotted the pure white robes of the Librarians themselves. He was glad, for the sake of his self-control, not to see the green-eyed Librarian who had met them earlier. Perhaps she was still sulking in her room after Julia's set-down.

He accepted a glass of wine and ignored the narrow-eyed look Julia shot him. She spoke in a whisper, out of the corner of her mouth.

"Do you really think that wise, when you're on duty?"

He shrugged, not bothering to lower his own voice in

return. "I might as well get some entertainment out of this party."

He heard the audible click of her teeth snapping together as she bit back a retort.

"Cheers," Hrabanic said sweetly, and clinked his wine glass against hers, smiling into her furious, dark eyes.

The chime of their meeting glasses was still ringing in the air when another voice spoke behind them, as sweet and rich as the perfume that drifted across them. "Why, Niko Hrabanic, as I live and breathe..." Soft fingers laid themselves across his stiffening arm as all his muscles clenched in resistance. "I didn't believe them when they said I'd see you here. I thought that would be too much to ask of Fate—far too much luck for me to hope for..."

Hrabanic turned, grimly holding his smile in place. "Your Highness." He bowed as deeply as the clinging fingers would allow him. "Your servant."

"Not anymore, Hrabanic. Alas..." The Archduchess of Plötz regarded him frankly, up and down, and her full lips curved in appreciation. "But, my. Wherever you've buried yourself for the past few years, it certainly hasn't done you any harm. I cannot wait for you to tell me all about it." Her long eyelashes swept down to cover her vivid blue eyes; her fingers tightened around his arm. "Why don't we find someplace to be alone, away from this dreadfully tedious crowd..."

Julia cleared her throat. It was a delicate sound, but as effective as a knife in slicing open the bubble that had held Hrabanic paralyzed. He gave a start, and breathed again.

"Your Highness, may I present Madam Shevina? I am here in her em—"

"Hrabanic is here in my company," Julia said, and smiled brilliantly at the Archduchess. "What an honor indeed. Your Highness." Her curtsey was a masterpiece of brusque efficiency.

"Ah. The little tavern-keeper." The Archduchess nodded, her own smile poisonously sweet. "I do believe they mentioned something about you. How kind of you to look after Hrabanic in my stead for so long."

"Uh," Hrabanic began.

Julia spoke before he could finish. "Why, I believe I looked after him for my own sake, Your Highness." She raised one eyebrow at the Archduchess as she leaned into Hrabanic's side. "I'm sure you understand just how valuable an asset Hrabanic can be—at least, to a woman who knows how to keep him."

Hrabanic took a deep, consoling swallow of wine. The pop of bubbles against his tongue and throat was a desperately needed distraction from the duel in which he clearly wasn't allowed to participate. But before either party could score another hit, they were interrupted by a man striding towards them, clad in crimson and gold and glittering with diamonds.

"Your Highness," Hrabanic sighed, and bowed.

He should have asked for a second wineglass. One was clearly not going to be enough.

"Hrabanic." The Archduke's predatory gaze passed over

his wife without interest and narrowed on Julia for a moment before snapping back to his former swordsmaster. "What are you doing here?"

If he didn't already know the answer to that question, in full and explicit detail, Hrabanic would be much surprised, and also professionally disappointed in the work of the Archduke's spies. But under Julia's minatory gaze, Hrabanic only said mildly, "I am here in the company of Madam Shevina, Your Highness. May I present—?"

"Shevina." The Archduke reached peremptorily for her hand; she accepted the demand, and arched her eyebrows when he raised it to his lips. "I must talk to you. Perhaps..." He frowned, and his roving glance landed on his wife's hand, still curled possessively around Hrabanic's arm. His face cleared. "Hrabanic, I'm sure you and my wife have much to discuss. Why don't you two find somewhere private while Madam Shevina and I—"

"Forgive me," Julia said, "but I couldn't possibly allow that."

"I beg your pardon?" The Archduke's thick black eyebrows snapped together.

"You know how shy Hrabanic is in company," Julia murmured. "I did promise not to abandon him tonight. And oh, look!" She pulled her hand out of the Archduke's grip. "I'm afraid I'm being signaled by the Head Librarian. I will look forward to talking more with you later, though, if ever I happen to have a spare moment or two. Hrabanic?"

Hrabanic bowed to both of the stupefied royals, extracted

his arm from the Archduchess's clinging grip, and followed Julia as she sailed away through the crowd, her chin held high. When he caught up with her, she closed her own hand firmly around his arm. He slid a glance at her out of the corner of his eye, and found her dark eyes snapping with temper.

Hrabanic's lips twitched. He said, "Well, you've certainly reinforced all their beliefs about the manners of the lower classes."

"Good," Julia said. "They deserved it. And you!" She glared at him. "You lied to me."

"I did not."

"Oh? Then tell me again, to my face, that you were fired for sleeping with the Archduke's wife."

"I never told you that."

"It's what everyone else said, and you never bothered to deny it."

"I told you I wasn't fired."

"Oh..." Her word dissolved into a growl. "Damn you, Hrabanic. You're supposed to be the simple one, without any secrets or deceptions for me to worry about."

Hrabanic cocked one eyebrow at her. He was, he realized with some surprise, actually enjoying the party after all. The look on the Archduke's face came back to him again, and he had to restrain himself from laughing out loud. "Come now," he said. "Have you forgotten your own words so quickly? Everything in this building is an illusion. Remember?"

"And Julia should know that better than anyone else," said a man's deep voice, just behind them.

Hrabanic swung around, his hand moving instinctively to the hilt of his sword. But there was no weapon in the outstretched hands of the old man who faced them, smiling underneath the hood of his white robe.

"Julia. My dear child. It has been far too long."

"Sir." Julia took his hands, but did not step into what looked like an invitation to embrace. When she spoke again, her voice sounded unusually strained and uncertain. "May I present my companion, Niko—"

"Hrabanic, of course. A pleasure." The man nodded genially, without releasing Julia's hands. "We have a copy of your treatise here in this very room. Most enlightening. I've read it several times, now."

Hrabanic blinked. "I am honored, sir. And, ah...surprised. There were very few copies printed, and I had thought that those—"

"Oh, we never worry about such tedious matters as print runs, here." The old man smiled gently and waved at the walls of books. "Hasn't Julia explained yet? We keep copies here of every book or pamphlet written, whether it is printed or not."

"In all of Plötz? That must be—"

"My dear boy..." The old man shook his head. "Do not let your imagination be so limited. We are constrained by neither geography nor—much to our poor Archduke's chagrin—political boundaries. Nor do we need to purchase our copies."

Teeth showed in his smile. "Knowledge is power, you see. And we have a natural affinity for it."

"Ah." Hrabanic surveyed the walls of books. They were all bound in leather of an unusually pale shade, and gilded with gold lettering on their spines. Or...he frowned. Was the binding really leather? It didn't look quite—

"Hrabanic," Julia said, "this is the Head of the White Librarians." She took a deep breath. "My grandfather."

"So," Hrabanic said, as they walked back to their rooms that night. "When exactly are you planning to mention the rest to me?"

Now that they were away from the crowds that had filled the Diamond Room and the even larger Dining Chamber afterwards, Julia looked limp with unaccustomed exhaustion. "I'm sorry I never told you that the Head was my grandfather. But—"

"Not that," said Hrabanic. "What I want to know is when you were planning to admit to me why he summoned you here."

The walls of the corridor were covered in swirling, indefinable patterns of pale gold and illuminated by cool white light with no visible source. There were no shadows to hide Julia's guilty glance. She sighed. "I take it you've already guessed?"

"It wasn't that difficult. The new Head of the White

Librarians is about to be chosen, you are the current Head's granddaughter..."

"I don't want the position," Julia said. "It's why I ran away, all those years ago."

"And the reason you were allowed to survive, with all your dangerous knowledge of their secrets, was because you were still under your grandfather's protection."

"Yes," she said. "Grandfather wasn't happy when I left..." She shivered, wrapping her arms around her chest. "...But he didn't send his assassins after me, either."

"Until now."

"The assassin can't have come from him," Julia said. "He's the one who nominated me. He's been planning it all along, all these years when I hoped he'd given up on the idea. But I'm not the only candidate, you see." Her lips twisted into a half-smile. "And I may protest as much as I like about not wanting the position, but that won't make any of the others believe me."

"Not a trusting group of people, these Librarians."

"You noticed?" She snorted. "Grandfather has only one vote to cast, but he has influence, which is more important."

"I see. Much easier to have you removed before the vote, then."

"Much."

A soft, scuffing sound caught Hrabanic's ear. He paused, listening. It wasn't repeated. Carefully, he slid his right hand to the hilt of his sword and fell back into step beside Julia. "So, when is this infamous vote going to be held?" he asked lightly, and set his left hand against her back.

"Tomorrow afternoon," she said. "But—ahh!" Her voice broke off in a gasp as Hrabanic threw her forward with one hard shove.

He spun around, drawing his sword in a fast, whistling arc. The other man's sword would have stabbed straight through his back had he still been walking. Hrabanic knocked it aside with a solid parry and dropped into a crouch.

They circled one another. His vision tunneled until all that existed was their dance. The other man's movements were fluid and quick, darting in and out, pressing lightly against Hrabanic's defenses from all angles—not attacking, but testing. Hrabanic kept his defenses even, testing back. Right, left, over, under. His opponent's blows were equally firm from every angle.

Hrabanic pressed harder, moving their circle forward. He wanted it further away from Julia—*damn*! His shoulder stung with the punishment for that moment of distraction. Red blood tipped his opponent's blade. The man followed up with a determined attack, closing in on Hrabanic's wounded side. Hrabanic gritted his teeth and riposted with a series of stronger blows, forcing the circle to widen again.

A different kind of red flashed suddenly in his eyes—a jewel on his opponent's hand, catching the light. Hrabanic blinked. He fell back a step. The other man grinned and lunged, aiming straight for Hrabanic's gut. His move was too fast, too well angled for any standard defense.

But not for the whistling attack.

Hrabanic spun on one heel, out of danger and into position, whirling full circle. He swept his sword across in the lethal zigzag. *First direction*: the other man's sword was knocked askew, sending the man skidding a step in the wrong direction. *Second direction*: Hrabanic slashed up underneath the man's arm, forcing it up and away from his side. *Third direction*: Hrabanic's sword stabbed down in the famous whistling arc, through his opponent's armpit, and into the man's lung.

Done. Hrabanic pulled his sword free, panting. He was impressed, in a distant way, that the other man's sword did not fall from his hand, even as he convulsed and blood poured from his mouth. If anything, the other man's grip on his sword actually tightened as every other muscle gave out. It clattered with him to the floor.

For the first time, Hrabanic realized his left coat sleeve was damp, saturated with blood. It must have been seeping down from his shoulder. His best coat, ruined. A pity. He couldn't afford a replacement.

But some people could afford almost anything.

He stood watching, his sword still drawn, as the other man died.

Footsteps sounded behind him. Julia.

Her voice sounded far away. "You're hurt. We need to bandage—"

"They'll need to find someone to clean the floor," Hrabanic said. There was a widening, dark puddle around the other man's body. It glistened in the unnatural white light of the hallway, dark against the darkness of the man's black coat and hair, his pale face set in frozen anguish. He'd been young—perhaps twenty, perhaps a little less. Hrabanic remembered being that young.

"Hrabanic—"

He knelt, setting his sword carefully to one side of the pool of blood. He took the other man's hand and pulled it free of its final grasp. Hrabanic was aware of Julia's voice still speaking behind him. He ignored it.

The delicate gold ring, studded with a single ruby, slipped free of the other man's finger. Hrabanic closed his hand around it and stood, heavily. He wiped his sword clean and finally turned to face Julia.

Her eyes were wide. "What is it?" she said. "You look—"

He opened his fingers to show her the ring. The ruby shone dully, like blood. It had fit perfectly around his own finger, once.

"Apparently the Archduke and Archduchess have an alternate candidate."

Hrabanic woke in the middle of the night. He was immediately conscious of the sound of heavy breathing nearby. The room was pitch-black. Slowly, silently, he rolled toward the side of the bed where he had left his sword.

The shuffling of enormous feet sounded at the same time

as the breathing shifted, granting a scant moment's warning. Hrabanic threw himself off the bed, landing barefoot on the cool wooden floor. The next second, he heard the heavy bedframe shudder and collapse under the shock of massive weight. *Where the hell was his sword?*

There should have been some reaction in the next room—Julia couldn't have slept through the crash of that breaking bed. But all Hrabanic could hear in the darkness was a noisy snuffling and snorting and the unmistakable sound of ripping cloth—the sheets on his bed being torn apart by what sounded like gigantic claws. And then: the unmistakable sound of sniffing.

It couldn't see him either.

Hrabanic stepped back, balancing on the balls of his feet. He held his breath as he knelt down and felt on the floor around him for his sword. The side of his middle finger brushed against its sharpened tip...

He felt the shift in the air just in time. He hit the ground in a roll that carried him halfway across the room, gritting his teeth to hold back a cry as his injured shoulder pushed against the floor, and his wound reopened.

The creature landed with a thud. It was between him and his sword.

He and Julia had traded rooms that night. He'd insisted on taking the outer bedroom, as being most accessible to attack. If this creature defeated him, though, there would be no escape route for her.

Think, Hrabanic told himself. Blood soaked through the

bandage on his shoulder. Goosebumps raced along his bare arms. He held himself still in the darkness, kneeling on the balls of his feet, poised for a leap in any direction.

Whatever it was, it was large, but not intelligent. He could hear it snuffling around, still searching for him where it had sensed him the first time.

If he ran, he could probably escape into the corridor before it caught on. But that would leave Julia to face the creature alone...if she was alone right now. The creature had entered his room—or been placed inside it—through a thick and securely locked outer door. So who was to say that one extra door had kept Julia safe from other intruders?

There was still no sound from the inner bedroom.

"Damn it to all ten hells," Hrabanic snarled.

The creature, as he'd known it would, leaped. He rolled directly underneath it, feeling the wind of its passage as they crossed paths.

It must have felt their crossing, too. It let out a muffled bellow and turned, heavily and clumsily, in mid-leap, landing only a few feet away. Hrabanic completed his roll, snatched up his sword...

The creature leaped, roaring, toward him...

And Hrabanic felt the impact shudder through his arm and back as his sword pierced two feet deep in flesh. Hot ichor spattered across his chest and face. Then the massive, hairy body slammed down on top of him, knocking him to the ground and covering his mouth and nose in warm, rank-smelling, smothering fur.

It took almost a full minute to disentangle himself and his sword. He cleaned the sword off as best he could, in two quick swipes across the creature's fur. Then he lunged for the inner door.

He paused for one moment, his left hand on the door handle, listening. Still no sound, not even rustling. His right hand tightened around the pommel of his sword.

He kicked the door open.

Light exploded against his eyes, and his vision blurred. Quick, fierce panting filled his ears, and flaring red, purple, and golden explosions of light blurred before him. When his vision cleared, he saw two women in familiar night-gowns, with their hands clamped around each other's throats.

Both of them were Julia.

"Damn it!" said the one on the left. "It's me, Hrabanic. She's cast an illusion."

"Don't be stupid," said the one on the right. "Remember what I told you: everything in this building is an illusion. Kill her!"

"Use your damned sword!" said the one on the left, grunting with effort as she wrestled for position.

Hrabanic let the door fall shut behind him. He looked from one to another, both pairs of fierce dark eyes glaring at him, both arrogant hawk noses daring him to fail the test.

Aha. He spun around to check the gilded mirrors that lined the walls—

But they only repeated the same picture he'd already

seen. And eight different replicas of Julia's most irate expression were far too many for any sane man to deal with.

Hrabanic turned back to the reality, sighing.

"You did say that," he said to the Julia on the right. "And the Head Librarian heard me repeat it to you. I wouldn't be surprised if several other guests heard it too."

"Oh, for all the gods' sake," said the Julia on the left. "Would you get to work already? What have you got that sword for, if not to use it?"

"Um," said Hrabanic. He hefted the sword. "Would you two mind stepping apart?"

"And let her go?" said the Julia on the right, with a sniff. "That's not one of your brightest ideas."

"Are you mad?" said the Julia on the left. "She's got a knife."

"She's the one with the knife!"

"I don't see any knives," said Hrabanic.

Both women rolled their eyes at him with identical exasperation. "Illusions, remember?" Then they glared at each other.

"Oh, good," said Hrabanic. "Remind me to thank you again sometime for inviting me to your happy homecoming."

"Hrabanic!"

"Would you hurry? It isn't easy holding her off, you know."

"It's a good thing you always say I'm so brilliant and clever and quick-thinking in situations like this," Hrabanic said.

The Julia on the right laughed. "Oh, please."

The Julia on the left said, "Do you really think this is the moment for a joke?"

"Oh well," Hrabanic said. "It was worth trying. Why don't you repeat what you really told me, five nights ago, when you invited me. Tell me why you wouldn't leave me at your tavern."

The Julia on the right said, "Because you may not be the brightest man I know, but that sword arm of yours shouldn't be allowed to go to waste. *Will you kill her already*?"

The Julia on the left smiled. Her dark eyes glittered. "You know why," she said. "Because you—alone in my tavern, without me—are useless."

"Got it," Hrabanic said, and lunged.

The Julia on the right let go of Julia's throat to swipe at him with what looked like empty air. Hrabanic ducked and thrust his sword straight through her stomach. She fell to the ground, dark eyes wide, lips parted. No blood flowed from the wound. As her right hand opened, Hrabanic heard the unmistakable clatter of metal falling to the ground.

He turned to the Julia on the left. She was massaging her throat with both hands, wincing. As he met her eyes, she shook her head ruefully. "Did I really say 'useless'?" she said. "You were right, Hrabanic. That was low, even for me. You do have some uses, you know. What you just did was actually quite clever."

Hrabanic's eyes widened. He spun back around to the

fallen Julia, dying on the floor. "Oh, gods, I've made a terrible mistake—"

"Oh, thank you so much," snapped the standing Julia. "I am capable of being something other than unkind from time to time, you know."

"Ha," Hrabanic said. "Not likely. So how long do we have to wait for the illusion to wear off?"

"Until she's dead, I expect," Julia said. "So—aha."

The familiar nightgown had shifted into white robes, covered now with blood; the dark hair lightened to blonde; the nose shrank and straightened. Beside the fallen body lay a sharp, curving knife with an ivory handle.

"Who the hell is that?" Hrabanic said. "And why didn't the light go away, too?"

"The light came from me, not from her," Julia said. "I like to be able to see who I'm fighting. And this..." Her nostrils flared with distaste. "This was my strongest rival for the Head Librarianship. Unfortunately."

"Ah." Hrabanic raised his eyebrows. "Maybe I shouldn't have killed her after all."

"There wasn't much choice, given the circumstances." Julia looked him up and down. "What took you so long to get here, by the way? I could only hold her off with my own illusions for so long."

"That's why she sent a distraction to keep me busy. Not a human one, either." Hrabanic nodded toward his room. "It took me a little while to finish it off."

"It was probably another illusion."

"I think not! It left blood all over my sword—and my chest, too. Look!"

"I was trying not to," Julia said. "Don't worry, it'll all disappear soon enough. Amanka"—she nodded at the fallen Librarian—"was a very talented illusionist, you know, one of the best in the Library. That blood will have been part of the illusion. It'll fade in a few more minutes, once the last remnants of her power are gone."

"I'm telling you, it was real. I felt it."

"Hrabanic..."

He glared at her. "Your faith in me didn't last long, did it?"

"It's not a matter of faith, you stupid man! I am *telling* you, as someone who grew up in the White Library, that such a thing is categorically impossible. Therefore, the only option left is—where are you going?"

"Back to my room," Hrabanic said. "If it was an illusion, it will have vanished when she died, right?"

"Fine. If you need to see the evidence to believe me..." Julia sighed and followed him, casting light ahead of her. "Someday, though, despite all your stubbornness, you are going to have to admit that I actually do know more than you about—oh!"

"Oh, indeed." Hrabanic smiled and crossed his arms. "Now, do you want to go ahead and finish that sentence, Madam Know-it-All?"

Julia didn't answer. Her face paled as she stared down at the hairy lump of flesh—the giant legs folded awkwardly beneath the tiny chest, the great head lolling with its pig-like nose pressed against the ground and its hideously expanded jaw wide open, revealing a maw full of sharp, long teeth. Its four-inch-long claws trailed limply across the wooden floor.

After a moment, Hrabanic broke the silence. "What?" he said. "Aren't you going to think up some clever explanation? Or even take a moment to be impressed that I managed to get past him to rescue you?"

"I am impressed." Julia's voice sounded husky, suddenly fragile. "I've never heard of anyone surviving an encounter with one of these creatures, before."

"So..." Hrabanic frowned at her. "Why aren't you throwing yourself at me with relief and passion?"

"Oh, please." She rolled her eyes at him, and he was relieved to see some of the color creep back into her face. "You know me better than that, surely."

"Well, then, what's the problem?"

"The problem..." She took a deep breath. "The problem is that it wasn't an illusion."

"So?"

"All that a White Librarian like Amanka can summon and control is illusion. Which means..." She looked back down at the fallen monster.

"Ah," Hrabanic said. "All that an ordinary White Librarian can summon, you mean."

"Exactly." She smiled unhappily. "These creatures only respond to the will of the Head Librarian. So—"

"Maybe you aren't your grandfather's true candidate, after all."

* * *

"But it makes no sense," Julia whispered.

They sat together on Hrabanic's bed, Hrabanic's arm around Julia's shoulder, her hands clasped together so tightly that her knuckles had turned a sickly white.

"Why shouldn't it make sense?" Hrabanic asked. "Maybe your grandfather is still angry at you for running away instead of staying to be groomed as his successor. Or—"

"I could understand that," Julia said. "I could even believe he was manipulating all of us through my nomination, and he never meant me to win. But Amanka was the Archduke's niece. If she had won, the White Library would have ended up under the control of the political leaders of Plötz. That's the last thing Grandfather would ever want."

"Maybe he's changed his mind about that since you left."

"No." She shook her head. "You have to trust me on this. When he was training me as his successor—and he really did mean it back then, I'm certain—that was the one message he hammered into my head, again and again. The Library had to remain independent of the government to maintain its strength. It's the main point he's fought for in all his decades as its leader."

"Could someone else have sent the creature?—I know,"

Hrabanic added hastily, "you said he's the only one who could control it. But still—"

"That isn't possible. The creatures only respond to psychic power, and that level of personal authority can't be imitated. When a Librarian becomes the Head, they assume the power of all the books in the library, all the Heads who have come before them, all the knowledge and power of the Library itself. No other librarian's strength could even compare—so no other librarian could communicate with the creatures, much less control them."

Hrabanic groaned and clapped his free hand over his eyes. "Then maybe it just never happened. Maybe this whole damned trip has been an illusion, and we're actually still in bed back in your tavern. Hell, it makes as much sense as anything else that's happened over the last five days!"

Julia began to shake inside the curve of his arm. He dropped his hand and looked at her with alarm. But she was laughing—at first silently, and then out loud, in an infectious roll of pleasure that ended with both of them locked in a tight embrace.

"Oh, Hrabanic," she murmured into his chest, through her laughter. "I am glad you came with me, you know. I am."

"I know, sweetheart," Hrabanic said. "It's my brilliance and virility that does it. That, and the way I comb my moustache—have you noticed it yet? No woman can resist me."

"Hmm," Julia said. "Well, perhaps that explains it, after all." She leaned up and kissed him, and their laughter mingled in the kiss. Then she sat back, her eyebrows drawing together. "About all these women who can't resist you."

"Ah," Hrabanic said. "Perhaps I should amend that statement. What I actually meant to say—"

"Never mind that," Julia said. "Let's talk about the Archduchess."

Hrabanic winced. "Do we have to?"

"That was a woman's ring on the assassin's finger, out in the hallway tonight," Julia said, "and you recognized it."

He grimaced and shut his eyes against her gaze. "Yes," he admitted.

"Well?" Julia's impatient sigh ruffled against his chest. "Come now, Hrabanic. I'm not going to eat you for it, you know. You might as well be a man and tell me everything."

Hrabanic opened his eyes and glared at her. "Yes, I recognized it," he said. "And yes, I used to wear it. It came from the Archduchess. I gave it back to her when I left."

"Hmm." Rather than the sparking irritation he'd anticipated, Julia's eyes were filled with an even more dangerous look of speculation. "So, I take it, she always gives the ring to her current favorite?"

"It is a mark of her favor, yes," Hrabanic said. "And, ah...it implies more than a, um, purely courtly degree of favor."

"Which the Archduke knows about and thoroughly approves," Julia finished for him.

"Yes," Hrabanic said, and cut the word off with a hiss.

"I see." She gazed up at him narrowly for a moment, and his cheeks heated. Then she surprised him with a grin. "I think," she said, "that perhaps it's time to pay a social call on your old employers."

* * *

Ten minutes later, the Archduchess opened her door to his knock.

"Why, Hrabanic," she purred. "I was hoping you would—oh." As Julia stepped after him into her luxuriantly appointed room, her face twisted. "I see you're not alone."

"Hrabanic is rarely alone, nowadays," Julia said. "It's one of the great advantages of having an unmarried woman for his lover. That, and self-respect and independence."

Hrabanic rolled his eyes up to heaven, but didn't bother to argue.

The Archduchess wrapped her silk robe around her sheer nightgown and glared at Julia, who smiled back with barbed sweetness. Hrabanic felt himself turn effectively invisible, left safely outside the dangerous bubble of focus that had taken shape around the two women.

"Is this considered a usual hour to pay calls, among your particular social circle?" the Archduchess inquired. Her narrow eyebrows, plucked into perfect arcs, rose as she regarded Julia's mannish clothing. "Or were you still out carousing yourself, and forgot that it was past most civilized people's bedtimes?"

"Oh, I generally carouse all night long," Julia said. "But as for 'civilized' people..."

Hrabanic coughed. The bubble broke. Julia slid him an irritated glance but cut herself off, taking a deep breath. "We came," she said, "to return something that was lost. And to speak to your husband."

"He isn't here."

"Imagine my surprise." Julia raised a single, un-plucked eyebrow, and smiled. "Hrabanic?"

He reached into his pocket and took out the ruby ring. The Archduchess blinked. Then a radiant smile lit up her face.

"I wondered what had happened to that," she said. "They told me it was missing from Christo's hand when they found him. My dear, did you retrieve it for yourself? You know it's only been waiting for you all this time, no matter what this"—her gaze passed over Julia and dismissed her—"this *person* has been telling you. All you ever had to do was ask." She reached out her hand. "Come—"

"It's an odd way of showing favor, sending an assassin to stab him from behind," Julia said.

The Archduchess laughed. "As if poor Christo could ever have defeated Hrabanic. What nonsense!"

"Then, I take it, it was your husband who ordered the attempt?"

The Archduchess narrowed her eyes. "I have no knowledge of tedious politics."

Hrabanic coughed again, even more pointedly. Both women shot him identical looks of irritation.

"You already know that your swordsman is dead," Julia

said, "but you may not know yet that your *husband's* candidate for Head Librarian—of whom you, of course, would know nothing at all—is also dead. Hrabanic killed her half an hour ago. And the current Head Librarian betrayed both her and me." She crossed her arms. "Now, are you interested in hearing what we have to say?"

The Archduchess blinked rapidly. Her lips pursed. Then she tied a belt around her robe, her posture shifting from invitation to honed steel. "I'll take you to my husband," she said. "You may have something worth discussing, after all."

"So, Amanka is dead." The Archduke scowled, resplendent in his crimson silk dressing gown. "And you say she had one of the Head Librarian's creatures with her?"

"Unmistakably." Julia nodded. She sat in the seat across from him and the Archduchess; Hrabanic stood behind her, his arms crossed, ready to draw his sword at any moment.

"I don't suppose there's any chance the Head could simply have transferred his support to Amanka?" the Archduke asked.

"No." It was the Archduchess who answered him, her voice firm. "All of my spies were in agreement: Amanka was loyal to us. The Head has been actively working to turn the other Librarians against her, in preparation for tomorrow's vote."

"So he must have meant her to fail, when it came to the

final attempt. He had a high estimation of Madam Shevina's ability to protect herself against Amanka, it seems. But Hrabanic would still have been dead, killed by the creature, and without his protection..."

"I'd have been dead soon afterward, killed by any simple, non-magical assassin he chose to send after me," Julia said. "Or, if I had lost the fight, the same fate would have come to Amanka. Either way, it would leave only one candidate for tomorrow's vote: Lafka. She was always my grandfather's toady. I should have expected him to reward her, in the end."

Her voice was steady, and her expression gave nothing away, but Hrabanic moved a step closer to her, so that she would feel his support against her back. He saw the Archduchess's blue eyes narrow. Let her make of it what she would.

"I have no desire to be Head Librarian," Julia said. "But I'm surprisingly reluctant to let my grandfather win, after all."

"I don't blame you." The Archduke studied her. "And how do you feel about the way the Library has held itself aloof from the needs of Plötz for so long?"

Hrabanic could feel the tension radiating from Julia's shoulders. But she said, "Far less convinced of its rightness than I used to be...especially if that helps me survive tomorrow's vote."

The Archduke grinned. It was the wolfish grin Hrabanic remembered well; the grin of the man who'd just gotten exactly what he wanted. Beside him, the Archduchess's lips curved into a satisfied smile. The Archduke held out his hand to Julia, who leaned forward to take it—

—And Hrabanic yanked her chair back, out of reach.

"Wait," he said. He'd seen those expressions on both faces before. He *knew* them. "Wait!" he repeated.

"Hrabanic, what—?"

"You had better send your servant out of the room if he's going to cause trouble," the Archduke growled.

"Hrabanic knows better than to involve himself in political matters far above his head," the Archduchess murmured, rising and gliding towards him. "Perhaps the two of us can retire to a different—"

But Hrabanic shook her roughly away, and Julia frowned up at him, ignoring both of the others. "What is it? What's wrong?"

"Tell me," Hrabanic said, "exactly how the Head Librarian controls those creatures."

"I told you. He holds the power of every book in the Library, and they respond to that power, in his shape, and—"

"But Amanka was a mistress of illusion."

"Yes, but she couldn't create the true aura of authority and...oh." Julia's lips parted. "*Oh.*"

"You were raised too well by your grandfather," Hrabanic said. "You have to think beyond his prejudices. The truth is, there are other forms of power beyond the power of books and knowledge." He looked across her, past the Archduchess's alarmed fluttering, straight into the enraged face of his former employer. "The Archduke's political position gives him plenty of it."

Julia rose to her feet without speaking. The Archduke started forward.

"This is nonsense," he said. "Hrabanic never did know when to keep his mouth shut. He's a decent swordsman, but when it comes to thinking—"

"He's good at that too," said Julia. "Who knew?" Her voice was dry and even. She looked the Archduke up and down, and her lips twisted into a sneer. "What fun you must have had, pretending to be my grandfather. You always wanted control over the Library; was it satisfying to wear Amanka's illusion while you ordered about Grandfather's creatures? To pretend you really were the most important man in Plötz?"

"You—impudent—little—"

"Careful," Hrabanic said. His sword was in his hand. He saw the Archduke's eyes fix on it; the Archduke's face purpled with the effort of holding back a storm of words. "You wouldn't want to make another mistake in judgment right now," said Hrabanic. "Not when you've lost all your best swordsmen."

"It was a beautifully laid scheme," Julia said. "I must admit, I wouldn't have imagined anything so clever originating from you, Your Highness. To organize matters so that even if your candidate lost, I would turn against my own sponsor and voluntarily come under the wings of your protection..."

Hrabanic coughed. Julia's lips twitched. "Ah," she said. "But it wasn't your scheme at all, was it?" She turned to the Archduchess. "What a pity you were stupid enough to lose Hrabanic's loyalty," she said. "Perhaps it will comfort you to know that I plan not to make that mistake myself. But I can promise you both that no matter who wins tomorrow's vote, the White Library will grant no favors to the Archduchy of Plötz. And after your little game tonight, I doubt any other Archdukes will be allowed to return here in the future. Hrabanic?"

"Julia?"

"I think it's time to end our social call," Julia said. "Staying too long with ill-bred company grows tiresome, you know."

"Indeed," Hrabanic agreed. "Deadly dull."

He waited for her to leave the room, then backed out after her, holding his sword ready under the Archduke's burning gaze. As he finally pulled the door closed, he remarked, "It's a pity we can't lock it from the outside."

"Unfortunately..." Julia said, behind him. Her voice sounded strained. "I'm afraid our social round isn't over for the night yet, after all."

Hrabanic spun around. Lafka stood in the center of the hallway, her white robe glowing in the sickly white light and her large, green eyes fixed malevolently upon them.

"The Head Librarian wishes to see you both."

* * *

The Head Librarian's study was a tiled octagon, barely twelve feet at its widest but lined with shelves that rose dizzyingly high, stacks upon stacks of books. Even when Hrabanic tipped his head back, he could catch no glimpse of any ceiling, only more and more bookshelves rising up forever.

"More damned illusions," he muttered under his breath.

"What?" Julia blinked and followed his gaze. "Oh, no," she said. "Not this part. Grandfather told you they have every book that's ever been written, didn't he? As the Head Librarian, he has absorbed all of them." She sighed. "It's part of what makes him so unnerving. That and his manner of treating people, of course. I always hated the way he'd summon me here and then leave me waiting like this."

Hrabanic glanced around the empty study. Lafka had ushered them inside and then left with a last, murderous glance, closing the door behind her. "Do you think he already knows what's happened tonight?"

Julia said, "I'd be surprised if he didn't. When I was a little girl, I believed he even knew the contents of my dreams." She tapped her fingers against the closest bookshelf. "Damn it. I was so certain I'd escaped this place. I could have sworn he'd given up his plans for me. When the messenger arrived to tell me I'd been nominated, I didn't even believe him at first. I—" She cut herself off abruptly as a hidden door swung open from the opposite wall of shelves.

The Head Librarian stepped inside, holding a book in his hand. His bald head gleamed in the bright white light of the room. His narrow lips stretched into a smile.

"My dear girl. You've done it, haven't you?"

"I beg your pardon?"

"The Archduke's candidate is safely out of the way—and you were quite right after all. I didn't believe you, you know, when you claimed your swordsman here would be able to defeat the creature even when taken by surprise. I am impressed, sir," he added, with a nod to Hrabanic. "My granddaughter certainly chose wisely when she persuaded you to assist her in her candidacy."

"Grandfather..." Julia's face paled. "That's not true," she said to both of them. "Hrabanic, don't listen!"

"To which part?" Hrabanic asked. He was rather pleased to hear his voice come out evenly, rather than in a roar. His hand tried to reach for the hilt of his sword; he restrained it, gritting his teeth. "The part where you and your grandfather were plotting together after all? Or the part where you agreed to send that creature into my room while I slept, without any warning?"

"I did try to warn you earlier," said the Head Librarian. "You may recall me telling you that Julia was herself living proof of the power of illusions. It is what makes her so ideally suited for the role she was born to play. She, you know, was the one who came up with the plan twenty years ago to keep herself safe from early assassination attempts by pretending to leave our Library and renounce her claims. Didn't you ever wonder why, if such a thing were actually true, I would ever have forgiven her?"

"The question did cross my mind," Hrabanic said. He

couldn't restrain himself after all. His right fingers closed over the hilt of his sword.

"Hrabanic," Julia said, in a thin voice. She reached out to him, but her hand fell back as she met his eyes. "Hrabanic, you mustn't believe him. You can't."

"Julia," said Hrabanic, "you were the one who told me every word spoken in this building is an illusion. Remember?"

He could see the deep breath she took. He'd never heard her sound so uncertain before. "Please—"

"You don't remember?" Hrabanic said. "Well, I do." He withdrew his sword in a smooth, curving arc. "So," he said to the Head Librarian. "Why don't you answer a question of mine, now that I've been polite enough to listen to your poison. Are you actually Julia's grandfather? Or is there a reason I've never seen you and that Lafka in the same room since I arrived?"

Julia grabbed the closest bookshelf for balance. "*What*?"

"I wondered why she wasn't at that gathering today," Hrabanic said. "Seeing as she was one of the candidates—even if she was the most unlikely one."

"I—but you—"

"It's good to see you're capable of being flustered, sweetheart." Hrabanic kept his gaze on the Head even as he spoke to Julia. "Always comforting for a man to know he's not the only one who can be taken off guard from time to time."

"Hrabanic, you bastard," Julia said. "I really thought you believed him! Him—her—" She turned on the Head Librarian. "Who are you?"

"Dear child," said the Head Librarian. "Can you really tell me you would believe a disgraced swordsman, fired from his last position, over your own grandfather?"

"Hrabanic was not fired," Julia said. "And surprisingly, yes, I would believe him over just about anyone else I know. Even my grandfather...if he were here. You're right," she said to Hrabanic. "I didn't see Lafka at the gathering. That was entirely out of character for someone who's toadied up to my grandfather all her life. If I hadn't been so distracted, I would have noticed."

She turned her glare on to the Head. "You asked how much I remembered when you met me and Hrabanic at the front door this morning, Lafka," she said. "Well, I can tell you: I remember exactly how much you resented me for being favored by my grandfather. I should have known he'd be clever enough to see through you eventually—and that you'd be just the type to stab him in the back."

"The front, actually. While he was bound and gagged," said the Head. The features shifted and rearranged themselves; it was Lafka who stood facing them now in her own white robes, her green eyes brilliant with hate. The book in her hand had shifted, too.

It had become a sword.

"I didn't simply kill him, you see. I stabbed him as part of a ritual that transferred all his powers and effectively transformed me into the acting Head Librarian. It was a difficult procedure. You would have been impressed."

Julia's eyes narrowed. "And how exactly did you plan to explain those new powers to whoever won the next election?"

Lafka sneered. "That was never a concern. I only nominated you to take Amanka's eyes off me. Everyone knew I was the least likely candidate. All I had to do was manipulate the two of you into doing each other in before the vote—and rid myself of your swordsman in the process."

"You haven't managed that part," Hrabanic said. "Julia, get behind me."

"No, wait," Julia said. "She took all my grandfather's powers. That means—"

"Quite," agreed Lafka. "I have absorbed every book in this Library—including your own little book, with all your sword-fighting secrets. In fact, I think you might call me your best student." She grinned and dropped into fighting stance. "On guard!"

He'd hoped the robes would slow her down. They didn't. She darted and wove around him, faster than the Archduke's hired swordsman, stronger in her movements, preternaturally agile and aware. Every thrust Hrabanic made, she countered. Every parry she made sent him another step back toward the angled shelves of books, leaving him less and less space to maneuver.

His vision narrowed, became a tunnel. Sweat slicked his hands on the pommel of the sword. Time to dare everything. He twisted fluidly on the slippery tiles and spun himself toward her: the whistling attack, a whirl of speed. She knocked his sword away with a sharp, short jerk of her arm—the exact defense he had prescribed in his treatise. He thrust overhand with all his strength. For the first time, Lafka seemed to waver. She stepped back, raising her blade as if to parry, but without any strength behind it. It was a move he knew well.

He had invented it, after all.

Her blade swooped through the distance between them, straight for his unprotected side.

The Hrabanic Deception was always fatal.

Swirling colors suddenly leapt into the air between them —Julia creating one last illusion, attempting to save him. But as Hrabanic's own treatise had stated, a true swordsman could fight even with his or her eyes closed. Lafka's blade pierced the illusion—

And his own blade stabbed deep into her stomach before the tip of her sword could even graze him.

She dropped her sword. Blood trickled from her mouth. Her eyes remained fixed on him in outraged surprise until she crumpled to the ground.

Julia's illusion fell away. She was breathing hard as she met Hrabanic's gaze over Lafka's body. "But how—? I thought—"

"Nothing could counter the Hrabanic deception?" Hrabanic was too winded to laugh. He managed to grin at her anyway. "That's certainly what I wrote in my treatise."

"And?"

Hrabanic cocked one eyebrow at her. "You really think

I'd publish all of my secrets in a book? That would just be asking for trouble."

"Oh, gods," Julia said, and let out her breath in a shuddering sigh. "So *that's* the real Hrabanic deception! Poor Lafka. She spent too many years living in the Library to even suspect such a thing."

"I can't feel too sorry for her." Hrabanic drew his sword free and wiped it clean. The octagonal study was silent except for the brush of his blade against cloth. Then a sudden thought made him pause.

"Wait a moment. If she took the last Head's powers when she killed him..." Horror stopped his voice. He dropped his sword to pat his frantic way across his head and chest and sides. He didn't *feel* any different...

Julia's laughter made him look up from his explorations. "It's good to know you're still not perfect," she said. "You don't listen very well, do you? She stole his power in a ritual, one that she probably hunted down in one of the most obscure books in the entire Library. That kind of transfer doesn't happen by accident."

"No?" Hrabanic turned and squinted nervously at the air around him. "So all that power is just...floating around? Waiting to leap inside someone else?"

"I'm sure it hasn't taken root anywhere yet," Julia said. "So don't worry—you haven't just become the most powerful man in Plötz without knowing it."

"Huh." Hrabanic's eyebrows rose. "In that case...unless

you're planning to accept the election tomorrow, as the only official candidate still remaining in the White Library—"

"Gods, no!" Julia whirled around. "You're right. We can't just stand around here talking. We need to leave now, quickly!"

"Let's just think a moment, first. So, neither of us is the most powerful person in Plötz, we've both offended the Archduke and the Archduchess, and the White Librarians won't be too happy with you either."

"True enough." Julia took a deep breath. "And, unfortunately, all my savings are back at the tavern. It'll take some time to have Miriam send them to me in secret, and until then—"

"Do you think this might help in the meantime?" Hrabanic reached into his pocket and withdrew what he'd been carrying all night long.

Julia looked from the ruby ring to Hrabanic's face and broke into a smile. "Damn," she said. "Forced to eat my own words yet again. Hrabanic, you are a decidedly useful man to have around."

"I'm glad you've finally noticed." Hrabanic offered her his arm. "Shall we explore the wider world outside Plötz? I've been buried in a backwater for the last three years, you know. A wise woman once told me it was time to stop licking my wounds and move on."

"An excellent plan," Julia said. "But first..."

Two figures walked out of the Octagon Room. They were a well-known sight in the White Library: the Head Librarian and his most devoted acolyte, deep in conversation. When they walked together down the corridor, no one took any notice. When they stopped in the suite of rooms that belonged to the Head Librarian's granddaughter and her obstreperous bodyguard, the Librarians whose duty it was to observe such things only shrugged. Clearly, the Head had devised a new plan. Probably both visitors were already dead, and the Head was merely taking care of business by disposing of their possessions. When the Head and his acolyte walked out the front door of the Library twenty minutes later, still intent on their discussion, they were bowed out with all due deference.

It was only when it came time for the election, twelve hours later, that the voters finally realized that all candidates, including the current Head, were either missing or dead.

But by then, Hrabanic and Julia had more interesting things to think about.

Midnight

She was running with two minutes left before midnight. The skirts of her new dress rustled against her legs as she darted through the formal gardens towards the small pool at their center. Music trailed from the long, low palace behind her, played by high, sweet pipes and smooth-as-silk strings. She ran barefoot across the grass, holding one shoe dangling from her hand.

Wind blew through the branches of the cypress trees, but no ripple disturbed the glassy pool, even when the girl knelt beside it and breathed her words against it.

"The prince danced only with me, all night long. You were wrong—I'll never regret it! And I know he'll find me and kiss me to finish the spell, because I've left one of my shoes on the steps of the palace. Once he finds the other shoe here, he'll know exactly what happened. He'll kiss me no matter what I look like!"

She dropped the second glass slipper and fell to the ground as clocks began to chime in the distance. Her dress shifted back into weeds and leaves.

The palace clocks struck midnight as a small green frog hopped into the pool, still croaking. Ten minutes later, a weary gardener, humming along to the dance music from the palace, swept away the fallen leaves and scooped up the glass slipper to give to his youngest daughter.

Clasp Hands

The smallest witch hung over the banister, her whole body forming an arc of yearning, as the first of her mother's friends arrived for their annual feast.

"Bella!" It was Aunt Calliope, bursting into the house in a cloud of snow, wrapped up in a six-foot scarf. She was already unwinding the scarf as she spoke to her hostess, midnight-blue wool and white stars swirling around her round, comfortable body. "Terrible weather! That traffic, can you believe it..."

But the smallest witch knew better than to listen to what Calliope said in those first, guarded moments. She looked instead, with her eyes half-closed, until she saw what was hiding underneath: the glimmer of gold filling the air around Calliope, and the tiny owl who hid, buried deep in Calliope's curly brown hair, blinking out at the smallest witch with a deep yellow gaze.

As the owl's eyes blinked twice, Calliope looked up. "And Katy!" She beamed and blew a kiss up the stairs, her long scarf dangling from her fingers. "Look how big you are! Is your mama finally letting you stay up this year?"

"Absolutely not!" said Katy's mom. The black-and-gold leopard on the back of her sweater seemed to arch and stretch in warning as she whisked Calliope's scarf away and hung it over Katy's favorite coat hook, the one shaped like an eagle's head. "She's allowed to wave hello to everyone, but then she has to go to sleep. School tomorrow—and *don't* give me that look, young lady!"

"Oh, poor sweetie," Calliope said, and made a sympathetic face. "Just another year or two, though—oh, look!" She whirled around. "It's Frigg! Can you believe I actually got here before her, for once?"

The door opened again, letting in more whirling flakes of snow, but none of them seemed to touch Aunt Frigg. She stood like a queen in the center of the doorway, glittering in white cashmere, framed against the dark night sky.

Katy didn't have to close her eyes to see the silver glow that surrounded this aunt's tall figure. Frigg had never bothered to hide what she was—not to Katy's sight, at least. As she took off her sleek, knee-length coat, Frigg didn't say a word...but she looked up at Katy with eyes that said: *Soon.*

Katy shivered with delight. Aunt Frigg had always, always been her favorite.

She clung to the banister as all the rest of them arrived, as wine glasses clinked and soft music played and her mother plugged in fairy lights against the dark. She slid down to her knees on the carpet upstairs, peering down through the bars of the stair rail at the living room below as the air filled with sparkles and women scattered across couches and chairs. More stools had to be dragged out from the closet, just like always, before the entire group could be seated.

"Why don't I ever remember how many we are?" Katy's mother demanded, and Katy mouthed the familiar words along with her while the other women cackled with laughter and sent showers of gold into the air with their wine glasses.

Everything else had changed this last year, until she had echoed and ached with loss, but this one night could be counted on to always be the same. She'd been waiting for it for weeks, squeezing her eyes shut against the dark, reciting all the familiar rites of the evening as if she could bring it on early by sheer willpower...as if the empty spaces in her house and heart could fill already in anticipation.

"Tonight," Katy whispered to herself. "Tonight, I'll bring them back."

Dishes gradually spread across the tables below, filling the air with scents of cinnamon and sugar, cooked meat and exotic cheeses. Laughter sounded, coffee brewed in the kitchen, and less than half an hour in, as always, Aunt Jessamy turned off the classical radio with a cry of disgust. "Come on, Bella, live a little, won't you? Join the *last* century, at least!"

As half the women shouted in protest and the other half shouted in agreement, she stuck in a CD of her own. A woman's voice suddenly filled the room, shrieking and wailing over pounding drums until even Katy's mom was dragged up by the others to dance along to the wild music. Aunt Frigg danced like a white tiger, all cool, elegant grace and power. Aunt Calliope stamped with joy until the furniture rattled, and she shook her long hair until it whirled around her and her owl fluttered free, up to a high shelf where it could look down at everyone.

Longing built in Katy's chest, the loneliness that had built and built over months, until it filled her throat and she couldn't resist any longer. She slipped down one step, two steps, three...

"Oh, Katy!" Her mother broke free and hurried to the stairs, shaking her head. "What are you doing still awake? You should have gone to bed by now."

"But—!"

"No buts," said her mother, and she walked Katy all the way to her room with a firm hand on her shoulder. "Come on. You've seen everyone, and now it's time for sleep for little girls."

"I am *not* a little girl," Katy muttered. But her voice was drowned out by the cries from downstairs.

"Aw, poor Katy."

"Good night, Katy!"

"We'll miss you, Katy!"

The chorus of familiar voices only ended as the door

closed behind her. Katy's chest burned as she padded to the bed and slipped inside. She could *feel* her mother listening as she pulled up the covers, laid her head on the pillow. She clenched her hands as she forced herself to lie still.

Next to her bed, the dull gold locket lay on her bedside table—her grandmother's locket, with a picture of all four of them inside.

"Almost time," Katy whispered to it. "She can't make me be alone any longer."

She waited until her mother's footsteps had moved away from the door. Then she slid out of bed, pulled up the rug, and pressed her ear against the floor.

"Is Katy really all right?" That was Calliope's voice. "It must have been a tough year for her, what with your mom and, well, Dan...it's hard to go from four to two."

"She won't let it break her." That was Frigg, her voice cool and certain. "She's one of us."

"Oh, she's better off without Dan anyway." That was Aunt Hannah, her words making Katy's shoulders tense. "Good riddance! Better no father than one who doesn't care. We *all* know that."

"Ohhh..." And *that* was Katy's mother. "I hope so. I mean, you're right, and she is strong, but..." She sighed, and Katy, listening, scowled. "All I want is to keep her safe, but if you could see the way she looks at me, like she thinks I'm completely inept, or...no!" There was a slapping sound, her voice turning brisk. "I've done more than enough moaning to you guys already. Tell me all about your love lives instead."

"*Well*...!" began Calliope with gusto

The other women dissolved into laughter.

"Turn up the music!" Jessamy bellowed. "And pass the wine!"

Men—and women—were dissected and dismissed. Jobs were complained about. New careers were suggested. Wild plans for treks across the world were devised.

If she hadn't been careful, Katy might have fallen to sleep with her cheek pressed against the floorboard, the way she often had in the past, as the comfort of their familiar voices echoed below her, promising everything wonderful that waited in the far-off future.

But that had been back when she still trusted her mother to guide that future for her.

This year, she wouldn't let herself fall asleep, tucked away from everything important. This year she stayed awake until the voices quieted. Until the food was all put away and the real business of the night began.

She waited until midnight, until the clock chimed twelve. Then she eased the door open with trembling hands, careful not to make a sound. The light in the hallway had been turned off. She crawled, whisper-soft, across the carpet, carrying her secret supplies in her hands. She peered down through the bars of the stair rail into the living room below, where the fairy lights had been extinguished and only twelve points of lights shone in the darkness: the candles that had been lit around the central coffee table.

Katy pulled out a match from the matchbox she had

stolen, shielding her own candle with her hands. But she knew her mother wouldn't see it, and neither would any of her friends. Not now. Now they were holding each other's hands in a ring around the table, with their eyes shut, and power rippled through the air like muffled thunder.

It made Katy's skin prickle and her eyebrows itch: the feeling of it rising all around her...and the feeling of her own power, rising within her to meet it.

I'm old enough, she told herself fiercely. *She can't make me wait any longer.*

"*Enter,*" the women below breathed, as one.

"*Enter,*" Katy whispered, and struck her flame.

Light erupted in a blazing sheet of flame around the table downstairs. The air shivered around Katy as she watched, holding her breath.

Then light exploded behind her eyes.

She cried out, dropping her candle. It fell somewhere into the blackness, but she couldn't see it anymore. She couldn't see anything but the light that flooded everything now, the internal fire that filled her eyes with flames.

"Little witch." A deep voice rocked through her whole body, echoing through every bone. **"Little witch, calling me all alone. Little witch without a circle to protect her."**

Katy couldn't feel the floor beneath her, couldn't hear her mother or her aunts down below. She'd been swept away from everything, but there were some things she still knew for sure, things she'd repeated and repeated in the last horrible year of nights, until her pillow had been damp and cold and she had fallen asleep with her hair pasted to her face by tears.

"I don't need my mother's protection," she snapped. "I'm old enough to decide things for myself."

A deep, rolling chuckle rocked through her body. **"Are you, little witch? And what would you decide?"**

Katy couldn't feel her hands or arms anymore, but she knew what she'd held looped over her wrist a moment ago. She had watched the others, all these years, memorized the ritual her mother had tried to keep so secret. "I have an offering for you," she whispered. "My grandmother's locket."

"Oh, how delicious," murmured the voice. **"Such a clever little witch, offering me that which holds your heart. But should you give up such a treasure, do you think?"**

"It's all I have," Katy said. "But..." She drew a shivering breath. "It's not a gift. I need them both back, in exchange. Gran and...and Dad, too."

For a moment, Aunt Hannah's words echoed in her ears, sending sudden disquiet shivering through her: *Better no father than one who doesn't care...*

She set her jaw. Dad had cared. He *had*. It was only her mother who had made him go, who had turned him hard. She had fought with him late in the night every night, when she'd thought that Katy was sleeping. She had refused to call him back, no matter how Katy had begged, until Katy *couldn't* love her anymore.

She hadn't even saved Gran from dying!

"I need them back," Katy whispered. "But I'll give you the locket in exchange."

"Ah, little witch," the voice whispered back, **"I'll tell you a secret. I'll take the locket, as you say, and you'll never be alone again...but that's because I'll be taking you, too."**

"What?" Katy's breath stuttered in her throat. "You can't do that! Tonight—"

"—Is the night," the voice agreed, **"the only night in the year when I can be called by the wise and the powerful for favors. But you've forgotten one thing, little witch. You had no circle to protect you when you called. And there's nothing so sweet to the palate of my kind as the pure and tiny flame of a little witch who hasn't grown into her power yet."**

"No!" Katy yelled.

It was no use. Her voice disappeared into the crackling flames.

There was no one close enough to hear her. There was only the voice, laughing all around her.

"Try to escape, little bird, if you like. But I promise you'll never manage it alone."

Katy burned with the truth of it. She *was* all alone. She had been all year long: as she sat by her grandmother's empty hospital bed...as she watched her father's car drive away...and as she ran to her room afterwards, slamming the door against the sound of her mother's angry voice behind her.

A small pair of yellow eyes suddenly blinked at her through the flames. When she looked again they were gone. But in the distance, she heard a soft whisper...a sound like the sound of owl's wings flapping.

Katy stared harder, desperately trying to see through the flames to the room beyond. For a moment they flickered. Then they snapped back into place. She was locked away from the house around her, just as she'd been kept away from her aunts and the party tonight.

"Oh, little witch," the voice sighed. **"I am glad that you called me. It's a long time since I've been so entertained. What fun it will be to devour such strength."**

Katy blinked.

Wait.

Her mother had called her strong, too. And Aunt Frigg had said: *"She's one of us."*

One of them: her wild and wonderful aunts, who had come every year of her life to fill her house with magic and wonder; who made her rigid mother actually laugh and dance and relax.

Katy *had* been stuck upstairs, as always, when they'd lit their candles that night. But the power in her had recognized their power when it rose to meet her, just as she had known all of their voices by heart through the floorboards. Because...

"I'm a witch," Katy whispered. "Just like them." And

they'd been coming forever, for all of her life. So... "I have *never* been alone."

She opened her mouth. She yelled through the flames: "*Mom! Everyone! I'm here!*"

A black-and-gold leopard leapt, screaming with rage, through the fire.

A brown owl fluttered after the leopard, growing as it flew until its great, billowing wings filled her vision. A white tiger followed after it, powerful and cold, while a giant, slithering snake opened its vast mouth wide behind them to show its dripping fangs to the flames. A raptor with jeweled claws led the rest of the animals, letting out a harsh battle cry in Aunt Jessamy's voice.

Katy recognized every one of them.

Hissing, yowling, hooting and snarling, they threw themselves around Katy and pressed her between them in their circle. They beat back the flames with claws and teeth. As Katy felt their strength rise around her, she felt something new rising in her own chest...something with teeth and claws of its own.

She opened her mouth, and it growled through her throat, filling her with feral joy.

She tipped her head back and let it out in a roar.

"Next time, little witch," the voice sighed, as it faded. **"Next time you call me on your own..."**

But Katy didn't listen, not anymore. The house was taking shape around her. The creature behind her eyes was fading, and every muscle in her body ached with effort. She lay in the center of the coffee table, curled in a circle between the candles, and as she opened her eyes, she saw Aunt Frigg extinguish the very last flame with her fingers.

"There," Frigg said, and she wiped off her hands with an expression of distaste. "That's the last time he'll try *that* trick again, I think."

"*Katy—!*"

That was her mother's voice behind her, but Katy had never heard it like that before. When Gran had given her last gasping breaths, Mom's voice had sounded as dry and thin and papery as if it might shred at any moment. When Dad had slammed the door behind him for the very last time, Mom had screamed after him with rage.

But Katy had never, ever heard her mother cry.

Her skin prickled with fear as she turned, pushing herself up on the coffee table, following that awful, unfamiliar sound.

Her mother's eyes were the green of the leopard who'd raged at the flames. "I almost lost you," she said fiercely. "Don't you understand? I can *not* lose you, too!"

The rest of the women around them held still and silent as Katy stared into her mother's leopard-gaze. Memories shifted and clicked into place.

"Mom," she whispered. "This is for you."

She lifted her grandmother's locket and dropped the chain over her mother's head.

Magic exploded in the air around them.

Her mother let out a choking sob and snatched Katy to her chest, where the locket glinted gold.

Aunts flooded into action around them, hugging and kissing and exclaiming and scolding, until the house echoed with their voices.

Aunt Jessamy turned on the music again, while Calliope plugged in the fairy lights.

"It's still a school day tomorrow," Katy's mom protested. But she didn't lift her face from Katy's hair as she said it, and her arms didn't loosen around Katy's shoulders.

"Bah," said Aunt Hannah. "Who cares about missing one day of school when our circle is finally complete?"

Katy pulled back. "Really?" she whispered. "Mom?"

She didn't have to turn to see her aunts' wild, mischievous, frightening grins all around her. They were candles lit within her chest, filling up the last of the empty spaces.

Her mother sighed. She bit her lip. Then she gave a rueful smile and pulled Katy up to stand in front of her.

"Well," she said, "I suppose it is only once a year..."

And the smallest witch danced with her circle all the rest of that night, whole and complete in the darkness.

Crow

A crow flew into Ruth's mouth one Sunday afternoon during lunch.

She'd just opened her mouth to agree with her mother when the crow launched itself through the air, shrinking to the size of a peach stone as it flew, until it popped straight into Ruth's mouth. She gagged and grabbed her throat.

Her mother didn't notice.

"You have really got to get yourself organized. Honestly, Ruth! The pins are coming out of your hair again. Can't you hold it back any better? You don't want people to think you have bag lady hair. And this garden is a mess. Look at those weeds!"

Ruth opened her mouth to say, *Yes, Mother*, but she

couldn't push the words through her throat. The crow flared its wings and choked her again.

She slumped back in her wicker chair and took a long, cold sip of water. It didn't dislodge the crow. She could feel it preening under the shower.

Her mother left at two o'clock as usual, looking dissatisfied. Ruth wandered back into her house, holding her throat lightly, afraid to squeeze too hard. She stopped in front of the hallway mirror and winced at the sight.

Her mother was right. Her hair had escaped the pins again. Curly, red spirals sprang out from the bun she'd so carefully pinned up that morning.

Ruth tried to mutter, *I look like a bag lady*, but the crow stifled her words. She stared at the reflection of her face, pale above her muted gray shirt.

This never would have happened to her mother. She never would have allowed it to happen.

I am a mess, Ruth thought, but she didn't even try to say it out loud.

"You look terrible," her boss, Dani, told her the next morning. She dropped a six-inch stack of papers on Ruth's desk. "You're all right, aren't you?"

Ruth opened her mouth to say, *Yes, I'm fine*, but the crow opened its beak. Her voice emerged at the same time as the crow's "braaak!" and somehow, the word that came out was,

"No!"

"What?" Dani frowned. "Uh...do you want to talk about it?"

Ruth shook her head vigorously, covering her mouth with her hand.

"I wanted you to do Marlene's work again today. Are you up to it?"

The crow jabbed Ruth's throat with a sharp claw, and she choked. Her mouth fell open.

"NO!" the crow shrieked through Ruth's throat.

Dani snatched up the stack of papers, eyes wide. "Fair enough," she muttered and backed away.

Ruth watched Dani whisper with one of the other secretaries on the opposite side of the room. Both of them snuck nervous glances at her. Ruth cursed the crow in her throat. She'd never turned down extra work before. How could she? That would make her look unhelpful, and no one liked women like that. It was one of the first rules her mother had drummed into her.

She ducked into the bathroom and opened her mouth wide in front of the mirror. When she peered into the dark cavern of her throat, she glimpsed the crow's beady eyes staring out at her.

"What are you doing here?" she whispered. "What do you want?"

But the crow didn't answer her.

Dani sidled up to her at 4:45, holding one of the letters Ruth had typed.

"Um...I just wanted to tell you, good job," she said. "You've always done a very good job."

"Really?" Ruth blinked. "I mean...thank you." The crow settled back into her throat, content.

Fifteen minutes later, Ruth headed for the bus stop. Halfway there, the crow jabbed her throat, and Ruth choked.

"What? What do you want?"

She turned around. She had stopped just in front of a clothing shop.

Ruth froze. Wild colors filled the window, the kind she'd always loved but never worn. Her mother's warnings echoed through her head. Nice girls, respectable girls, wore white or black or gray, and they buttoned their blouses right up to their chins. Only loose girls, cheap girls wore rainbow colors, because they were trying to show themselves off. Respectable girls...

The crow ruffled its wings impatiently.

Ruth took a deep breath. Was she really going to listen to a crow?

She stepped through the shop's door as lightly and carefully as a ballet dancer, touching her neck for reassurance.

That Sunday, when Ruth's mother arrived for lunch, her mouth opened wide in horror.

"My God! What have you done to yourself?"

Ruth stepped back to let her mother into the house. Her

emerald green skirt billowed around her legs as she moved, and her thin, peach-colored silk tank top let the breeze through to cool her skin.

Ruth's mother fumbled in her purse. "For God's sake! What were you thinking? Here, I have some pins somewhere. We'll just—"

"No," said Ruth and the crow together. Ruth shook her head, and her red, curly, springy hair shook with it, unbound, crazy and wild and wonderful. She gestured towards the back door. "Lunch is ready outside."

"Well. I don't know what you expect me to say." Her mother pursed her lips. "I hope you aren't wearing costumes like this to work!"

Ruth thought of the peacock blue suit in her closet and smiled. She opened the back door for her mother.

"You certainly haven't taken out any of those weeds, I see."

"Nope," Ruth said. She looked out across the garden, blazing with color—yellow dandelions, purple wildflowers, green climbing vines. "I decided not to."

"What?" Her mother sank into her usual chair. "Ruth, is something wrong with you? You're acting crazy today. Why on earth wouldn't you want to get rid of those nasty dandelions? Don't you want to organize your garden?"

"No," Ruth said. She felt the crow rustling in her throat, preparing to speak. *Don't worry,* she thought. *I can handle this one myself.*

Ruth looked straight into her mother's angry, frightened face.

"I like it this way," she said.

True Names

I'm so tired and frustrated, I could bust. Between Emmy caterwauling every time I set her down, the dogs breaking into the pantry again, and every inch of my big round belly tugging at me like fire every blessed time I turn, I'm hardly halfway through the housework by the time the sun starts to set. Any minute now, Sam and his brothers'll come piling in from the farm, expecting their dinner, and you know Sam'll be making his usual comments about how his own ma always had dinner and a smile at six, come rain or shine, and that with five growing boys all pulling at her skirts.

This isn't what I bargained for, I'll tell you that. When I let Sam sweet talk me into moving out here to the back of beyond to be his wife, it was all about the romance of the wild, the two of us standing at each other's sides against mountain lions and poisonous snakes, and me learning to be just as fierce against them as any man. Days like today somehow never got mentioned in any of his stories, back then.

But wanting and having are two different things, as my own mama always told me, and tonight's dinner isn't about to go cooking itself just because Carrie L. Gibbons, Carrie Landry as was, wants to sit down on the floor of her own kitchen and cry her eyes out like the brainless girl she used to be.

Emmy's clinging to my shoulder like a baby monkey, one plump fist stuck inside her mouth to gnaw away her teething pains. Her eyes look big and suspicious in her little pink face, and I don't dare set her down now, not when her screams of outrage might trigger even louder wails of my own. So I waddle around the kitchen with only one hand free, lighting the oven and slicing up the steak, doing my best to ignore the aching of my heavy belly and back, and when I hear the dogs start barking outside, I curse under my breath because I know it must be Sam and the others heading in already to find me lacking—especially when the barking cuts off after no more than a minute.

But then the doorbell rings.

Now, that doorbell hasn't rung more than four times in the last two months. None of the men on the farm would think to ring it any more than they would fly, and the neighbor women all just give a knock and a holler as they open the door themselves. We're close as cats around here—with only ten families farming out this way, if we didn't talk to each other, we'd have to whistle Dixie for company. It's only the preacher's wife from out East, on her rare visits of state, who's fussed enough to ring the bell; and even she's got to be slaving over her own man's dinner at this time of day.

The bell rings again while I'm still standing rigid as a rock in pure astonishment, right in the middle of the kitchen with a frying pan in my hand. I look at Emmy on my shoulder, and she looks back at me, big-eyed.

"Well, darlin'," I say, "the only way to know's by seeing," and I wipe my free hand on my apron as I head for the door.

It isn't the preacher's wife outside, but a dapper little man with the last of the day's sunlight shining on his slick, copper-colored hair and a fancy leather sales case by his side, made of some kind of mottled snakeskin. The dogs have always barked at strangers, but not this time. This time, they're sitting way, way back, watching him from a respectful distance. They stay right there even after they see me, though Red, the oldest, lets out a soft little whine.

I'm so startled by the way they're acting, I haven't said a single word of greeting. But the little man's smile is as bright as the fading sun over the mountains.

"Ma'am," he says, and he gives me a bow the likes of which I've never seen before. "Herbert Huggins, at your service. Hot day, isn't it?"

I hadn't thought so, before, but I realize he's right—it is hot, much hotter now than it was this afternoon even at the height of the day, and now that I've noticed it, the heat presses down against me like a branding iron until I can't hardly breathe, and the sweat pops out all across my skin.

The heat doesn't seem to be affecting Herbert Huggins, though. His neat, tan-colored suit is almost the same color as the dry ground around us, with not a single tell-tale sweat-stain in sight, and he looks every bit as comfortable in it as a lizard sunning himself on a rock. His smile gets even toothier as he points and says, "That's a mighty fine baby you have there, Mrs.—?"

"Gibbons," I say, and I make myself smile back—but when I look down, I see my free hand's crept up of its own accord to cradle Emmy's head, and I'm pulling her tight into my chest, after spending all day trying to get myself free of her.

I must have pulled her too tight; she lets out a squawk, and Herbert Huggins's lips turn down in sympathy, like a sad-faced clown.

"Ah, the little ones," he sighs. "Now, the truth is, Mrs. Gibbons, I'm here today to help you out with some new discoveries in domestic science—innovations that will no doubt make all the difference in the world to a hardworking lady such as yourself. But I surely do hate to see you or your lovely daughter suffer any discomfort from this terrible heat that has come upon us. So perhaps we'd be better off sitting in your own comfortable kitchen—which is neat as a pin, I am certain—rather than bandying words in the open air. Ma'am?"

He gestures like a gentleman for me to go ahead of him, and trapped in his flow of words like a fish caught up in too strong a current, I turn to walk straight down the hall.

But as I turn, I see the dogs: see Red, the oldest, staring at me.

If Sam's cursed Red once for his lack of brains, he's cursed him a thousand times—and it's not three hours since I had to chase Red and the others out of my clean pantry, hollering unladylike imprecations at the bunch of them.

But I see Red staring with all his might, while he sits quiet and still ten feet away, and something inside me wriggles free from that current that's trying to carry me down the hall without thinking.

"I can't," I say—and hearing the truth pop out of my mouth, I can't believe that I'd forgotten it, even for a moment. I stop and turn back with my big round belly blocking the door, holding Herbert Huggins and his sales case safe outside. "My husband and his brothers'll be back any minute, and I haven't even started cooking dinner. I'm sorry, Mr. Huggins, but—"

"No need to fear, Mrs. Gibbons. I ran into Sam and the boys on my way in, and they said I should go straight ahead. Why, Sam bragged all about your cooking skills, and said I might just as well stay for dinner." As I blink, Mr. Huggins adds, "After our conversation, Mr. Gibbons gave me permission to use his given name."

"Oh." I look back at Red. "Well, I suppose . . ."

"The heat, Mrs. Gibbons," says Herbert Huggins, and he sets one hand on my shoulder to nudge me gently down the hall.

I might have said something else—something's nagging at my brain—but a knife of pain stabs up through my belly as he touches me, and I double over like a tree struck by lightning. I have to bite down hard on my lower lip to keep myself from crying out; it's a good thing Emmy's clinging so hard to my shoulder.

"Oh, dear," Herbert Huggins says, all kindly concern. "I do hope you're not unwell, Mrs. Gibbons. Is it—?"

"It's nothing," I say, and I straighten like an old woman, feeling every bone pop in my back. I don't like the look in his eye as he watches me. It reminds me of a rattler, waiting to strike. "I'm fine," I say, brisk as a sweeping broom, and I hurry ahead of him to the kitchen, feeling his eyes on my back the whole way there.

"May I ask," he says, as he follows me in, "how long it will be before you and Sam have another little charmer come to join your family?"

He can ask, but I don't have to answer . . . or, at least, not with the truth. "Less than two months!" I say, like it's the best news in the world. It's more like four months, actually, but I've swelled up so fast this second time, you'd never guess it—and even though Sam'd surely call me crazy for thinking this, less time feels safer right now, somehow more secure, under Herbert Huggins's hungry gaze.

I nod at the chairs gathered around the kitchen table, and I reach back for the frying pan. "You can take a seat anywhere you like, Mr. Huggins. I'm just going to start frying up potatoes to go with the steak for dinner. If you want to tell me about those domestic science innovations of yours—"

"Soon," he says as he sets his leather case down on the table. He straightens the creases in his trousers, finicky as anything, before he sits. "Soon," he repeats, smiling. "But it can wait on coffee."

I pause with my fingers just brushing the pan. "Coffee?"

"Sam said you make a real smooth cup of coffee. Almost as good as his own ma's, he said."

And that's when it hits me, what's been niggling at the back of my mind.

Herbert Huggins saw Sam first, out on the farm. But the farm is nowhere near the road he should have traveled. The road comes straight to our house, with the farm spilling out behind. There's nothing but bare rock and mountain behind that, and no one foolish enough to live there.

But I didn't see a motorcar pulled up outside. I didn't even see a horse.

"Are you all right, Mrs. Gibbons?" Herbert Huggins's eyes are bright and beady and fixed on my face. Again, I think of a rattler, curled up gray against gray rock and rattling its tail softly, while it holds its jaw wide open.

I swallow hard on the thought, and I lift my hand from the frying pan. "Coffee," I repeat, and I try to sound perky. "Coming right up!"

Any minute now, Sam and his brothers'll be home. All I have to do is wait.

I start a pot of water boiling, and I'm trying to move like I'm as graceful and strong as those sleek mountain lions that come prowling down around our house at night, but I swear, my belly feels like it weighs a hundred pounds, and I can't help grunting with effort as I lift the pot, more like one of Sam's great cumbersome cows from the farm.

"I do hate to put you to extra work," says Herbert Huggins. "Can I lend some assistance by holding your sweet baby for you?"

"No, thank you," I say back, just as sweet and smooth as syrup. "It's no trouble, really."

And even Emmy must realize something's wrong, because she doesn't let out a single squeak when my arm tightens around her.

"So, these innovations—" I begin, and I'm so eager to turn his mind away from trouble, I actually reach right across the table like I have no manners, to open up his sales case myself for some distraction.

He snatches it away before I can touch it, something nasty flashing in his eyes. "Not yet, Mrs. Gibbons. I told you, not until after coffee!"

I have to stop myself from dropping my eyes and backing away like a cow being herded without a peep of protest. *Show no fear*, Sam told me on our first trip 'round the farm together. That's how you deal with danger out here, whether it's a big old bull trying to turn itself master or a snake paralyzing a mouse with the power of its gaze until the poor little thing can't even remember how to run away. So I keep my head held high and my eyes fixed on his as I say, "So you did. I just forgot."

"Never mind." Scowling, he sets the case down on the floor, out of my reach—then adjusts it another few inches, as he eyes the hot oven like it's right about to leap at him. I swear, he makes as much fuss setting down that case as a tomcat hunting out the perfect spot of sun to lie in. Finally, though, he lets it go and smoothes down his slick, coppery hair as if he's calming himself with the gesture. And when he looks up at me again, I wish he hadn't.

"So tell me, Mrs. Gibbons. What brought you out here in the first place, to such an . . . isolated locale?"

I don't like the way he says "isolated," like he's running his tongue up and down the word. So instead of giving him the quick answer—which would be Sam—or the long answer, which might still start with seeing Sam across that crowded dance floor, but would have to go winding past all five of my married sisters along the way, and even take a pause to confess how my daddy's house felt smaller and smaller every day after he re-married, with my own mama less than six months in the grave . . . instead of giving him any of those true answers, as sorry as they've all turned out to be, I just say, "You seem pretty cozy around these parts yourself. Have you been out here before?"

His tongue darts out in his sudden grin. "Oh, I've been around these mountains a long time."

"Is that right?"

The water's starting to boil on the stove, so I lean over to drop in the coffee grounds, measuring them out real careful, the way Mama taught me, and twisting to keep them out of the way of Emmy's grabbing hands. But I can still hear the way his smile deepens as he talks.

"Hasn't your husband ever told you about the dangers in these hills?"

Mountain lions, rattle snakes, the adventure and romance of the wild. . . . "He's mentioned one or two," I say, and I keep my voice light as air. "I guess every new place has some dangers."

"Ah, but this is an old place, Mrs. Gibbons . . . and I've been out here even longer than your husband, if you can believe that." He pauses and then adds, soft and measured: "I was in these mountains before any man ever thought to farm here."

My hand tightens around the coffee scoop, but I don't turn. My mind's whirring like an engine, and all I can think to say is, "Is that so, Mr. Huggins?" But my voice is shaking like a leaf, ignoring all of Sam's wilderness lessons.

"Indeed it is so," he whispers, right behind me now, breathing on my bare neck. "Does that surprise you, Mrs. Gibbons?"

I'm staring out the window with all my might, my free hand still holding the coffee scoop half-tipped over the boiling coffee, and every purple band in the twilit sky is telling me that Sam is late, late, late. "*It's past six, Sam, damn it,*" I want to yell, but instead I say softly back to him, "I guess I am surprised, Mr. Huggins. I wouldn't have taken you for an elderly man."

"Would you care for another surprise?" he hisses right into my ear.

No, I think, *no*, and I'm frozen still, like a trembling little mouse who thinks she can stay safe by not moving—but he's already whispering the truth into my ear:

"Sam and his brothers aren't coming home."

That does it. I've got the heavy pot in my hand, and I'm yelling a fierce battle cry as I turn and throw the whole damn pot of boiling coffee over his head.

He staggers back, but I keep the empty pot high. I can hear the sizzle of boiling water working on flesh, even over the hammer of Emmy's screams of outrage, and it makes me sick to my stomach.

But when Herbert Huggins lifts his head, there's not a mark on his smooth face, and I realize there are more dangers out here in these mountains than even Sam knew to warn me against.

"I've lived in these mountains a long time, Mrs. Gibbons." His lips peel back from his teeth into a mockery of a grin. "I preyed on the creatures who used to rule these hills, and I know all about the creatures who've moved here now, so arrogant and so slow-witted. They think of themselves as strong and fierce with their bows and arrows, their shotguns and their plows, but these new ones'll tell me anything I ask, only for fear of seeming 'impolite.' Why, when I asked Sam Gibbons for his name, he told me straight off, just like all four of his brothers had before him, and then I had him exactly where I wanted him, in my power. But more than that, he told me something else, too. He told me your name. And now I'm telling you, *Carrie Gibbons,* you may not move from that spot!"

My feet root to the ground like they've been painted there, and I can't even turn, though my daughter is screaming to high heaven on my shoulder, and Herbert Huggins's hungry gaze is fixed right on her.

"I've been here a long time," he says, "but the taste of a young child, from any species, is still very sweet indeed." His tongue darts out, quick as a lick of fire, and he turns to look down at my fat belly. "And the flavor of a babe not yet born . . ." His eyes narrow to slits, flashing yellow. ". . . now, that is beyond perfection."

Emmy bangs her fists against my shoulder in her rage, the baby inside my belly kicks so hard I almost lose my balance, and that is when I realize the truth. "You're wrong," I whisper.

"Wrong?" He blinks his slitted eyes. "I told you, you can't—"

I hurl the empty pot right at his head, so he has to duck, and I throw myself forward, pushing my big, cumbersome body right past him.

"I am not just Carrie Gibbons," I gasp, and I pull open the oven door, letting out a billow of heat that knocks me back.

Every predator has a weakness, Sam taught me that, and I've only seen one weakness, so far.

I grab his sales case with my free hand.

"I am still Carrie Landry," I tell Herbert Huggins, and I throw the leather case straight into the flaming oven.

There's a flash of light, and there are screams the likes of which I've never heard before in my life, but I have been a mother for over nine months already, and I have learned to listen to screams without flinching. When they're all over, there's nothing left on the floor before me but a little wriggling striped snake, glaring up at me with beady black eyes and hissing with all its might.

In a few minutes, I'll have to call for the dogs, and we'll go together out into the darkness to see if there are any remains left of my husband and his brothers. There'll be hard decisions to be made, and harder times to go through, and a lot of tear-filled nights along the way. None of this is what I bargained for, and that is the simple truth.

But right now, I tighten my grip around Emmy's little round body, and I lift my frying pan with my one free hand.

If there's one thing Sam taught me, it's how to deal with snakes.

Good Neighbors

It wasn't so bad living next door to a notorious necromancer, most of the time. The cottage came dirt-cheap for me and my father because of the location. Of course, the locals all whispered and shook their heads when they saw our wagon, piled high with luggage, rolling through their town along the way. A few kindly souls even ventured out to warn us, that first day, in case we'd somehow mistaken that black monstrosity of a castle down the road for a mere eccentric's folly.

Once they'd accepted that they couldn't talk us out of moving in, though, they left us alone, shaking their heads even more dolefully—but moving quickly, too, to get safely behind their high town walls before darkness arrived. That was when the great doors of the castle would open wide to let the bats and the hellhounds and the undead minions stream out unchecked.

Luckily, I've never cared to go rambling at night. I have better things to do when the sun goes down, mostly involving small tools, a set of good gas lamps, and my own private workshop. I'm only too happy *not* to have any shock-able neighbors peering in through the windows as I do them.

In my new home, iron horseshoes planted three feet from the windows kept the undead minions and so forth at bay, leaving me to putter away, safely undisturbed, for the first three and a half months after moving in. Dad worked happily through his latest puzzle book, and the seasons shifted from summer to autumn outside the iron-laced windows of our cottage.

But some things can't be ignored after all...and when I stepped out of the cottage one morning to find a moaning, human-shaped creature lying on the grass beyond our horseshoes, his horribly mismatched legs separated and twitching on the ground beside him, I realized I couldn't ignore our sinister neighbor any longer.

"Oh, for *goodness'* sake!" Hissing with frustration, I turned and stomped back inside, forgetting all about the nice hike down to the swamp that I had planned to get my ideas moving for the day.

Dad was still sitting at the kitchen table, working out a particularly tricky acrostic. He didn't look up as I passed him the first time, but when I came stomping back out of my workshop and started back towards the front door, carrying a clanking bag of tools by my side, he raised his eyebrows. "Working in the sunshine for once, Mia?"

"Not by choice." I sighed.

By rights, I knew I ought to go hammer on the gates of that ugly castle until some responsible party came out to take care of the problem for me...but whoever had created that poor creature had nothing *responsible* about them.

"Shh," I whispered as I knelt down by him. His bleary eyes blinked helplessly up at me, yellowed and watery from the too-bright sun. His sickly-white skin was already starting to burn. "I'll take care of this," I promised him as I took out my sharpest knife, "and you'll feel much better soon."

I'd never leave a creature helpless and vulnerable on my own property, and there wasn't a single craftswoman's instinct in my body that would allow him to leave as mangled as he had arrived.

It took ages to get the measurements exactly right, what with all the distracting twitching. I wasn't used to sealing together that kind of meaty matter, either. Once I was finally finished, though, he stood firmly on two feet once more, and if those feet didn't match, well, at least the legs above them did. Now that they were evenly sized, he wouldn't trip over them anymore, and my stitches—with a bit of extra help—were tight enough that even if something else made him stumble, they wouldn't come loose and leave him helpless again.

By then, the exposed skin on his face and hands was peeling terribly, but he still shuffled eagerly before me, pawing at my hands and grunting as I put my tools away.

"Yes, well..." I patted his arm, forcibly resisting the impulse to check the stitching in his throat as well. "It was nothing. Really. Just go home now before you burn any worse, and don't let anyone stitch you up so badly ever again."

That was that, as far as I was concerned...but I should have known better from the start.

Wicked necromancers aren't known for leaving mysteries alone.

An hour later, I had just returned from my invigorating hike down to the swamp and had a whole new pack of ideas all jostling for position in my head. I was busy scribbling notes as I heated a kettle on the stove when a sudden clatter sounded at the kitchen window and made me start.

Outrageously, when I looked up, I found that a sharp-eyed crow had bypassed every one of my protections just by tossing a hard pebble at the iron-framed glass above my mostly-ignored little window box. The moment the creature caught my eye, it opened its beak to let a piece of paper flutter to the ground just beyond my buried horseshoes.

Rude!

I pointed forcefully at the ugly scratch that it had left on our nice thick windowpane.

The crow flapped its wings and cawed even more forcefully back at me, kicking one clawed foot towards its waiting message.

Enough! I abandoned my kettle for the privacy of my own workshop. I'd dealt with more than enough of my neighbor's intrusions for one day.

Luckily, Dad thought to turn off the stove before we had any more disasters. When I finally emerged to look for food, several busy hours later, I found him sitting on the sagging couch by the fireplace, holding that small slip of paper in his hands and studying it thoughtfully with his puzzle book and pencils set aside.

"How did *that* get in here?" I demanded.

He looked at me, calmly, over the rims of his spectacles. "So you've already seen our neighbor's invitation?"

"Pah." I rolled my eyes as I opened the lid of the cheerfully humming new icebox I'd created last month. There was more to its design than would have been easily explainable to anyone who'd insisted on examining it closely, but it looked ordinary enough from a distance to be safely stored in our windowed main rooms rather than hidden in my workshop. "You know I'm not interested in any social invitations—*especially* when their messenger damages our window to deliver them."

"Hmm." Dad's skeptical tone made me glance back at him—only to find his gaze moving thoughtfully to the window and the grass outside, which I'd so carefully lined with iron horseshoes on our first day here. "Did you leave any path for him to knock on the front door?"

"What kind of a question is that?" The ice box lid hung open behind me as I swung around, a cold chill skating up my spine through my coveralls. "We moved out here to get *away* from nosy neighbors, remember? Or have you already forgotten...?"

My words trailed off into a horrific silence. Shame suffused me like toxic gas billowing up to overflow a beaker.

Of course he hadn't forgotten. How could he?

I opened my mouth to apologize—but he shook his head, stopping me.

"Here." He held out the slip of paper as he rose, metal supports shifting smoothly all along his legs. "You should at least read the invitation before you make any decision."

Biting my lip, I took the paper from him.

Your presence is requested tonight at eight o'clock.

Ha, I thought. But I kept my mouth shut under Dad's steady gaze.

He sighed as he looked up at me. "Even the strongest iron can't keep the world out forever, you know."

Maybe it couldn't...but I could send a message of my own.

No one would ever hurt my family or our home again. The townsfolk nearby might all cower when those great gates swung open, but I never would. I knew how to send flying messengers, too...and wasn't it useful that all of those respectable townsfolk hid behind their high walls at night?

They wouldn't see a thing.

At eight o'clock on the dot, I was sitting comfortably in my workshop with a pot of fresh, hot tea before me as my cloud of mechanical messengers answered our neighbor's invitation with a rapid-fire barrage of hard pebbles against every narrow window in the black castle's upper walls. Every single piece of visible glass was hit at once with a pebble from my garden designed to leave a scratch *exactly* like the one left on my window earlier that day.

The answering howls of the castle's denizens were so loud, they filtered all the way down the road, through the window-less walls of my workshop.

I smiled as I poured myself a cup of tea and settled back into work. *Message received and acknowledged.*

My perfect satisfaction lasted all the way until the next morning, when I looked out through the kitchen window.

"*Unbelievable*!"

There wasn't one undead minion lying in sad pieces on the grass outside today. There were *seven*...and they were the most mismatched group imaginable, an appalling jumble of horrifically misassembled limbs.

That first one had obviously stumbled into my wards by accident. But for this many to arrive today? My neighbor must have sent them all against my wards on purpose, trying to overwhelm me with sheer numbers in punishment for rejecting his almighty summons.

The arrogance of it was breathtaking. Clearly, he had no idea of how strong my wards really were...but all the same, I couldn't let these poor creatures pay the price. They'd already suffered enough.

Taking a deep, calming breath through my teeth, I turned towards my workshop to gather up my tools.

"You'd better bring your tea along with you," said Dad, without bothering to look up from his puzzle book. "It'll take you a bit longer this time—and it'll do you good to work out in the sunshine for once."

It took quite a bit longer, actually...and the next morning, there were even more.

As I looked around on that third morning at the dozens of twitching body parts scattered across our grass, all waiting to be evened out and reassembled, I told myself that I should feel real satisfaction in this visible triumph of my careful wards. Better yet, my infuriating neighbor *had* to feel the sting of humiliation each time I not only failed to cower at his fury but actually sent his minions back to him in better shape than before. *That* had to prove my lack of fear without a doubt.

And yet...

It wasn't only the lost hours that nagged at me as I spent my third day in a row on painstaking repairs. It was the sense that I was missing something vital in my challenge. For an inventor, there could be no greater frustration.

I was still gnawing over it in mid-afternoon, well after I'd sent the last minion shuffling on her way, her skin blistering with temporary sunburn but her limbs permanently perfected. I'd seen different minions today than on either of the first two days; for all that the numbers thrown at me had grown each time, none of the minions I'd seen had ever returned to my property a second time. Something about that bothered me intensely. Instead of walking out my prickly tangle of thoughts or retreating to the sanctum of my workshop as usual, I planted myself on our own front step to stare at that ugly black castle and brood.

That was how I saw the townsfolk coming.

It was a flicker of movement in the distance that first caught my eye—a flicker that clarified into a large clump of people moving together...with torches flickering in their grasps.

I didn't even realize I was moving until I'd already leapt to my feet, my heart doing its best to escape my chest.

Burning timbers.

And my father's cry as that flaming beam had fallen on him, trapping—

"*No.*" The word came out like a vow...or a prayer. I forced air through my chest and blinked hard, focusing on the space around me here and now.

It was a new space. A *protecte*d space, because no one here knew us, not like the town where I'd grown up—or those neighbors whom I'd always thought I'd known, before torch-light had turned all of their faces into masks.

This time, we hadn't given our respectable neighbors any reason to think we were different from them. I'd hidden everything about us too well.

The door opened behind me. Metal clanked as Dad stepped to my side, watching the procession in hollow-cheeked silence.

"We're safe," I told him, my eyes fixed on the line of torches. "They're not coming for us."

"I know." He didn't move.

His legs had to be paining him from so much time standing upright. The metal supports that I'd created might make it possible, but nothing I did could make it easy...or make it up to him for what had happened.

"You can go back inside now," I told him softly. "Weren't you working on a new puzzle in there?"

He shook his head, a sigh whistling through his teeth. "Mia...I don't think *that's* the most urgent puzzle to solve."

My father hadn't set his mind to anything but puzzles on paper ever since our old house had burned down. He'd never once blamed me for it, even though we both knew that my inventions were the ones that had brought those torches down on us that night, turning ordinary, respectable acquaintances into an angry, frightened mob.

No one ever got so frightened of regular metal-working, the kind he'd mastered long before my birth...but from the moment I'd first fastened my toddler hands around one of his tools, my inventions had always turned somehow into *more.*

"I'll put the icebox in my workshop," I promised. "They'll never see it. I'll put some extra flowers in our window box, too. I'll even make sure that they match and look good. I'll—"

"*Mia.*" That was all that Dad said. But I'd seen that look on his face a hundred times across my life, from my very first lesson decades ago. It meant: *You're not paying attention. Start again.*

So I dragged my head out of my burning memories, and remembered what I'd been thinking just before I'd been interrupted.

Sometimes, a challenge looked obvious but contained secret complexities behind that shiny surface...like a locked workshop hidden behind a respectable flowery window box.

Our neighbor didn't bother with window boxes or any other such pleasantries to appease the respectable folks. His big black castle shouted exactly what he was: *Wicked.*

He'd sent his minions to attack me twice in a row, hadn't he? Really, I should be grateful that the mob was coming to burn his ugly castle down.

But then again...I'd never seen a single minion twice. *That* was what had nagged at me earlier. If he wanted to overwhelm me with numbers, why didn't he send the minions that I'd made strongest, the ones most likely to succeed? Instead, he sent mangled minions to my property each night, I fixed them...and then he went ahead and sent me even more badly-built minions right on the verge of breaking, even though he had to know what would—

Oh. Oh! My jaw fell open in outrage.

The sheer *audacity* of the man—!

"He did try to invite you over and be sociable about it," Dad said mildly.

"Ha!" I shook my head, still stunned. "You *know* I'm not interested in socializing with neighbors. That's why we moved here in the first place."

I'd learned the hard way that it was *never* safe to reveal my own truths to the respectable folk around us....

But my own closest neighbor nowadays didn't even pretend to be respectable—and despite everything that I'd assumed, he actually did care about those poor creatures he was stewarding, after all. Had he even been the one who had built them so badly? All I knew was that he was looking after them now...even when that meant sending them to a cranky, unsociable neighbor to be fixed.

"I can't." I whispered the words. Then I repeated them, my gaze jerking back to my father. "I can't! After the last time I let other people see..."

"Did I ever teach you to worry about window boxes?" Dad shook his head chidingly. "Remind me, Mia. Who put your first tool in your hands and taught you exactly how to use it?"

Tears stung my eyes, blurring his familiar, beloved face. "You did," I whispered.

I'd always wanted so badly to make him proud.

Now, his mouth was bracketed by white lines of pain... but his smile still shone with pride as he patted the metal supports that I had built him. "Haven't I been telling you to do more of your work out in the sunshine?"

By the time I joined the twenty-person-long, torch-bearing procession, they had already reached the great black walls of the castle and were milling around in front of it. I recognized their leader from the group that had visited us on our first day in the neighborhood: the town's mayor, a tall, upright man with a close-shaven face, a rigidly straight nose, and a fanatic's zeal in his blue eyes. Mayor Hall's face broke into a fierce smile as I walked up to join all of them, pulling an open wagon packed full of metal behind me.

"We hoped you'd join us, friend! I'm only thankful that you've survived 'til now. The last people who owned your cottage fled the very day after the necromancer arrived. We've all feared terribly for your safety, but don't worry—we'll end this creature and his monsters now. The sunlight weakens them, you see, and they all have a terrible fear of fire."

I shifted closer to the door of the big black castle looming over us. Everyone would be asleep in there for hours, but I lowered my voice anyway. "What happens when they're not afraid?"

"I beg your pardon?" The mayor frowned, glancing around at his supporters.

"When they're out and about and not frightened," I said patiently. "*Do* they actually eat people? Ever? Or do they just wander around moaning and getting some exercise?"

His brows snapped even tighter together. "What kind of a question is that? They're monsters! If they haven't eaten anyone yet, it's only a matter of time. You should be grateful that we're saving you! Unless..." His eyes narrowed. "You haven't been corrupted by the necromancer's dark magics, have you?"

Grumbles broke out behind him. Suspicious gazes heated my skin. Torches rose higher in anticipation.

"I've never spoken a word to him," I said as I took a final

step and planted myself between the torch-wielding group and the big black door that protected all the minions. "But I do believe in being a good neighbor—and I don't particularly like fire, myself."

"Now, see here, young lady—!"

I snapped my fingers. Twenty arm-sized mechanical mosquitoes lifted from their limp, resting pile in my wagon and rose into the air, wings snapping out around them with loud *clicks!* As the townsfolk all stumbled back in surprise, high-pitched buzzing burst out from my inventions to fill the air with humming menace.

Each mech-squito held a sharp metal rock in its skinny, multi-legged grasp. Each of their long, metal snouts dripped with the water I'd pumped into them, just waiting to be deployed now.

"Luckily," I said, "*my* creatures are more than capable of dealing with a bit of fire."

"But that's—that's—!" Mayor Hall was stammering too much to even create a full sentence. Behind him, though, more and more cries flew out.

"Witchcraft!"

"Unnatural!"

"Spellcraft!"

"Abomination!"

I lifted my right hand. The mech-squitoes followed its lead and flew into a V-formation, visibly preparing.

"One," I said, loudly and clearly, "two..."

That did it. The crowd turned and ran, their torches streaming trails of hot smoke in their wake.

Only their leader turned back, twenty feet away, to point one shaking finger at me. "You're next," the mayor snarled. "You may have fooled us before, but now that we know what you really are, you can't stay awake to guide these *things* forever. So—"

A man's voice spoke calmly from a window high above me. "Isn't it fortunate, then, that my creatures *do* stay awake all night? And *they* believe in looking after our neighbors, too."

As I spun around to stare up at him, the famous necromancer nodded politely down at me.

He was just *unfairly* handsome for someone wearing a rumpled and ragged old crimson bathrobe, with sleep-stubble covering his pale cheeks and his black hair standing up in all directions.

...And he had absolutely, definitely been eavesdropping. "You've had that window open the whole time, listening in on us?" I demanded.

"I find it safer to leave my windows open, nowadays." His lips quirked as he looked down at me, an unsettling warmth in his dark eyes. "I have to protect my precious glass from my new neighbor, you see."

"Ugh!" The mayor let out a frustrated groan, turned, and ran the rest of the way, following his own followers back towards the respectability of those high town walls.

I didn't look after him for long. My attention was firmly

focused on my own outrageous neighbor, who had propped his elbows on his windowsill and was sending down a lazy smile that sent all *sorts* of suspicious reactions tingling through my skin.

"May I invite you in for tea?" he asked idly. "Or will you attack my home again if I dare?"

"I just *saved* your home," I reminded him.

"In that case..."

He gestured elegantly, the crimson bathrobe falling away to reveal one pale, lean wrist. The great black door to the castle swung open before me with a long, ominous creak. Darkness awaited me within.

"I'm not fixing any more of your creatures for free," I warned him as I hesitated on the threshold. "You can't trick me again."

"I did *try* to organize proper payment." He sighed wistfully. "If only *someone* had been kind enough to accept my social invitation..."

I let out a long-suffering sigh of my own. He and Dad were going to get on just fine, I could tell.

Still: "I don't socialize," I informed him.

"Neither do I, ordinarily. Won't it be fascinating for us both to try?" He raised one jet-black eyebrow, a dangerous gleam in his eyes. "Unless, that is...you're too frightened?"

My shoulders snapped perfectly straight. As my mechsquitoes swarmed furiously around me, I bared my teeth up at him in a ferocious smile. "Of course," I said sweetly, "I'd be *delighted* to be neighborly."

Bad neighbors had tried to kill me before, so I knew perfectly well how to deal with them. As my new neighbor's low laughter wrapped around me from above, inciting a whole host of aggravating new sensations, I realized that dealing with my first *good* neighbor might be an even bigger challenge.

Still... As I recalled the wicked gleam in the necromancer's eyes, my lips curved into a secret smirk of my own.

This time, I wasn't missing any pieces of his puzzle...and for the first time in my life, I didn't have to hold back a single jot of my own power. *No more hiding behind window boxes.*

Head held high, I stepped into the necromancer's black castle, my own unnatural magical creatures buzzing around me.

Challenge most definitely accepted.

Love, Your Flatmate

From: Emmeline.Heatherton@gmail.com
To: faevix@hotmail.com
Subject: HELP

Mum,

I understand that you didn't actually believe there would be a lockdown when you agreed to let your friend's daughter stay at my flat 'for just a week.' (Remember that promise? I do. I also remember that you *didn't ask me first.*) (You also remember, *I am sure*, that I sent you SEVERAL ARTICLES about that possible lockdown in the weeks beforehand. But...moving on. *Deep breaths.*)

I know that cultural exchange is healthy. I'm glad that you and Lady Silvana had such a wonderful time as flatmates all those years ago, and I understand that humans and fey have different attitudes because of our different lifespans and expectations. I *get it*, okay? As you've always reminded me, I haven't done much travelling, but it's not like I've made my assumptions about the fey based on trashy shows like *Fey Nights*. I grew up on your anecdotes, remember?

So many lovely anecdotes. SO many...

But Maxi and I are never going to be BFFs and penpals for life like you and Silvana. I'm sorry, but it is just *not going to happen*. It's not only that we have nothing in common. It's the amount of time that she spends in my bath every day, running the hot water over and over again...and the fact that she has NO IDEA how much my water bill will cost and – let's face it – she *doesn't even care*, no matter how hard I try to explain to her that a junior editor's salary is not going to cover it, *especially* if I end up laid off by the end of all of this – and frankly, it's not as if I'm getting much work done in the meantime...

Not to mention the endless harp and flute music playing in the air around her *all the time*, so I *never* get a break to listen to my own music or think about anything else but her – oh, and the fact that my living room is now *covered in leaves*! Dear God, even if I could focus on my work, I can't even find most of the manuscripts on my desk under all of her rampaging greenery. I'm having to take all of my Zoom meetings in my bedroom now - and YES, don't worry, I took down all of those fabulous girl-band posters from behind my bed, because I am an adult professional and I understand the concept of maintaining appearances. Some of us actually *have* jobs, unlike spoiled fey aristocrats who swan around taking baths and listening to pretty music all day.

I might have survived a single week with Maxi. Possibly. I truly cannot take much more.

I know she can't stay with you two at the moment, but please, please, *please* will you use your connection with Lady Silvana to find out when the border between London and Faerie will finally reopen? *I am begging you.* I need to know when this will end!

Love, your desperate daughter,

Emmeline x

* * *

Posted on the door to the bath in Emmeline Heatherton's flat:

Quick Note: My water company will not accept money that turns into leaves as a monthly payment. Also, we both need time in here every day. Just a polite reminder! :) E xx

* * *

From: MaximilianaMorgana@feymail.com
To: HLSilvanaMorgana@feymail.com
Subject: Aid in my time of need?

Dear Mother,

Are all humans so impatient and so tediously focused on their useless little strips of paper money? Or is Emmeline Heatherton particularly greedy? She has spoken of little else since I arrived. I'm not certain she understands the concept of relaxation, much less art or pleasure.

You may have marvellous memories of your nights spent carousing in London with Emmeline's mother, but I cannot pretend that my own memories will be nearly so pleasant. Not only are we restricted to Emmeline's uncomfortably small residence for most of every day, but she hasn't even bothered to create the most minimal of gardens in her home. I've done my best to create one for her as a polite gesture in return for my accommodation (such as it is), but her reaction when she awoke to find a beautiful silver apple tree from Faerie growing from her bedroom carpet was...I must say, *anything* but grateful.

Honestly, I give up on even attempting any meaningful *rapprochement* with a creature who has so little in common with me, no matter how deceptively appealing her snub nose, freckles, and (rarely seen but admittedly astonishing) smile may be. Instead, I have turned my thoughts to my next symphonic creation in the hopes that I may perfect it by the time that I'm finally allowed back into the serene halls of home. Unfortunately, I have so little space to myself that I've been forced to spend hours every day hiding underwater inside Emmeline's small white bath simply to achieve some semblance of isolation for artistic focus...a necessary habit that has apparently driven my temporary hostess over the edge into madness. Can you even imagine any fey being so petty as to place a cost on *water*? It is inconceivable.

Please tell me that the border with Faerie will soon reopen. I can easily promise that I am not infectious, as I *of course* stay well away from humans on my single allowed daily walk, and my landlady and I are hardly maintaining kissing contact.

I understand that trials are meant to strengthen our inner resources, but I cannot imagine many fey facing such a trial as Emmeline Heatherton's 'helpful' little talks on human money. Just the sound of her voice – adorable though I first thought it to be – is beginning to make me twitch in despair at the lectures ahead.

Yours in tribulation,

Maxi xx

* * *

Note that appeared on Emmeline Heatherton's laptop keyboard, written in golden ink on a leaf that puffed into a shower of glitter after being read:

I do beg your pardon, but would you terribly mind putting on headphones when you listen to your own music? I'm afraid it is disturbing my concentration. As you would put it: just a polite note! :) M xx

* * *

A series of texts between phones:

Emmeline: Hi Maxi, of course I'd be glad to buy myself a pair of headphones - but to be quite fair, perhaps you could buy yourself a pair to use for your music as well? Or we could take turns and each play our own music for an equal amount of the day? Just a thought! :) - E x

Maximiliana: I'm afraid there may have been a cultural misunderstanding. I am attempting to create a symphonic harmony that will enlighten the ages, soothe the immortal soul, and fulfil my life's vocation. Are you genuinely claiming that it is every bit as important for the flat to echo to the deafening beats and banshee screams of your favoured rock 'music' when you – unless I'm very much mistaken? - are not even the originator of that sound? – M x

Maximiliana: How is it possible that those hellish drumbeats are now even LOUDER? The windows will surely break at any moment.

Maximiliana: Are you now ignoring me AND all of the ancient laws of hosting? I am very much surprised that your mother would raise you in such ignorance of tradition.

Emmeline: I'm afraid I couldn't hear the sound of your text arriving on my phone, Maxi. What a shame. Perhaps you should turn your own music down? Then I'll be more than happy to do the same with mine.

Emmeline: Dear God. Have you actually added TRUMPETS to that mix?

Emmeline: I'm fairly certain that those ancient halls of yours will EXPLODE if you add any more elephants. Won't your mother be proud then?

Emmeline: There have to be laws of guesthood, too. Are you even going to answer the damned door? Or is THAT beneath you, too?

* * *

From: Emmeline.Heatherton@gmail.com
To: faevix@hotmail.com
Subject: I'm going to kill her

FYI, I was just given an official warning from my landlord because of your old friend's daughter. Apparently, the building operates a three-strikes-and-you're-out policy...and I've just hit the first strike.

This is not something I have ever had to be told before. I have *never* been so humiliated in my life.

Please tell me you've at least asked Silvana when that border will reopen. I need to know how much longer this torture will last!

Emmeline x

From: faevix@hotmail.com
To: Emmeline.Heatherton@gmail.com
Subject: Re: I'm going to kill her

Darling, please try to calm down. I know you've always had a tiny little issue with anxiety, but I really do think you're taking it just a bit too far. No one's going to evict you during a lockdown! Really, just *try* to take your mind off all those worries and let yourself relax for once.

Your father and I have taken up making our own cocktails every evening, and it is *such* a soothing hobby! I've attached our five favourite recipes for you to sample, too. Enjoy!

Love,

Mum xxxxxxxxxxxxxxxxx

* * *

Diary of Emmeline Heatherton

I can't believe I was bellowed at by my slimy landlord with every neighbour in the building listening in...and now my mother wants me to solve all of my problems by getting plastered!

Perfect. Just perfect.

I officially give up on everything – including bloody cultural sensitivity. I gave myself a headache watching Fey Nights on my phone last week to be polite, but I'm not doing that again. I'm watching tonight's episode on the big telly in the living room, and I don't care what Maxi thinks of it. (It's not as if I could take out my headphones to watch it in silence – not after everything else that's happened today. Those headphones are LOCKED DOWN until she's gone. That is non-negotiable!)

If she gets too offended by all of that trashy fun and rampant on-screen fey-human sexing (in the most implausible locations), she can just find herself another damn flatmate who thinks that glowing green eyes, cute pointed ears and shimmering, hypnotising hair make up for EVERYTHING ELSE about her personality!

...OK, and maybe I will make cocktails, too. Why not? What's the worst that could happen? I might finally relax near my new flatmate? Ha. That is never going to happen!

Diary of Emmeline Heatherton

Oh. My. God.

What was I thinking? What the hell am I going to do? What do I even say when she finally comes out of the bath?

This has got to be the most awkward morning-after in the history of the universe.

What if she tells her mum – who tells mine – what happened?

Oh. My. God.

No more cocktails ever again. Especially not while watching Fey Nights.

Oh, God.

Oh, no! Another note.

Deep breaths, Emmeline. I am a strong, courageous woman. I can read whatever she has to say. After all, it can't be any worse than everything that we said to each other yesterday afternoon. Right?

Right. I'm going to open it.

Now.

* * *

Note that appeared on Emmeline Heatherton's bed, written in golden ink on a leaf that puffed into a shower of glitter against her bare skin after being read:

For the purposes of improving our mutual cultural understanding, would you consider summoning up those Fey Nights online archives again and bringing them in to watch together in the bath? M xx

* * *

Diary of Emmeline Heatherton

Well.

I

Obviously

Oh, what the hell. I have to wash this glitter off my skin now anyway, right? At least this way, we'll save money by bathing together.

A sign posted on the refrigerator door of Emmeline Heatherton's flat:

Agreed Schedule of Events from Now Onwards:

9 a.m. – 3 p.m. Maxi's music takes precedence in the flat because it is her actual job (which probably should have been mentioned earlier, to avoid misunderstandings), while Emmeline will focus on editing so as not to lose her own job.

3 p.m. – 5 p.m. Emmeline's music has precedence in the flat, and Maxi will NOT make any negative comments about it if she ever wants to watch *Fey Nights* together again.

Supper will be cooked on an alternating day-by-day basis.

Addendum in golden ink:

I agree to open my mind and restrain musical critiques – but ONLY if you agree to share every manuscript you edit in the vein of Fey Nights...and preferably by reading them out loud. – M xx

* * *

A series of texts:

Emmeline: You know, your music is really growing on me... for some reason. x

Maximiliana: Would you care to provide me with more inspiration for it? x

Emmeline: Promise you'll reheat the bath water with your own magic this time, for the sake of my poor water bill?

Maximiliana: To make you smile? DONE. xxx

Emmeline: I'm coming. xxx

* * *

From: Emmeline.Heatherton@gmail.com
To: faevix@hotmail.com
Subject: Re: Good News, Darling

Hi Mum,

Thanks so much for letting me know about the border! Unfortunately, I won't be able to take you and Dad up on your invitation to Skype-with-cocktails in celebration of the big reopening, because – for once! – I won't be here. Maxi's bringing me along for her big performance in her mother's halls, and really it would be *so* rude to miss it when her new symphony is actually dedicated to me.

Luckily, I had plenty of holiday time saved up from work,

so you don't have to worry about that. (You always told me I should take more time for travel and adventures!) I've asked one of my neighbours to water the new cluster of apple trees in my living room, so those should be perfectly fine as well (as long as my awful landlord doesn't hear about them).

I *think* I'll only be in Faerie for a week...but we both know what happened last time that promise was made about a fey-human visit, don't we? ;) Anyway, Maxi's promised to introduce me to some of her favourite fey authors while I'm there, because we have surprisingly similar tastes when it comes to lowbrow entertainment. So – who knows? Perhaps I can leap up the publishing ranks in a rather different way than I'd expected.

Btw, Maxi's still learning (slowly) to appreciate human music, but she's turned out to be an enormous fan of cocktails. Her very favourite is your Devon Special. Mine is one that she invented herself – she calls it the Emmeline Surprise. Perhaps I can bring her along with me next time we're allowed to visit in person at your house? Then she can teach you the secret of how she makes it. She won't tell me any of the ingredients! She's so ridiculous, she actually claims—

Sorry, Mum, I have to go. *Fey Nights* is about to start, and it's become a vital part of our mutual cultural understanding.

Love,

Emmeline xxx

House of Secrets

My father's house is full of secrets. They cling to the thick, dusty curtains that he keeps tightly drawn all day and night, muffling the sound of his friends' low, intent whispers and blocking out the sunlight. I can hear the dull echoes of carriages outside, rattling past at all hours, but I never see them. Since I arrived here eight days ago, I've become a creature of shadow, as dim and hidden from the outside world as everything else in this house.

Back home in the country, where I lived with my nurse, the sunshine poured in all day long. Bessie's cottage might have been a tiny, insignificant thing compared to my father's great house in town, but hers led out onto fields and woods where I could wander to my heart's content. The local girls were forbidden to talk to me, but the wind brushed against my skin like a caress whenever I stepped into the meadows, and distant bells always seemed to ring in the air whenever I walked in the woods, although Bessie claimed she couldn't hear them. In the summers, I spent nearly every day outside, coming home only for required meals, or when Bessie managed to pin me down to study my letters.

"You're the daughter of gentryfolk," she always told me, "no matter who your poor mother might have been. I'll not have your father disappointed when he finally summons you to live with him."

Back then, of course, my father was only a name, scrawled hastily at the bottom of his brief, infrequent letters: *William Norton, Esq.*

William Norton, Esq., hoped that my health was well and that I was behaving for my nurse. William Norton, Esq., would summon me to town when I was older, for my coming of age.

I always tried to think of that as a promise rather than a threat. Bessie certainly presented it that way, spinning me stories of glamorous society balls and handsome, eligible young men. I might not be invited to the dances in our local village or courted by any respectable young men here, but things would be very different in town, she promised me.

"He'll want to marry you off proper," she said, "pretty thing that you are. A fat enough dowry will excuse almost anything with those folk. And he obviously cares for you, or he wouldn't have sent such lovely cheques all these years, only chucked you into an orphanage like the gentry do when they want to forget their own misdeeds. You, he's remembered."

And remember he did, for just eight days before my seventeenth birthday, his dark, polished carriage appeared in front of Bessie's door. When I first spotted it, on my way back from the woods for our mid-day meal, I actually stopped breathing for a moment.

I was finally going to meet William Norton, Esq.

I hadn't brushed my hair since I'd first woken that morning, and I hadn't taken the time to pin it up properly even then. Why would I? There was no one in our village to impress, for I was shunned by everyone respectable and Bessie never allowed me to mix with the rest. I'd ventured alone, as usual, into the woods...and of course my hair had slipped loose of its plaits in a dozen different places by midday, falling in messy brown strands across my dirt-spotted cheeks.

But I needn't have worried. William Norton, of course, had not come himself to fetch me. He had sent a servant in his place, a young man only a year or two older than me, but with skin that was as dark a brown as my eyes, so that I stopped and stared in open-mouthed surprise when I first stepped into Bessie's cottage, as if I were the most mannerless of yokels. I caught myself a moment later, slamming my mouth shut, but I could see from his steady gaze that he'd noticed my shock, and I bitterly regretted it.

I knew only too well what it was to be unlike everyone around you.

Stepping forward, I dipped a curtsy and smiled despite my hot cheeks. "Are you a visitor, sir?" I did my best to sound polished and confident as I spoke. The truth was, I hadn't practice at talking to guests, for we rarely had any. The only people who ever visited our cottage were the occasional older women neighbors who came to gossip with Bessie over tea and study me critically from the corners of their eyes, searching for any evidence of inherited immorality.

"I come from your father, Miss Norton," the young man said, and he pulled a letter from inside his plain brown coat. "He has sent me to bring you home."

At that, I went still with my hand already half-held out. Distantly, I heard Bessie's voice rising in horror.

"By herself, sir? Without a maid, or any other female to accompany her? But surely – "

"You may read Mr. Norton's instructions in his letter." The young man's deep, soft voice reverberated through the small cottage room. "I do promise to keep her journey safe."

Stepping forward, he pressed the letter into my hand. There was nothing to do but open it.

Lily, read the letter, in that familiar, impatient scrawl, *My man Achilles will see you safe to Manchester. Start at once. Yrs sincerely, William Norton, Esq.*

"Achilles," I repeated blankly as I looked up, the letter hanging off my hand. Something very odd was happening in my stomach.

Ladies weren't supposed to mention stomachs. I was almost certain I remembered Bessie telling me that, once. I'd never paid much attention to those lectures, though. I had never really believed, until now, that they would ever apply to me.

"What does it say?" Bessie bustled over to join me.

But I was still looking up into Achilles's dark eyes, trying desperately to keep my balance as my world twisted sickeningly around me. "You...have a remarkable name," I said inanely. It was all that I could let myself think about, in that moment. Anything else about that letter would have overset me completely and sent me tearing out of the house into the freedom of the woods like a true madcap and a coward, too.

I realized, vaguely, that I was shivering.

Bessie snatched the letter from my hand and let out a gasp of disbelief. "*Start at once?* But we've had no letters of warning, no preparation. Why – "

"No." Steeling myself, I turned away from my father's man, who hadn't offered any answer to my foolish statement. *Just as well.* I forced a smile for my good nurse, who had looked after me so well for so long, and I locked my gaze away from the back door of the cottage with its too-tempting pathway to escape. "We have had warning, though, haven't we, Bessie? He always said he would summon me one day, when I came of age."

"Yes, but..." Bessie stopped and drew a deep breath through her teeth. "Well! He is your father, so there's no more to be said about that. But I won't send you off without a proper meal, at least. Not to mention your hair – your clothes – !"

I put one hand, guiltily, to my disheveled plaits.

For the first time, I thought I glimpsed the hint of a smile on Achilles's face, if only for a fraction of a second. "I'm certain we can wait that long," he said gravely.

Of course, it took scarcely five minutes to pack everything I owned and change into my "best" gown – which meant the one gown that had never been ripped by tree branches or stained with mud, because I only ever wore it to church. It could never have been called fashionable even by country standards, and I couldn't help noticing now, under Bessie's worried gaze, that I had certainly grown since she had sewn it last year.

Still, Bessie fussed for ages over my hair, pinning it all up into a crown fit for a queen. A queen probably wouldn't have eaten yesterday's stew, reheated in the pot over the fireplace, but I devoured two large bowls of it, savoring every bite. My father's man ate it, too. He said hardly a word, and that only when spoken to, but if he felt a city-dweller's disdain for country food, he didn't show it in his demeanor. And Bessie talked enough for all of us.

"Of course you really ought to have more suitable clothing – but then, I'm certain your father will see to all of that, especially before he introduces you to any eligible young men. He'll take you to a proper dressmaker, no doubt, to fit you out like all the other fashionable young ladies. By next week, you'll be glittering like a diamond! Why, there'll be balls and salons and fancy breakfasts, and – and I wager you'll soon forget all of your time here, and you'll forget me, too."

"Never!" I said, and I set down my bowl to wrap my arms around her strong shoulders. "I'll never forget you. And I'll visit." *Somehow.*

Achilles didn't say a word. But he bowed to Bessie on our way out as deeply as if she were a fine lady, and he helped me into the carriage with a strong, steady hand.

He didn't join me inside it, though. He sat with the coachman in front, leaving me to sit in solitary splendor on dark velvet cushions, looking out through windows that were made of real glass, as we rode away from my old life and left Bessie behind.

Life would be far better in town, of course. Bessie had always said so. It would be a glittering, glamorous improvement, and any young lady ought to be grateful for the change in her circumstances...especially a young lady who owed so very much to her father's generosity already.

I would have to work very hard to repay him and to make him proud of me somehow. I had no idea how I would do it.

But I tried my best to feel hopeful instead of frightened as my father's carriage rattled along the road, joining more and more vehicles along the way, while my head ached more and more with every passing mile. The thick smoke that filled the air of Manchester, belching from the chimneys of the hulking factories, was not the most promising of welcomes. Tall, grim buildings closed in on us from every side, each house pressed tightly against the next without a single spot of greenery in sight. I had to press my handkerchief against my mouth and nose to stop myself from retching at the foulness of the air. Still, I told myself not to take it as an omen, even as I clamped my hand around the handkerchief, desperately trying to breathe in any final remnants of the clean scent of home.

My father was a man of means. Surely he must at least have a garden that I could escape into, even if there were no fields or woods.

By the time the carriage finally rolled to a stop, four hours after I had entered it, my head was pounding, and my bones ached. When the door swung open, it took me a long, numb moment to blink out at the dark stone house before me and realize what was happening.

We had arrived.

Achilles had been holding out his hand for at least a full minute, by then.

I took a deep breath, fighting through the fog that seemed to have wrapped thicker and tighter around my mind with every moment since we'd entered the dirty city.

"Forgive me," I said, and lowered my handkerchief. I clenched it in my bare hand – Bessie had moaned in despair at my lack of gloves that fit, but there was nothing to be done about it – as I shuffled forward on the velvet seat cushions, out of the smothering warmth of the carriage.

Achilles helped me out of the carriage just as he had helped me inside it, but this time I had no attention to spare for the feel of his warm skin brushing against mine. An iron gate stood closed before us, and beyond it, stone steps rose up to a house more grand and intimidating than any I had ever seen before, for all that its grim stone sides were covered with soot from the dirty air.

I'd never even seen a house with more than two storeys before today. Every storey in this house was lined by windows...but every single one of the windows that rose level upon level above us was completely closed off by dark curtains, as if it were shutting its eyes tightly against my arrival.

My father wants me, I reminded myself. But my fingers tightened around Achilles's hand with a convulsive grip.

He removed my hand, perfectly gently, and opened the gate for me, as if he knew my particular weakness. "Miss Norton."

"Thank you." I forced a smile, paltry though it was, and moved forward, careful to raise my bare hands high so that not so much as a hint of skin could brush against the gate. Protected by my plain dark skirts and petticoats, I only felt a brief wave of warmth against my legs, quickly extinguished by the lurch of my stomach as the door swung open at the top of the steps.

A tall, grey-haired man looked down at me as if he were measuring me for purchase and finding me wanting.

Swallowing, I came to a halt. "Father?"

The man looked past me to Achilles. "The master has been asking for you." Then he looked back at me, his grey eyes as chilly as a winter sky. "I will show you to your room, miss."

"This is Horsham," Achilles murmured into my ear. "Your father's butler."

He moved forward behind me, and automatically, I moved, too, picking up my skirts and starting up the heavy stone steps.

Still, I hesitated at the very opening of the house. The air outside might be thick with soot, but the hallway before me looked as dark as a cave and far less appealing.

"I should go to my father," I said. "He wanted – "

"He desired me to show you to your room," said Horsham, and turned his cold gaze upon me until I gave in and stepped over the brink.

Achilles slipped past me, and the door shut behind me with a thud, closing me in. I blinked and blinked again in the warm, stuffy darkness.

Horsham lifted a candle from a small side-table and pointed to a tall staircase, half-hidden in the shadows. "If you would..."

I looked, somewhat desperately, at Achilles. Unsmiling, he gave me a low bow, then turned and disappeared into the darkness at the end of the hallway. Even his footsteps were muffled by the faded carpet.

Unhappily, I followed Horsham up the steps.

The air outside had made me cough, but inside the house, the taste was almost worse – so old and stale and over-warm, it made my head swim. Inside my third-storey room, at the very back of the house, it tasted worst of all, as close and thick as if the windows hadn't been opened to air the room out for years.

I started for those windows the moment that I stepped inside. I was nearly suffocating, by then. I reached for the thick, black curtains and yanked hard...with no effect.

Something was holding them in place.

"Ahem." Setting down the tall candle that he had carried, Horsham cleared his throat. "The master prefers that all of the curtains in the house remain closed during your time in residence."

"But – "

"It is the master's preference," he said inexorably, and closed the door.

I lasted nearly two minutes before I tried again. But the curtains didn't budge, and this time, my hand brushed against something hot and agonizingly painful along the way. Gasping, I stumbled back, nursing my injured palm, where a welt was already forming.

The curtains had been nailed shut...and the nails, of course, were made of iron.

Cupping my hand against my chest, I backed toward the canopied bed. Dust puffed up from its covers as I sat down, my gaze still fixed on the dark curtains.

It hurt to breathe.

It hurt far worse to think.

But my father couldn't know my sensitivity. Of that, I was certain. He knew so little about me, how could he know that odd detail?

Although perhaps Bessie might have written to him about it, when I was a child and she'd first discovered...

No. I would not believe that that cruelty had been intentional. He'd cared for me all these years, seeing to it that Bessie and I had enough for all we needed when any other man would have discarded me. He couldn't possibly wish me injury now...even if he was too ashamed to let any of his neighbors glimpse his bastard daughter in his house.

And that was the thought that repeated itself in my head as the hours passed and the candle sank lower and lower in its stand.

Perhaps the worst part, as I sat there in that close, dimly-lit room, was my increasing certainty that this room, placed as it was at the back of the house, must overlook a garden. The house was too large, and too far from its neighbors, not to have at least a small green patch behind it. More than that: I felt an itchy sensation tugging at the edge of my awareness, as if I could actually somehow sense the garden tantalizingly nearby, rustling and vibrant and full of everything I needed and couldn't have.

With my curtains nailed shut, I couldn't even look at it.

Still, Bessie had raised me to be strong, and I would not let myself disappoint her. I had learned my letters for William Norton, Esq. I had left my home for him, too. Now, it was time to find out what he wanted from me in payment for all his years of cheques and distant fatherly support.

But no matter what Bessie had promised, I was growing

coldly, grimly certain that it wouldn't be balls and dressmakers after all.

I heard male voices underneath the floor of my room at one point, and I tensed, but they moved on after only a few minutes. Horsham brought me a plate of cold meats and a slice of bread some hours later, when the room had grown even darker, with no sunlight left to fight its way through the curtains. Still, I did not change into my nightdress. I was waiting for my father's summons...and I fell asleep still waiting and still fully dressed, long after the candle had finally worn down to a nub and disappeared entirely.

When I woke, it was still fully dark. But I was finished waiting.

I was glad that I had not undressed. All I had to do was feel my way across the room to escape, as I should have done hours earlier. I had been enclosed in the darkness for so long, by then, that shadows did not worry me.

I remembered my way to the staircase, and down the stairs. But I hesitated at the bottom, one hand clinging to the dusty stair rail.

The thought of meeting Horsham unexpectedly, in the darkness, was unpleasant. The thought of meeting my father...

I hardly even knew how to name the mixture of emotions that churned through me at that idea. But I did know one thing for certain: I would not sit obediently in my room any longer, like a butterfly pinned to a greedy boy's wall. I had to find my way outside, to breathe.

I started down the pitch-black hallway, one hand brushing against each wall, in the direction of the greenery that had called me from my prison.

I bumped, hard, into a human body less than a moment later.

"Aaah!" I jumped back, my pulse galloping in my throat.

"Miss Norton?"

I was too startled, at first, to even recognize that voice. Then I heard the snick of a tinderbox being lit, and I saw Achilles's face in the glow of a candle set on the side table. He straightened, setting down the tinderbox. "I beg your pardon, miss. I heard a noise and came to investigate. I didn't mean to frighten you."

"Of course." I set one hand to my throat, but I couldn't slow my pulse. The air was too old, too filled with dust. I felt as if I were choking on it. "I was looking for the garden," I told him. "Would you please direct me there?"

An expression I couldn't decipher passed over his face. "You needn't use the word 'please' with me, Miss Norton. I am your father's servant."

More of the society manners that I hadn't learned, no doubt. I sighed. "Please," I repeated.

He didn't argue against the word, this time. Instead, he paused so long that I had time to note that he, too, was still fully-dressed, despite the fact that it must surely have been the middle of the night.

I pointed past him, into the deeper darkness. "Is the door unlocked?" I prompted him. "Or will I need a key?"

"Forgive me, Miss Norton." He sighed. "Your father gave me specific instructions that you remain within the house."

"But..." I stared at him. "I cannot even visit the garden? At *night*?" My chest was tightening more and more, until I could barely even suck in enough breath for my words. "Who could possibly see me now, to shame him?"

Achilles's face tightened, as if with pain. "There would be no shame," he said quietly, "but I owe your father my loyalty...and *I* would see you." He met my gaze squarely. "I am sorry, miss."

I clamped my lips together, before any intemperate words could burst out.

There was clearly no sense in trying to push past him; the hallway was a narrow one, and his wide shoulders nearly filled it.

"I cannot go back to my room," I told him plainly, when I was finally able to speak again.

He looked at me a moment, then nodded, as if some question had been answered. "I was instructed not to allow you to leave the house," he said. "But would you care to explore it?"

It was an odd tour that we took through my father's house that night, in the stale darkness. There were two different grand receiving rooms on the ground floor, along with a dining room, but none of them looked as if they had been used in years. Higher up in the house, on the first storey, we walked through a library crammed full of leather-bound books on folklore, mythology, and science, all jumbled together. It was the first room I'd stepped inside that showed any signs of recent use. We also passed one room whose door Achilles did not open. Hushed male voices sounded inside, too low for me to decipher any words, but with a tone of urgency and anticipation that made the skin at the base of my neck itch with an odd discomfort.

"Your father has guests," Achilles said quietly, and ushered me onward.

He would have deposited me at last in one of the receiving rooms, to sit alone like a fine lady, but I would not let him. We ended in the kitchen instead, in the very basement of the house. The air, at least, was fresher here, closer to the earth. And there was some semblance of familiarity, if not coziness, to the great hearth in the corner, though there were no friendly, sweet-smelling herbs hanging from the ceiling here.

There was far less food than I would have expected, actually. I'd never been invited through the front door of the local squire's house, back home, but I'd been inside his kitchens once with Bessie, so I knew what a gentleman's pantry ought to look like, and just how crowded it ought to be. Achilles had lit a second candle when we'd stepped inside this kitchen, chasing away some of the shadows that might have hidden the scarcity all around me as I sat down at the sturdy wooden table in the center of the room.

"Is my father's cook away?" I frowned at the bare counters.

Achilles was leaning into a cupboard, his voice muffled as he answered, "Your father has no cook, Miss Norton, and no servants apart from myself and Horsham. We generally take turns with the cooking as needed, or have meals delivered from a local pub." He straightened, holding the remains of what looked like a savory meat pie. "I have found us something to eat, though, if you're hungry."

"I am," I admitted, and dug in heartily, though the welt on my hand ached with every movement, and the food itself tasted bland and chewy. Still, I remembered what he'd told me, and I said politely, "It is very fine."

"Thank you," said Achilles, "but I'm afraid I couldn't claim credit, even if that were true." Humor gleamed in his eyes as his full lips curved into a half-smile. "This pie came from the pub's landlady, not my own hands. Mine would have been even worse, I promise you."

My shoulders relaxed for the first time in hours as I laughed, caught in his warm gaze. "I can cook a little," I told him, "but they wouldn't be elegant recipes."

His eyes flared wide, as if I'd insulted him. "I think not," he said, with finality. "You are a gentleman's daughter."

"Am I?" I hadn't realized, until now, just how much fury had been simmering inside me all those hours as I sat in my darkened bedroom, alone. "My father was very urgent in his summons, but he seems not to care to have me here now."

Achilles's expression turned blank, as if he were drawing another set of curtains against me. "Your father...is most preoccupied."

"With what?" I pointed at the empty kitchen counters. "What exactly does he care for? He keeps a fine house in town, but he doesn't bother to employ a cook, or even a maid to fight the dust. Why not? It can't be for lack of money, surely."

Achilles winced. "Miss Norton..."

"Does he not care for the state of his own home?" I demanded. "Or is he hiding something else besides me, and can't afford any witnesses?"

At that, Achilles stood, leaving his plate half-full. "I beg your pardon." He bowed with stiff formality. "I have work to do, Miss Norton, and I cannot leave it undone any longer. Shall I show you back up to your room?"

The pie in my stomach seemed to curdle at the sudden chill in his voice, but I kept my chin lifted as high as if I really were the lady he had called me. "That won't be necessary," I told him. "I can find my own way back."

And I did, picking my way through the still house by the light of the candle he had left me.

There were no voices sounding through the door of my father's study this time. But as I stood with my ears pressed to the door, I heard a soft swishing sound, again and again, as of pages turning in fierce study...study far too intense, apparently, to allow for the distraction of a mere daughter's arrival.

My own words from the kitchen, so full of splendid confidence and outrage, echoed in my ears, spurring me on to some brave confrontation, a demand for answers. And yet...and yet...

I stood alone in the darkness of the hallway, shut out of my father's study and my father's notice, as I had been all my life. It felt all too sinkingly familiar. And as I stood there, I couldn't help remembering every disdainful look I had ever been given when I'd ventured out with Bessie from the safety of our house and woods; every parent who'd warned their daughters not to play with me when we were small; and every mother who'd stood protectively before her son, glaring at me as I'd walked past them in church, ever since I'd grown into a woman's shape.

I could not face any looks like that again. Not now. Not after this long, strange day...and especially not from my father, after all those years of waiting for his notice.

My hand fell away from the door handle. As I turned and left for bed, exhaustion weighed down my bones until I nearly staggered.

Tomorrow, I would be stronger. Tomorrow I would confront him. I promised it to myself as I lay down in the big canopied bed. It sagged underneath me, soft and smothering, and it made me miss my narrow cot in Bessie's cottage with a physical ache of longing.

The last thing I thought, before I drifted into unhappy sleep, was: *If he doesn't want me here, not really...perhaps he'll change his mind and let me go home?*

It was home that I dreamed of, that night. But I wasn't in Bessie's safe, cozy cottage, after all. Instead, I found myself standing in the night-dark forest nearby, one hand set on the familiar bark of an oak tree, while sweet, high-pitched bells rang around me in jubilation. Voices laughed and called to me from the shadows of the trees beyond, in a language that I very nearly knew. Every rolling syllable tingled against my skin like a promise. Music played in the distance, beckoning me to dance among others, for the first time in my life.

I was more than invited. I was welcome.

I picked up my skirts and started forward into the free, green darkness...

...And woke, coughing, with dust filling my throat and choking me in my too-soft bed.

There was a large china pitcher of water on a stand in the far corner of the room, clearly meant for my ablutions. I had to down nearly a quarter of it before I could finally stop coughing. Even after I had finished, my eyes still leaked, stubbornly, in their corners.

That fresh night air had felt so real.

I would have ripped apart the stifling curtains that hid the window if it hadn't been for the cursed iron nails that held them...and the unfamiliar sensation of sinking lassitude that ran like melting lead throughout my veins, once I had finally finished coughing.

Even plants could grow without sunlight, Bessie had told me, but they grew white and limp when they were so deprived.

My head pounded as I dragged myself toward the door, but I fought the urge to collapse back into bed. I was no plant, despite my name; I was a human being, and I deserved answers from the man who'd ordered me here.

I found him standing just outside, his hand upraised, preparing to knock on my door as I opened it.

"There you are," my father said briskly, dropping his hand. He looked me up and down, eyes narrowed, while I gaped at him in the shadows of the unlit hallway.

His hair, unlike mine, was black; his lips were thin, and they compressed even tighter as he studied me; but his eyes and nose were nearly identical to those I'd glimpsed in reflections all my life. It was odd to see those familiar brown eyes narrowed in calculation. There were specks of red in the whites of them, as if he'd stayed up late too many nights and woken up too early...or perhaps not yet been to bed since I'd heard him in the middle of the night. But rather than displaying any of the exhaustion that I felt, he seemed gripped by nervous energy, tapping one foot against the carpet and one impatient finger against the pile of books that he carried under one arm as he nodded twice, firmly.

"Yes, yes," he said, "Achilles was quite right. I should have foreseen it."

"Father?" I put one hand to the doorway, but it wasn't only my physical balance I had lost.

"Never mind," he said, "you'll feel better soon, I'm sure. I'll have Achilles bring you something." He took the top book from his pile and flipped it open as he turned away, his voice growing abstracted. "Unless you'd rather sit downstairs, of course. He said you didn't care for your room. Not very girlish, I suppose. No feminine frills and fripperies...well..."

"I want – I *need* to go outside!" With a surge of effort, I broke through the leaden fog that had settled around me and started forward, my head pounding harder than ever. "Please!"

"Yes, yes, I understand." He flapped one hand impatiently. "I should have thought of it. Achilles will see to everything."

"So I *can* go out to the garden?" I sagged against the faded paper on the closest wall, limp with relief.

He looked up from his book, something cold and grim skimming across his expression. "That would not do at all," he said. "No, you'll need to stay inside, my dear, for your own safety. But Achilles will take care of things."

"My *safety*?" I stared at him. "But – !"

But he was already striding away, and when I tried to follow after him, my legs slid out below me like dead stalks, leaving me collapsed and alone on the carpet.

I had run through woods and meadows all my life, and climbed trees for the sheer joy of movement. But as I lay slumped on the floor of my father's house, I couldn't find the energy within me to move at all.

Achilles found me there some time later, long after the fog had overwhelmed me entirely.

I heard his voice before I saw him. "Miss Norton!"

It took me a moment to open my eyes, and another moment to focus though the dizzying swirl of colors as everything blurred before me. Finally, though, Achilles's features swam into place, strong and clear. He knelt before me, his forehead creased with worry.

"How long have you been lying here?" he asked.

I tried to shrug, but I could only manage a tiny shift in my shoulders. "Since..." I drifted off, my voice fading.

"I should have come earlier," he muttered. "Forgive me. I was in the garden. Your father desired me to gather these for you." He nodded over one broad shoulder; then, when he realized that I couldn't see past him, he shifted aside to clear the way.

A massive green bundle of long grass lay on the carpet beyond him. He must have tossed it down when he'd seen me. It was like a vivid piece of the outdoors itself, with dandelions and other wildflowers scattered among the long green stalks.

At the sight of so much abundance, my tight chest finally loosened. For the first time in hours, I took a deep, invigorating breath.

Watching me carefully, Achilles scooped up a handful of the piled greenery and passed it to me. "I'm afraid it's hardly an elegant bouquet. There is no gardener in residence to grow roses for you."

"Oh, no, these are far better than roses!" I pressed the mass of slim green stems against my nose and mouth as tightly as I could, breathing in their vibrancy. Tingles of pleasure shot into my lungs and out through all my limbs, like bright stars of captured sunlight. As sudden energy flowed through me, I pulled myself up into a sitting position, bracing myself against the floor with one hand.

It was surprisingly easy to move, after all; I let out a startled laugh. "May I have the rest, please?"

Achilles was frowning even more deeply now, but he silently passed me more and more stalks of grass and leaves and wildflowers, until they filled both of my arms and I could taste their fresh air and bright green life in every delicious breath I took.

I jumped to my feet, kicking my long skirts out of the way when they sought to tangle me. Nothing could stop me from moving now. I gave a twirl from sheer giddy delight, clasping my treasure to my chest....and then realization hit.

"Oh!" I came to a standstill, cradling the greenery more gently in my arms. "But we'll need water for these, or they won't survive the day!"

Achilles rose slowly from the floor, his dark eyes wary. "Shall I bring you a vase for them? You needn't stir yourself –"

"Don't be absurd!" I started down the stairs, my thrice-mended petticoats rustling around me. I couldn't help it; a full-blown laugh burst out of me as I looked back, a moment later, to find him staring after me, stock-still at the top of the third-storey landing. "Well?" I demanded, exhilaration flooding through my lungs. "Can't you keep up?"

"I don't believe I can," Achilles said quietly.

But he couldn't have meant it literally, for he was at my side only a few quick strides later, his eyes hooded and his expression startlingly grim, as if he were contemplating issues far too unpalatable for such an unexpectedly delightful morning.

I gave him a mischievous grin, hugging my greenery to

me, as we reached the next landing. "I'll race you to the kitchen!"

He started to utter some protest, but I ignored it. I hadn't stretched my legs in a run for nearly twenty-four hours. I couldn't wait a moment longer. I tore down the staircase, whirled around the bannister on the first storey landing, raced down the final flight of steps toward the darkened hallway below...

And as I leapt onto the ground floor, triumphant, I nearly ran into Horsham, who stood before the closed front door with two men I'd never seen before.

Their eyebrows rose as their gazes fixed on me. The exhilaration in my chest turned cold.

My father had worked so hard not to let anyone know of my existence.

"Oh!" I grabbed the bannister, forcing myself to a stop. "I beg your pardon. Gentlemen." I ducked an awkward curtsy, still clinging to my mass of greenery. "I only..." But my powers of invention dried away under Horsham's cold, disapproving glare.

Proper young ladies did not run down staircases, giggling, and throw themselves down the last few steps. And my father's daughter was meant never to be seen.

But the two men behind Horsham had no disapproval in their expressions.

"Well, I *say*!" The man on the left was in his middle age, I thought; at least as old as my father, if not a few years older, with a finely embroidered waistcoat and the comfortable mass and weight of a man who'd known expensive dining all his life. He gave me a leering smile that made my hand clench on the bannister, as I fought the ignoble urge to back away. "Is she the one, then?"

"The...?" I gave Horsham a panicked glance, but his lip only curled, faintly, in response.

The other man was younger, with a lean build and spectacles on his bony face. But his eyes were intent behind his spectacles, and his face was alive with calculation. "Oh, yes," he murmured. "Oh, I can see it. Ye-e-es..."

I'd been so transfixed by their attention, like a mouse cornered in the open by a pair of snakes, that I hadn't even heard any footsteps behind me. So it came as a shuddering relief when I heard Achilles's voice suddenly speak behind my shoulder. Better yet, with his voice came the sudden awareness, like a rush of warmth, of his strong, steady presence just beside me as he joined me at the bottom of the staircase. "Gentlemen." He nodded with cool politeness. "Mr. Norton is awaiting you in his study."

"Oh, but we're enjoying ourselves right here!" The older man let out a sniggering laugh. "We've only just met this fine young lady. I'm sure Norton won't mind waiting a few more minutes, eh, what?"

I tensed, and felt Achilles shift closer. But the two men were moving closer, too, until I was hemmed in on all sides.

"I do have a few observations I would like to make first," said the younger man. He reached out as if to touch my face with his long fingers. "For example – "

I jerked back. But Achilles was already moving.

"Forgive me." He blocked the man's hand with one solid arm and slipped his other hand beneath my elbow in a silent gesture of support. "Miss Norton has a prior engagement. If you would excuse us, gentlemen..."

The younger man's eyes flared wide, and again, I thought of snakes. I could only too easily imagine a forked tongue flashing in affront from between those white teeth.

His friend glowered, big shoulders tensing as if for battle.

For a moment, I thought they would refuse to move. But as Achilles drew me gently and inexorably forward, they finally stepped aside, making way for us.

My skirts brushed against the bigger man as we passed, and my skin crawled. But I held my greenery close for comfort as Achilles's hand dropped away from my arm, and I followed his lead in walking slowly and calmly down the hall, with my head raised high...

...And it was the other man's coldly intent gaze that left an icy trail along my back.

"Bloody cheek!" growled the bigger man, as they finally started up the staircase. He stomped up the steps in Horsham's wake, huffing as if his waistcoat were too tight. "Norton ought to have a talk with that man of his about the way he addresses his betters! If you ask me, he's starting to get notions above his station, and I'll be happy to tell Norton that myself. Why – !"

His friend's voice interrupted him, too quietly for me to make out the words as they walked higher up the stairs. But I heard the hissing undertone in his voice, and it made my jaw tighten even more.

I waited until they had moved entirely out of hearing before I finally stopped walking and let out the full-body shudder that had been building inside me all the while.

"Ohhh." I drew a deep breath and then released it, shaking my head. "What vile creatures. Why on earth did my father invite them here?"

Achilles did not respond, except to look away from me.

I eyed him guiltily in the half-darkness, wishing I could read his expression better. Neither of us carried a candle, and only just enough dim light filtered through the closest thick curtains for me to make his features out. "Will you be in disgrace for rescuing me from them? I never meant – "

"No," Achilles said curtly. "Do not concern yourself." His shoulders looked stiff with tension as he turned back to face me, his dark face tightly set. "You have nothing to apologize for, Miss Norton."

"But if they complain to my father – "

Achilles shook his head, cutting me off. "Your father has found me useful for many years. He will not dismiss me for one morning's irritation to his friends."

His friends. My face twisted with distaste. "I cannot think highly of my father's taste in company."

Achilles sighed, his shoulders slumping. "I believe he finds them useful, too."

Something in that word made a chill prickle through me, even in the stuffy warmth of the narrow hallway. "Does my father calculate everyone's worth by their usefulness to him?" I asked.

And silently, I added: *Exactly what use does he intend for me?*

Achilles gestured forward without answering. "You wished to find a vase, Miss Norton."

I looked at him a long moment before I finally nodded and gave in. "Very well," I said. "Will you escort me?"

He went still as I closed my hand around his strong arm. For a moment, he said nothing, only looked down at the point where my fingers curled around the sleeve of his plain black coat, absorbing the warmth that emanated through it. Then he said, his voice sounding strained, "Miss Norton. I am a servant, not a gentleman."

"And yet," I said, "you rescued me from the two *gentlemen* who were visiting my father." I met his gaze squarely, daring him to disagree. "So, will you escort me to the kitchen?"

He opened his mouth, as if to speak. Then he closed it again, his dark eyes searching my face.

"Very well," he said quietly. "But only this once."

Ten minutes later, we were sitting at the long wooden table in the kitchen, where my greenery sat in a tall vase. I was eating bread and cheese for my breakfast when he said, abruptly breaking the comfortable silence: "I met your father when I was nine years old."

I set down my bread, waiting.

He didn't even seem to see me, his attention directed

inward, at something that drew his brow into a frown. "I was...my mother and I..." He stopped.

I put out my hand until it hovered only an inch from his on the table between us, but he did not take it. Instead, he drew a shuddering breath and straightened, drawing away from me. "I never knew my father," he said plainly. "He and my mother did not marry."

"Like my parents, then." I picked up my bread again. Something in his mood had infected me; instead of lifting the bread to my mouth, I began picking the end into crumbs with nervous fingers. "I never knew my mother, either. My father sent me to live with Bessie when I was born."

"You were better there," Achilles said. "He made the choice that was best for you, and gave Bessie what she needed to support you. My father..." His shoulders shifted as if he were trying to release some heavy weight. "He took no such care with us. My mother did...what she had to do for our survival. But in the end, it wasn't enough. When I was six, we went into the workhouse." His generous lips tightened until, for a moment, they looked nearly as thin as my father's. Then he opened his mouth again on a sigh. "I might not have survived it, if not for your father. He came in one day and chose me out of everyone there, all of us desperate for escape. I've never been beaten or locked in again. Only because of him, I am free."

Unlike me, I thought. But I didn't say it out loud.

Instead, I asked, "What of your mother? Did my father take her in, too?"

Achilles's features twisted. "My mother was...not well, by then. And Mr. Norton had come looking for only one servant, a young and agile boy to run his errands." He took a deep breath, his right hand knotting into a fist. "She told me to go, to take the opportunity to escape. I saved all of my earnings. But when I went back..."

"I understand," I said. And I did. I closed both hands around his fist.

A cough sounded behind me.

Horsham stood watching us from the doorway.

I yanked my hands back, my whole body flooding with scorching heat. Achilles stood up so quickly, his chair clattered against the floor.

Horsham watched it all with cold eyes. "Mr. Norton desires your presence," he told Achilles.

Two hours later, as I sat alone in my father's library, I heard footsteps hesitate outside the door. Unease slid along my spine. I held still, unmoving, not even daring to release my breath. If it was one of my father's friends, come to find me alone...

Finally, the footsteps moved on. I sagged with relief. A moment later, I heard someone run quickly down the staircase. Through the curtained window, I heard the front door open and close, and then a carriage rattled off down the street outside.

With a sigh, I lifted up the book of ancient mythology that I had chosen, trying my best to summon up any dregs of interest in the long, rolling phrases and unfamiliar names, as the sudden burst of panic drained out of me. But it wasn't until much later that I realized what had actually happened.

Achilles had been sent away by my father...and I did not see him again.

It was Horsham who brought me my greenery from then on. It might have been carelessness or cool calculation, but always, he seemed to wait until my very last strands were drooping in their vase, and I was lying, nearly as lifeless, in a sluggish, aching torpor on my bed – or, if I had managed to drag myself in search of help before my legs gave out, on the carpet or stairway outside my room. But it was useless to ask for them to be brought any earlier; they came when he chose to bring them, like my meals.

At least the greenery he brought was enough to let me breathe, and move. But there were no more lush armfuls of the long grass from my father's untended garden, only small, carefully-sliced chunks that barely pierced through the thick, dusty air of the house. I didn't dare step far from them, but I was equally frightened to clutch them too close, for fear that they would die even more quickly.

And, of course, there were no more friendly moments of warmth or companionship to be found in the kitchen. It was cold and empty the first time I visited it at night after Achilles's departure, in lingering hope of finding him returned. The second time I visited, I saw a candle flickering through the doorway, and I started forward joyfully.

But the man who stood at the cupboard was leaner than Achilles; and when he turned, I saw my father.

He looked nearly as startled as I felt. Of course, it was only my second meeting with him since my arrival, four days earlier – and this time, with my vase in my hand, I was capable of real movement and speech.

I realized as much even before my shock had faded. Grim determination took its place.

This time, he would not find it so easy to walk away from me.

"Father!" I said.

"Ah...Lily. Yes." He gave me a quick, perfunctory twist of his lips that might, perhaps, have been intended as a smile. "If you'll forgive me..." He raised the plate of bread that he'd pulled from the cupboard. "Only collecting fuel for the scholarly endeavors," he said, starting forward. "So..."

I placed myself, unmistakably, in his path. "Don't leave," I said. "Not yet." *Not this time.*

He frowned. "Lily..."

"I need to talk to you," I said.

"Talk?" He blinked, as if the word were foreign to him.

"You summoned me here," I told him, "but I still don't know why. What is it that you want of me?"

His nostrils flared. He let out a sound somewhere between a laugh and a "harrumph." "You needn't bother yourself about that," he said.

"But I do." I would have crossed my arms if I could have. With my vase tucked securely in the curve of my left arm, the best that I could manage was to set my free hand on my waist and tip my head back to look him squarely in the eye, as sternly as possible. "I do concern myself, Father. And I have a right to know."

"Hmmph." His eyes narrowed, moving from my face to the vase in my arm. "Determined to have all the answers, are you?"

"Yes," I told him.

"Well, then." His cheeks creased. It might have been the first real smile I'd seen from him, but somehow, it didn't make me feel any better. "It's only four days until your birthday, isn't it?"

"Um..." My eyes widened. "Yes?"

He nodded, his smile turning secretive. "An important birthday, too, particularly in your mother's family. Your coming-of-age, they would term it."

"Would they?" I blinked at him. Was he really going to offer me a début, after all? For one mad moment, there in the darkened kitchen, Bessie's tales of glamorous balls and dashing suitors floated in my head.

I dismissed them in an instant. But by then, he had taken the opportunity to brush past me while I was distracted.

"You'll find out everything on your birthday," he said as he strode for the door. "Of that, I promise you."

"Wait!" I hurried after him, reaching out to grab his coat sleeve. "Father, I have to ask you something else."

His expression was openly impatient this time, as he tried to tug his arm free and I stubbornly clung to him. "Well, girl? Out with it."

"Achilles..." I swallowed, feeling heat gather at my throat. I couldn't avoid this, though, not with any justice. "Please, Father. Tell me: Did you send Achilles away because of me?"

His eyebrows rose. The new smile that curled his lips made my face burn, even as he finally stopped trying to pull free. "Concerned about him, are you?"

I plowed doggedly forward, clutching his sleeve. "He did nothing wrong, Father. I don't know what Horsham told you, but – "

"I haven't dismissed him, if that's what worries you." Father snorted. "He's far too useful for that."

"Oh." I let out my breath in a sigh of pure relief. "Thank goodness."

"No, he's merely taking care of some business for me in Leeds for the next five days. Then he'll come back to serve me for many years longer." Father shook his head gently. "I'd hardly blame any man for making *that* mistake. Why, I made it myself, once. With some creatures, it's simply unavoidable. But a man with any sense will understand that, in the end, and find a way to turn his error into something useful."

Useful. The word rang heavily in my ears.

"What use am I to you, Father?" I whispered, holding his sleeve tighter than ever.

"On your birthday," he said, "I'll tell you."

There was only a brief widening of his eyes to alert me.

Then, with a sudden lunge, he knocked the vase out from under my arm.

I dived for it, my breath catching in my throat...

And when I looked up again, I was alone.

I dreamed again, that night. I wasn't in the forest near Bessie's cottage this time, but hovering just at the edge of it, while the long grasses of the meadow rustled behind me.

Chiming voices beckoned me deeper into the trees. A clever wind tugged at my skirts, trying to pull me in.

Everything in my body yearned toward that lush green gathering. But when I tried to step forward, my throat clenched...

And the next moment, I woke up, gasping for breath, in my bed.

I couldn't see anything in that pitch blackness, thick with dust and hopelessness. But I did not need sight, then, to know that the paltry strands of grass had gone limp and drooping in the vase that I had set beside the bed.

I could barely summon the energy to roll over and stare in the direction of the impenetrable curtains that hid the garden from me, and my freedom.

The memory of those enchanted voices was already fading in my head.

Horsham did not bring any more greenery to me for another twelve hours.

That was three days ago. This morning, I found an iron bar set across the inside handle of the front door.

Today is the day before my seventeenth birthday...and apparently, there will be no escape.

I'd spent almost all the years of my life waiting with hope or with fear for my father to summon me. But when I saw that iron bar this morning, I knew with cold certainty that I could not afford to wait any longer.

Bessie forced me to learn my letters against my will when I was a child, only because my father was a gentleman and he deserved to have a daughter who could read and write like a lady. This afternoon, as I crept into my father's study, with every escape route from the house barred against me, I silently blessed my old nurse with all of my heart for her foresight. For as I pawed, faster and faster, through the books and papers piled on his desk, from anatomical drawings fit for a surgeon to well-worn books on myth and ritual, reading the notes scrawled in them by William Norton, Esq.'s, familiar hand, I finally understood a great many things about myself...

...And about the man who had fathered me.

"Lily." His voice sounded in the doorway and startled me into a gasp. Oddly enough, he didn't look angry to find me poking through all of his careful notes – years' worth of notes, based on their scribbled dates; notes and books he'd been accumulating for the last seventeen years, at least.

...Ever since he'd found out what a useful seed he had planted.

He looked dryly amused as he walked toward me, shaking his head. "You couldn't wait until tomorrow to find out, eh? I suppose there must be some of me in you, after all."

"Half of you," I rasped, through a dry throat.

But he'd clearly never seen me as a true daughter.

I picked up an ancient-looking pamphlet that started near the bottom of the pile: more folklore, like the books that filled his library. I only hadn't realized, until today, that he was actually reading about me. "So this is why you never told anyone who my mother was."

His thin lips twisted into a wry smile. "Would your good country nurse have believed me?" He slid the book from my hands, as if it were a gift I'd been offering him. "You should be grateful that I didn't choose to tell her the truth. Those superstitious country folk think of your mother's people as lesser demons, you know. Even Horsham believes in all that rubbish, and he's been a city man for nearly thirty years now. Why, you'd have been tortured all your life if they'd had any hankering of it. Barred from the church. I spared you all of that."

"Grateful," I repeated.

Iron nails studded the window in the small, cramped room. There was nowhere I could turn to breathe, as my chest tightened more and more.

"What happened to my mother?" I whispered. "Why were you the one who raised me?"

He shrugged as he set the book back on his desk. "Childbirth is always a dangerous business," he said. "Especially for them. Humans are rougher, tougher sorts, you know. That's why so few creatures like you come safely into the world – and even fewer survive long enough to come of age." Something like a smirk flitted across his face. "If you think you're a small, slim sort, you should have seen *her*. She managed to bring you to me before she gave in for good, though, before she could even tell her own family." He shook his head in what looked like amused disbelief. "Her kind always did like a good, romantic impulse. Named you, too, with her last breath, as she passed you to me."

My mother named me. I nestled that thought tightly into my heart, holding it private and safe where he couldn't see it touch me. I had far more urgent truths to elicit from William Norton, Esq., and I was running out of time.

"Why didn't you send me back to her family, then?" I asked.

Of course, I'd seen the notes he'd scribbled, by then. I could hardly fail to know the answer.

But apparently, I was still a child at heart, in that moment. Because somehow, I still wanted my father to prove that I was wrong after all.

Instead, he settled down in the great armchair before his desk with a sigh of contentment. "What use would they have had for you? Whereas I – ! Why, there are men who've spent their whole lives searching for a creature like you. You have no idea of the power a true scholar can harvest from your mixture, if he knows exactly what to do and when to do it... and the riches a sensible man can earn, too, if he's willing to share that harvest with his friends!

"But for now, if you don't mind..." He waved briskly toward the door as he picked up the top sheet of paper. "It isn't your birthday yet, after all."

Not until midnight tonight. My *coming of age* in my mother's tradition, according to my father's notes. The moment my blood will come into its power.

That is when the ritual will begin.

Apparently, Horsham knows my habits by now. When I retreated into the library, half-blind with grief and rage, I found a plate of cold pie waiting there, beside my accustomed chair.

I doubled over, clutching the back of the closest chair for balance as I tried desperately to keep my gorge down.

I should have run away the moment I saw my father's carriage in front of Bessie's door. But there is no forest to escape into, here in the city. Only in my dreams.

If my father is right about my coming of age, those recent dreams must have been more true than I'd realized. After all, my mother's people should be more and more able to sense my affinity to them with every moment that the clock ticks down. They'll finally recognize me as their own.

But the iron that holds me a prisoner here holds them out, too. Whether the other side of my family wants me or not, they cannot save me now. No one else can.

Now, I can hear the tall clock downstairs tolling half past

eleven o'clock, as I sit waiting in my room at the last, in the endless dark. My hands are raw and weeping from my first attempts to break past the iron nails on a downstairs window, soon after my meeting with my father. Horsham forcibly escorted me up here half an hour later, after he discovered me battering at the thick curtains with a kitchen knife, my hands wrapped in layers and layers of toweling for protection. Before he locked my bedroom door behind him, he confiscated every last bit of greenery from me but a single handful of grass, leaving me just enough air to breathe.

There was no need to leave a guard at the door, after that. And everyone knows there can be no escape through a third-storey window.

I haven't enough energy left to try to barricade my door. But even now, huddled on the floor beside my tightly-curtained window, measuring out every breath and harboring the last precious remnants of strength, with my puny bit of greenery resting in my hands, I still haven't given up...

...For I didn't walk straight to the window when Horsham locked me in. I picked up the big china water pitcher, first, from the stand by my door, though it felt like a lead weight in my hands.

I've spent all my life feeling dutifully grateful for my existence, only waiting for my father to decide exactly what use to make of me. Now it is time to claim the rest of my life for myself. From now on, I will make my own choices, no matter how bitter they may taste.

When I hear the front door of the house open and close,

and men's voices starting up the steps, I don't feel even a moment of panic. All that I feel now is a ferocious sense of resolution. After all these years, my waiting is finally at an end.

I am ready.

Slowly, I heave myself to my feet. With the last of my strength, I pull my arms back.

Then I fling the pitcher at the center of my curtained window.

Glass shatters. The sound is muffled behind the curtains, but it echoes through my bones. It is the sound of my salvation.

Footsteps sound on the staircase below, men's voices raised in drunken laughter, but they're too late.

I take a last, deep breath of my greenery, for strength. And then I let my whole body pitch forward. Even the burning pain of the iron nails is not enough to hold back the force of gravity.

Fire blazes along my skin. Cloth wraps around me. I burn as I fall from my bedroom window, wild and free, no tame plant to be harvested for any man's use. I am Lily, and even if my father was right and my mother's people have no use for me...well, then at least I can still choose my own ending.

The curtains, with their cruel iron nails, fall away from my face. I take one desperate, elated gulp of the outside air, cherishing my final taste of freedom...

And cool hands grasp me from every side, as steady as a heartbeat, as transparent as clear water.

I'm not falling anymore. I'm flying, carried by a dozen gentle arms, slower and slower until they set me on the ground of the abandoned garden. Wild greenery erupts before me, and long grass pokes up under my skirts, tickling against my mended stockings and welcoming me home.

The sound of ringing bells fills the night air, wild and joyful and finally intelligible to my ears.

Home. Darling. Lost child. Found!

Alight, ecstatic, and alive, I twirl around and around in my father's darkened garden, my skirts lifting around me in the caressing breeze. Hands stroke my hair, my cheeks, and my arms, and even my rawest burns ease at their touch. I laugh out loud in wonder and disbelief.

No wonder my father never dared let me step outside as the days grew closer to my seventeenth birthday.

Just as I finish my final twirl, a familiar figure comes skidding around the corner of the house, his outlines revealed in the faint glow of light that bleeds outside through the thick curtains and the broken window upstairs.

"Miss Norton!" Achilles looks frantic, nothing like his usual unflappable self, as he drops the ladder he's been carrying to the ground. "Thank God I found you in time! What I've discovered – we must leave... Miss Norton?" His voice grows suddenly uncertain as I walk closer and closer to him, my skirts whispering around me like a promise. "Why are you smiling at a time like this?" he asks faintly. "You're in terrible danger."

"Not anymore." My skin glows as I point into the darkness of the hedges and trees that gather at the back of my father's untended garden. More and more tiny, sparkling lights appear amidst the branches as we watch. Golden bells ring triumphantly in my ears. "I'm just preparing to finally go home," I tell him, "for my coming-of-age début."

His dark eyes widen, and he falls back a step. "You saved yourself," he says softly.

"But you came to save me, too." I glance down at the ladder he's brought, to carry me from my window like a knight in a fairytale, and I shake my head in amazement. "I thought you such a loyal servant, you would never question anything my father did."

"Well..." He shrugs uncomfortably, then gives half a laugh. "You said my name was remarkable, once."

I tilt my head, trying to read him in the darkness. "Yes?"

His lips twist in a wry grin. "My mother gave it to me for strength," he says. "But apparently, every Achilles has his particular weakness, too."

My whole body hums with delight, in the dark green vibrancy of the garden, as I reach out to take his hand.

Before I can, shouts sound overhead. "There she is!" It's one of my father's despicable friends, leaning out of my broken window with a group of men clustered behind him. "She's with your damned servant, Norton! By God, he deserves a good thrashing for this!"

"There's no time for idle talk," my father raps out. "Gentlemen, *now*!"

Their heads disappear from the window. I don't need to

hear them to know that they're thundering down the three flights of stairs, heading in our direction.

Achilles steps back before my hand can touch him. "Go." He points to the gathering lights in the garden. "Quickly. Take your opportunity." His voice drops to a half-whisper. "You know I did, all those years ago."

The lights at the end of the garden beckon me home. My family's voices grow stronger and clearer with every moment. All I have to do is step into the lush darkness to join them.

Instead, I hold out my hand once more. "I'm not leaving you behind," I tell him.

"Me?" He lets out a bark of laughter, then points at his chest. "And what use would *I* be in Fairyland?"

I narrow my eyes at him, like Bessie at her very sternest. "You've been useful to my father for all these years," I tell him. "Don't you want to find out what use you might be to yourself?"

His breath catches. His strong throat works, so close to my lips.

"The first time we met," he whispers, "I took you away from the world that you knew."

"Now it's my turn," I say, and I close my fingers around his.

The striking of the clock echoes through the iron-bound walls of the house. Angry voices sound through the tightly curtained windows. My father and his friends are pounding toward us on heavy footsteps of retribution, duty, and authority...

But there won't be anyone left to greet them when they arrive.

Together, laughing with delight, as clumsy and as giddy as children, Achilles and I run hand-in-hand toward the lights in the wild green darkness, as midnight finally strikes and I leave my father's house forever.

Afterword

Thank you so much for reading Touchstones! I hope you've enjoyed these stories. Visibility matters hugely, so I would really appreciate it if you could take the time to honestly review it. Even a one-line review makes a huge difference.

If you'd like to keep up with my stories and books, the very best idea is to sign up to my monthly newsletter:

www.stephanieburgis.com/newsletter

You can also subscribe to my Patreon if you want to read stories like these early (and also take part in my monthly Dragons' Book Club).

www.patreon.com/stephanieburgis

If you enjoyed the romantic fantasy stories in this collection, you can read my Harwood Spellbook series of novellas and short stories (starting with *Snowspelled*), or read *Scales and Sensibility,* the first full novel in my Regency Dragons trilogy of fantasy rom-coms. (*Claws and Contrivances*, Book 2 in the trilogy, is coming in late 2022, and I'll be sending out preorder links to my newsletter subscribers ASAP!)

You can also read *Good Neighbors: the Full Collection*, which charts Mia and Leander's romance from beginning to end (including lots more metal magic, necromancy, midnight balls, and midnight expeditions underneath opera houses along the way - oh, and Mia's dad gets his own romance, too).

You'll find excerpts from all of my published books on my website: **www.stephanieburgis.com**

And of course you can follow me on Twitter and Instagram, too.

twitter.com/stephanieburgis

instagram.com/stephanieburgisinwales

Acknowledgments

Thank you so much to Ravven for the beautiful front cover to this collection! And thank you to Patrick Samphire for the wonderful spine and back cover.

Thank you to all of the wonderful editors who published most of these stories to begin with and gave me wonderful line edits along the way. Thank you to my amazing teachers at Clarion West, who taught me to learn to love writing short stories: the late and much-missed Octavia Butler, Bradley Denton, Nalo Hopkinson, Connie Willis, Ellen Datlow, and Jack Womack. I really appreciate your patience and your thoughtful critiques!

Thank you to Julia Kitvaria Sarene and Patrick Samphire for really helpful last-minute typo-catches.

And thank you so much to my patrons on Patreon, who make this and all of my other books possible. Specifically, thank you to Abigail Gawith, A. C. Bauer, Adrienne Joy, Alexis, Ali Baker, Amanda Taylor-Chaisson, Amy Bond, Anna M., Anne Nesbet, Ash Hopkins, Asha Hartland, Beatrice Berendonk, Brandi Blackburn, Brooke Johnson, Cara Scheffler, Catherine Neff, Charlotte Taylor, Cheresse Burke,

Courtney Havens, Creektaken, D. Franklin, d+tee, Dana Levy, Daniel Fishman, David Schwartz, Deb Horng, Deborah Dakin, Debbie Lee, Delia Sherman, Demet Charlotte Hoffmeyer-Zlotnik, Doreen Farrar, Edmond Hyland, Elisa Wiik, Elizabeth Chuter, Elizabeth Gentry, Emily Williams, Eric Schneider, Fiona Morton, Francene Lewis, Gabe Krabbe, Gail Morse, H. Nieuwenhuijzen, Haddayr Copley-Woods, Heather Holt, Intisar Khanani, Jacqueline Seamon, Jasmine Stairs, Jen Stiles, Jenn Greiving, Jenn Reese, Jenni, Jim Burke, Jim Dean, Joanna, Jody Myers, Julia Kitvaria Sarene, Julia Knowles, Julia Linthicum, Julia Rios, Kara Pekar, Kara Snow, Karen Kisner, Karen Riegle, Kate Elliott, Kate Proctor, Katharine, Kathy Martin, Katrina Middelburg, Kayden Harper, Kimberly M. Lowe, Konstanze Tants, Kyna Foster, Lab, Laura Bang, Laura Watkins, Lauren, Leanne Rabesa, Leng M., Libby Gorman, Lillian Tschudi-Campbell, Linda Duvall, Lisa Moore, Liz, Llinos Cathryn Wynn-Jones, Lora Timonin, Lucy, Lydia San Andres, Mariam Zama, Marissa Lingen, Mary Anne Anderson, Mary Grove, Mary Perthen, Mary-Anne Mitchell, Melita Kennedy, Melody, Meredith, Michael Bernardi, Michele Wellck, Molly Van Ryn, Morgana Kay, Mynda Cruz, Nancy Stone, Naomi Twery, Navessa Allen, Nicola, Nicole Hunter, Patricia Anderson, Rachel Halpern, Rebecca, Rebecca Joseph French, Renee Sweet, Robert Tienken, Rosemary Claire Smith, Roxanne Baechler-Gill, Rupal Patel, S Klotz, S.P., Sadie Slater, Sandstone, Sara Carmody, Sara Glassman, Sarah Anderson, Sarah Cannon, Sarah Fleming, Sarah

Fünke, Sarah Swarbrick, Sarah Thompson, S.B. Beasley, Scatha_B, Selina Lock, Shannon Haddock, Sharon Corbet, Solomon Foster, Sorrel Jones, Suna Dasi, Susan Franzblau, Susannah Cooke, Tahmi DeSchepper, Talia Lester, Tamara Case, The SF Reader, Vickie R., Virginia Farris, Vivian Behrman, and Ying Lee.

I appreciate every one of you.

Earlier Publications

The Wrong Foot: First published in *Daily Science Fiction*, November 8, 2013. Republished in *Podcastle*, March 21, 2014.

Undead Philosophy 101: First published in *The December Lights Project*, 2010.

A Cup of Comfort: First published in *Beneath Ceaseless Skies*, Issue 210.

Dreaming Harry: First published in *Unidentified Funny Objects*, edited by Alex Shvartsman, December 2012.

Offerings: First published in *Fantasy Magazine*, August 2009. Republished in Wax & Wane: A Gathering of Witch Tales, ed. David T. Neal, March 2016.

Dancing in the Dark: First published in *Daily Science Fiction*, May 2012.

The Disastrous Début of Agatha Tremain: First published in *Willful Impropriety: 13 Tales of Society and Scandal*, ed. Ekaterina Sedia, September 2012. Republished in *Inscription Magazine*, 12 May 2014.

The Art of Deception: First published in *Insert Title Here*, ed. Tehani Wessely, April 2015.

Clasp Hands: First published in *Daily Science Fiction*, May 2014.

Crow: First published in *The Town Drunk*, May 2007.

True Names: First published in *Strange Horizons*, 9 November 2009.

Love, Your Flatmate: First published in the anthology *Consolation Songs: Speculative Fiction For A Time of Coronavirus*, ed. Iona Datt Sharma, June 30, 2020. Republished in *Podcastle*, June 2021.

www.ingramcontent.com/pod-product-compliance
Lightning Source LLC
Chambersburg PA
CBHW020528310726
48979CB00014B/2249/J

* 9 7 8 1 7 3 9 1 1 7 6 1 0 *